Praise For
Anne Kelleher

THE GHOST AND KATIE COYLE

"A lighthearted, tightly paced story with entertaining characters. Thoroughly enjoyable."

—*Rendezvous*

"A spirited otherwordly romance that sub-genre fans will find very entertaining . . . Ms. Kelleher is rapidly ascending to the pinnacle of the supernatural romance field."

—Harriet Klausner, *Under the Covers*

A ONCE AND FUTURE LOVE

"This is a wonderful, tender, poignant, and chivalrous tale that will captivate medieval fans everywhere."

—*Romantic Times*

"Lordy this is wonderful; it's one that grabs you, and at the end you say, WOW!"

—*Bell, Book & Candle*

"Kelleher has written a beautiful story of timeless love. For a fascinating time travel trip of your own, pick up *A Once and Future Love* and enmesh yourself in the historical detail and engaging love story."

—*Romance Industry Newsletter*

"A spectacular medieval romance with a time-traveling twist."

—Harriet Klausner, *Under the Covers*

*L*OVE'S
*L*ABYRINTH

Anne Kelleher

JOVE BOOKS, NEW YORK

This is a work of fiction. Names, characters, places and incidents are
either the product of the author's imagination or are used fictitiously,
and any resemblance to actual persons, living or dead, business
establishments, events or locales is entirely coincidental.

TIME PASSAGES is a registered trademark of Penguin Putnam Inc.

LOVE'S LABYRINTH

A Jove Book / published by arrangement with
the author

PRINTING HISTORY
Jove edition / December 2000

The Penguin Putnam Inc. World Wide Web site address is
http://www.penguinputnam.com

ISBN: 0-515-12973-9

A JOVE BOOK®
Jove Books are published by The Berkley Publishing Group,
a division of Penguin Putnam Inc.,
375 Hudson Street, New York, New York 10014.
JOVE and the "J" design
are trademarks belonging to Penguin Putnam Inc.

PRINTED IN THE UNITED STATES OF AMERICA

10 9 8 7 6 5 4 3 2 1

For my sweetest Meggie Moo,
my pearl without price,
with love, beyond limit or reason . . .
Mommy

In the writing of this book, I have been deeply indebted to various scholars who, through the excellence of their work, enabled me to more readily anchor my imagination in solid fact. They include Anne Somerset, *Elizabeth I;* Alison Weir, *The Life of Elizabeth I;* Christopher Hibbert, *The Virgin Queen;* Antonia Fraser, *Mary, Queen of Scots;* and A. L. Rowse, *Shakespeare the Man,* which was one of the sources of the genesis of this story. My friend Josephine Putnam Vernon and I wrote the first draft of this story when we were still in high school. Both she and Lorraine Stanton have been to me the kind of friends Alison and Olivia are, and I hope I have in some small way conveyed the importance of those relationships in my own life through those characters. And finally, my deepest thanks go to my mother, who introduced me to the works of William Shakespeare when she directed a shortened version of *Macbeth* with my fifth grade class, thus instilling in me a love of the English language and an appreciation for its literature and its history that continues to grow to this day.

Prologue

A HEAVY PALL of smoke hung in the thick tavern air, wreathing the faces of the patrons who, for the most part, were too deeply engaged in the contents of their cups to either notice or be bothered by it. And certainly no one paid the least attention to the two men sitting in the corner, for the one was readily dismissed as a prosperous Puritan in his expensive but serviceable garments of unrelieved black, and the other as nothing more than a well-to-do shopkeeper. Master Christopher Warren leaned over the rough plank table and addressed his soberly dressed companion beneath the babble, which rose and fell all around them. "We've heard you've a mind to offer your daughter's hand to Lord Nicholas Talcott." He waited just long enough to observe the shock register on the other man's face, then leaned back against the grimy white-washed wall.

"Master Warren! How—how—" Sir John Makepiece sputtered and set his tankard down with a thud. "How do you know that?"

Master Warren allowed himself the reward of a small smile. "We have our ways, Sir John."

"You and Walsingham's crew—I've heard tales about you lot." The country knight looked disgusted, his Kentish accent growing thicker as surprise yielded to dismay.

"Have you, now?" Master Warren's face was bland, and his lips beneath his thin mustache twitched. "Don't be alarmed, Sir John. Everyone is well aware of your unimpeachable loyalty to Her Majesty."

"Then what business is it of anyone's to whom I betroth my daughter? That's still a father's prerogative—least, so it was the last I heard."

"And so may it always remain, Sir John." Warren raised his own tankard in a mock toast. "But because of your, ah, interest, shall we say, in the Talcott estates, some of us thought it prudent to approach you regarding this— this rather delicate matter."

"Involving Talcott?"

"Ah, you begin to see." The irony was lost on the other man completely, and Warren sighed inwardly. These country dolts were difficult to reach at times. It required the patience of a saint—of a mother, he corrected himself (after all, there were no more saints in this brave new Protestant world)—just to explain circumstances in a manner in which they would be understood. However, he reminded himself, if one took the time required, one's efforts were usually rewarded with a kind of dogged loyalty that was difficult to find anywhere else, let alone purchase. And certainly not at Court, he reflected, scanning the tavern's common room more by force of habit than out of any real concern he might be seen and recognized. This dingy tavern near St. Bartholomew's Hospital was the last place anyone connected with the Court would come. And Sir John Makepiece was a Protestant of highest repute—known only for his devotion to his family, his lands, and the new religion. It mattered not at all if Master Warren were seen in his company. And if, of late, Sir John's leanings seemed to be growing less than moderate, that only increased the chances that Warren could convince him to participate in the scheme to bring Lord Nicholas Talcott of Talcott Forest to a complete and final reckoning on the executioner's block. He shifted to a more comfortable position on the hard bench and leaned across the table once more. "What if I told you there could be a way to acquire the Talcott patrimony without the loss of your daughter's hand to an avowed Papist family?"

At that, Sir John looked even more taken aback, but, to his credit, conceded Master Warren, this time he took a quaff of ale and set his tankard down slowly before replying. "What are you talking about?"

"It's well known, Sir John, that you've had a taste for the Talcott acres for quite some time. You offered to buy them, I understand, some fifteen or twenty years ago— near the beginning of our Queen's glorious reign, after the death of old Lord Talcott"—*may his soul forever burn,* he added privately—"and were quite rudely spurned. Am I correct? And then again, about ten years ago, was it? There was another bit of unpleasantness, I believe, regarding property lines? And this latest—forgive me if I speak plainly—this latest scheme, to offer your daughter to Talcott . . . You're a rich man, after all. Talcott's circumstances are not much better now than they were at the passing of his father. But there may be another way—without sacrificing your daughter."

"How do you know all this?"

Warren shrugged. "Most of it is a matter of public record. It doesn't take a genius—or a spy—to see that you've coveted those lands as another man might a whore. And I'm merely offering you the chance to acquire them. Legally, of course."

"Of course." Sir John picked up the tankard and peered into it, as though searching the depths for the answers to the questions he wasn't sure he wanted to ask. He raised his watery blue eyes and met Warren's with the assurance of a man who knew he'd never walked any but a straight and narrow path. "I'm a godly man, Master Warren. I serve the Lord in all I do."

"As do all of us in Her Majesty's service, Sir John.

And that's what brings me here today. Talcott's the son of an avowed Papist, for all that he purports to have converted to our ways and forsaken those of his fathers. He—"

"He never struck me as a religious zealot. If anything, I'd wager the man has no religion at all."

"Even worse," Warren said smoothly. "We have reason to believe, however, that Talcott was involved with the plot to free Queen Mary."

"That Papist whore is one piece of mischief that's well laid to rest." Sir John's voice rose above the taproom chatter, and Warren leaned forward, gesturing for him to lower his voice.

"Aye, but you're wrong, Sir John. Would that it were that simple. We believe that Talcott is a spy, actively working with agents of Spain, for the King of Spain has sworn to take revenge against our own good Queen. And if we can prove it, his estates will be forfeit, and you, Sir John, as a loyal subject of Her Majesty, could reap an ample reward." Warren sat back, picked up his tankard, and let the words sink in, watching as uncertainty warred with greed across the knight's face. He suppressed a sigh. This might take longer than he thought, and might ultimately prove fruitless. Sir John, for all that he coveted the Talcott acres, was nonetheless known as a man of decent reputation. But there would be another way, Warren thought. If Sir John were an unwilling pawn, there was always a way to find another. He would bring down the Talcotts if it were the last thing he did in this world, or hunt down their shades in the next. Every night in fevered dreams his father's burned and bloody ghost cried out to him for revenge. His son would not rest in his own grave until he saw the proud Talcotts humbled, their name destroyed, their heritage stripped from them once and for all. Ever since he'd joined the ranks of Sir Francis Walsingham's fledgling secret service, he had worked for this day. He wasn't about to let the opportunity slip through his fingers. If Sir John was not to be tempted, there were plenty that could be.

"I'll do it."

The finality in the knight's voice startled even Master Warren. He took a deliberate sip of ale to regain his composure, then signaled for the landlord to bring another round. "Excellent, Sir John." He smiled and, glancing up while the landlord set two more tankards of foaming ale in front of them, found himself looking into the large, mild eyes of one of the other patrons. The deep-set eyes were fastened directly on both of the men, and instantly Warren was alert. He noticed that the young man was as plainly dressed as Warren himself, in a coarse linen shirt and leather jerkin, and that he toyed with a quill. A piece of parchment lay before him on the table. With a frown, and a muttered explanation to Sir John, he rose and approached the young man, who was now writing busily on the parchment. Warren eased behind him, ostensibly on his way to the jakes in the back.

The younger man did not look up as Warren peered over his shoulder, swiftly taking in what the young man wrote. He narrowed his eyes at the scribbled scrawl. Poetry. He shook his head as a wave of relief washed over him. He jostled the young man's shoulder when another patron bumped into him, and he seized the opportunity to get an even closer look. The young man glanced up, and their eyes locked and held. Warren had the immediate impression of a lively and searching intelligence and an impersonal curiosity that seemed to peer into the very depths of his mind. Instinctively he lowered his eyes, muttering a pardon. The young man shrugged good-naturedly and went back to scribbling verse.

Warren hurried back to his own table, where Sir John nursed his tankard filled with foaming ale. The little episode had unnerved Warren more than he cared to admit, and he wanted nothing more than to conclude this piece of business and be off. "Now," he said, leaning in close, as the knight looked up, "this is what must be done."

Chapter 1

"I'M TELLING YOU, Liv, that portrait was *you*," Alison O'Neill declared as she folded her tall frame into the cramped seat of the tour bus beside her friend. "I've never seen anything like it—it could've been a photograph."

Olivia Lindsley looked up from the accordion file full of dog-eared notes and faded manila folders on her lap and smiled. The painting hanging near the ladies' loo inside the English pub bore a certain resemblance, she'd had to admit when Alison had pointed it out. But she knew enough about sixteenth-century art to know that any likeness was more an accident of technique than any real semblance she bore to the long-dead subject. "Oh, I'm not so sure about that, Allie. A lot of portraits end up looking a lot alike because that's the way the painter knew how to paint people. And the mirrors back then weren't exactly the same quality we have today, so unless the artist was a complete incompetent, it didn't really matter."

"That portrait doesn't look like another portrait. It looks like *you*. It's got the same dark hair and eyes, the same arch to your brows, even that little half-smile you get when you're thinking."

Olivia laughed softly at her friend's insistence. "Did

you have a chance to ask the landlord who she was?"

"Oh, him." Alison dismissed the landlord with an airy wave. "Said he didn't know, but that the portrait had been there since Cromwell's time. What do *you* think?"

"Well," said Olivia softly, slipping the tattered manila folder that held her father's final notes on the subject of Shakespeare's Dark Lady into the file folder, "I'd say that the clothing definitely belonged more to the late sixteenth century, or possibly early seventeenth, than Cromwell's period. She wasn't dressed like a Puritan, that's for sure. I'd say it probably came from one of the noble houses around here, maybe to keep it safe from marauding Puritans, and was just left there and forgotten. There was so much upheaval during that period. Whole families were wiped out. There's probably no way to ever know who she was."

"That's a shame, then," Alison said, settling her long limbs into a more comfortable position. "Because maybe she was one of your ancestors."

Olivia laughed again. "That's even more unlikely, I'm afraid. The Lindsleys are Scots, and you know that my mother's family came from Italy. Besides, Dad and I spent a whole summer here the year you and I were sophomores in high school just researching the family tree. Remember? We never set foot in Kent."

"Humph." Alison waved another dismissive hand. The bus was beginning to fill with tourists, together chattering as loudly as a flock of excited birds. "I still say it could've been you."

"Well, no matter who *she* was, let's hope that the Talcott chronicles can shed some light on the identity of the Dark Lady," Olivia said, patting the folders on her lap. The folders were covered with notes in her father's cramped writing. "If I can find something that proves that Olivia, Lady Talcott, was the wife of one of the Talcotts of Talcott Forest, my father's work will be just about finished."

"And then what about you, Liv?" asked Alison, her

dark blue eyes gentle. "What are you going to do?"

Olivia shrugged and glanced out the window. The parking lot was crowded with buses and tourists speaking at least a dozen languages, and the August air was humid. The bus was stuffy, and suddenly she wanted to be on the way to the last stop on her self-imposed itinerary. "I haven't decided."

"But you did check into those schools you mentioned? The drama school at Yale? The ones in Manhattan?"

"Not yet. But I will. As soon as we get back. It's too late to enroll for fall now, anyway. And I really want to get this book finished and out of the way before I—" Olivia broke off.

"Before you move on," Alison finished. There was a short silence between the two friends as all around them the seats filled with the tour group, all talking at once, it seemed, about the lunch at the authentic English country tavern. "You know, Liv, I know how important your dad's work was to him. And I know how much it meant to him that you worked for him all these years. But ever since I've known you, you always talked about how much you wanted to be an actress. You're only twenty-four. It's not too late."

Olivia met Alison's concerned eyes with a smile. "Allie, I know that. You're right. Believe me, I have every intention of applying the minute I get this book done. It was Dad's lifework. I just can't let it die. And if I don't finish it, who will? In some ways, this is as much my project as it was his."

"I know, but—"

Olivia reached over and patted Alison's hand. "You're a good social worker, Allie. But please don't worry. Just enjoy the tour while I check out the family records. Okay?"

Alison gave her a long look. "Okay."

Olivia nodded in the direction of the front of the bus. "We'd better listen up. Mistress Mary is about to make a pronouncement."

Alison rolled her eyes as she turned her attention to the plump, gray-haired woman who stood in the aisle next to the driver, clutching a clipboard in one hand. Alison was making this trip so much fun, thought Olivia, she was beginning to wonder why she hadn't let her friend talk her into it sooner. She knew why, she thought, suppressing a sigh. Her father's death last November had abruptly ended nearly six years of intense research into the identity of Shakespeare's Dark Lady. Although many scholars accepted the view of noted Shakespearean scholar A. L. Rowse that the Dark Lady of Shakespeare's sonnets was Emilia Bassano, a woman loosely connected to the Elizabethan court, David Owen Lindsley—Olivia's father—believed that a cache of letters discovered at Oxford in the early 1990s offered a far more likely, albeit more mysterious, possibility.

During Olivia's final semesters in college, she'd begun to function as her father's research assistant, and in the last couple of years since her graduation, she'd worked exclusively for him. Her father had urged her to apply to graduate school and begin work on her own Ph.D., but Olivia had hesitated, held back by a dream of her own she scarcely dared voice. Only Alison, her best friend since they were both fourteen, knew her secret ambition.

Physically, the friends couldn't be more different, but in temperament, they complemented each other perfectly. Alison was tall and athletic, her strawberry-blond curls cut closely around her lightly freckled face, her eyes a dark gray-blue. Olivia, on the other hand, was petite, with dark hair that fell nearly to her waist, and an olive complexion she'd inherited from her Italian mother. They'd discovered each other in high school, when the extroverted Alison had taken the more reserved and quiet Olivia under her wing. "Under her wing" was a mild way to describe how Alison and her large Irish family had virtually adopted her, Olivia mused, thinking back to all the holidays and weekends she'd spent with the O'Neills. Her own father had insisted she accompany him on his summer sabbaticals, but he was relieved that Olivia had found a more congenial place to spend her Christmas and Easter breaks than the dusty, warm library of the house they inhabited during the school year. Content to stay in a residence provided for him by the university, he had never felt the need for a more permanent home. And in each other, the two girls had found the sister both had always wanted.

Now, at twenty-four, the two women were still the closest of friends, though their lives were clearly taking opposite directions. Alison had just finished her M.S.W. and had started working in the public school system of New York. She was excited about her work helping young teen mothers and fathers. Olivia, on the other hand, had decided to finish her father's final project before pursuing her own ambition to act. Her father's death the previous year had left her with enough money to safely support herself for a few years. A successful career on the stage might be one shot in a million, she knew, but she owed it to herself to try, just as she felt she owed it to her father to finish his final legacy. Besides, in the years of working with her father, she too had been intrigued by the mystery. It had been the works of William Shakespeare that had made her want to be an actress. She thought of her father, David Owen Lindsley, who would roll in his grave at the thought of his daughter auditioning at theaters in the dregs of New York City's off-off-Broadway streets. Professor Lindsley, three times a Ph.D., with eight languages to his credit—all dead ones—and a library filled with his own publications, had never encouraged or understood his daughter's aspirations to act. Although he'd supported Olivia in her study of sixteenth-century playwrights, he'd never for a moment thought that a serious career could be made on the stage.

She glanced up to see Alison slump further in her seat and swiftly cover her face with her open guidebook. "What's wrong?"

"He's coming this way," Alison hissed.

Olivia looked up to see a young man in his late twenties coming down the aisle, two cameras hanging around his neck, his pasty complexion matched by his thinning blond hair. "Him?"

"Yes, him," Alison whispered. "In the pub he acted like I was his new best friend." She fixed her eyes on the page and determinedly ignored the young man, who tried to make eye contact but was forced, by the press of other tourists, to take a seat farther back.

"People love you, Allie," Olivia murmured when the man had passed. "That's why you're such a great social worker."

Alison groaned and rolled her eyes as the tour guide, Mary Higgins, gave two short bursts on the whistle she wore around her neck. She had just enough time to mutter, "Let's hope I can convince all those fourteen-year-old moms to talk to me," when Mary Higgins held up her hand and began to speak. She had an interminably cheerful voice that seemed as though it would never falter, even when confronted by the most vexing of travel complications. "Listen carefully, everyone! We've got a schedule to keep!" The group began to quiet down, and faces peered from both sides of the aisle. "Now, let's see," Mary continued. "We'll arrive at Talcott Forest in just a few minutes. It's only"—she peered back at the driver—"what is it, driver? Fifteen miles? Yes." She beamed at her charges like a benevolent monarch on progress. "Now. There's been a slight change in plans. Instead of touring the house first, and then going off to change into our Elizabethan costumes . . ."

Next to Olivia, Alison squeaked, "What?"

"Ssh!" responded Olivia, listening intently.

". . . We'll be changing first and then touring—all in costume! The revel will begin as soon as we get there. So don't be surprised to see wandering musicians"—here she paused and looked around, her wide face ecstatic—"masked dancers, noble lords and ladies, and"—here she paused for an even longer moment—"quite possibly

Queen Elizabeth herself. It's well documented that our
immortal Gloriana dined more than once at Talcott Forest,
and I have it on excellent authority that we're likely to
be graced by the presence of Her Majesty herself. Now—
and this is most important so please give me your full
attention!" She looked meaningfully at a few people who
were carrying on whispered conversations. "The eclipse
is scheduled in just two hours and six—no, seven minutes.
On each seat, you will find a pair of special sunglasses,
like these." She held up a pair of cardboard sunglasses,
which had blue and red ribbons falling from each corner.
"As you can see, they've been specially designed so that
we will all appear as though we're attending a masked
revel! Now, it is very important—extremely important—
that during the eclipse you wear these glasses for safe and
proper viewing. Also, immediately following the eclipse,
we will be touring the maze. Now, the maze at Talcott
Forest is one of the premier examples of its type still
extant in England today. We are extremely fortunate that
the present Lord Talcott has such a keen appreciation for
the historical value of his home."

"Keen appreciation for the tourist dollars, you mean,"
muttered the guy Alison was trying to ignore. Olivia
glanced backward through the crack between the seats and
realized he'd found a seat right behind them.

"So! Are there any questions?" Mary smiled, obviously
not having heard the comment, or choosing to ignore it.
"Yes?" She nodded in the direction of a woman who was
frantically waving her arm.

"What happens if someone gets lost in the maze?"

"Oh." Mary smiled indulgently. "It's not that large a
maze. I understand you only need turn consistently to the
left—or maybe it's the right—to find your way out. And
of course we'll all be together. I'm sure it's not likely that
anyone will actually get lost. Anything else? No? Good.
Now don't forget to keep your spectacles with you at all
times. I believe we're all loaded up, so let's be off!" She
practically bounded up the aisle, which, thought Olivia,

was no mean feat for a woman who had to be nearing
sixty.

Beside Olivia, Alison groaned. "Are you sure we have
to change?"

"Oh, come on," said Olivia. "It'll be fun." She winked.
"You don't want to miss our immortal Gloriana, do you?"

"Not for one hot second. And I sure can't wait to meet
her wearing my funny glasses. We're going to look like
Masterpiece Theater meets Elton John. But it's easy for
you to say. You're going to be searching through records
while I'm out strolling around."

Mary plumped down into the vacant seat across the
aisle from the two friends.

"We're on our way!" She blew two short bursts from
her whistle. The bus doors unfolded, closed, and slowly
the bus pulled away. She craned her head over the back
of the seat in front of her, anxious as a mother hen with
wayward chicks. "Everyone settled? Good!" She favored
Alison and Olivia with a broad smile. "Did you two girls
have a nice bit of lunch?"

"Well, to tell you the truth," answered Alison, before
Olivia could speak, "I was so full from breakfast I
couldn't even think about food. But there was a very interesting portrait back there by the ladies' room—did you
see it?"

"Hmm." Mary frowned. "No, I can't say that I did."

"It looked just like Olivia."

"Olivia!" Mary beamed at them both. "You don't say!"

"Oh, the resemblance was remarkable," Alison was
saying as Mary turned the full force of her focus on Olivia.

"Fancy that! We must be sure to ask at the house if
they have any idea who it could be. They may know at
the house. They've done tremendous research into the
whole family history. And you girls do understand how
important it will be to wear your glasses?" Mary looked
as earnest as a kindergarten teacher. "After all, we don't
want any injuries!"

"You do remember, don't you, Mrs. Higgins, that I won't be part of the regular tour?" Olivia peered around Alison. "I'll join you for the revel after I've had a chance to look into the Talcott records."

"Ah, yes, that's right. I remember. You're the one who's doing the research into the Dark Lady, aren't you?" Mary leaned across the aisle and patted Olivia's arm. She favored both of them with another radiant smile, pulled her clipboard onto her lap, and adjusted her glasses on the end of her nose. "Thank you for reminding me. I'll just make a little note of that right here so I won't worry if you aren't anywhere to be seen until dinner. Now if you'll excuse me, I have some items to check off."

Olivia winked at Alison, who rolled her eyes toward the ceiling once more, settled back into her seat, and closed her eyes. What a good idea, thought Olivia. A nap was just what she needed.

The bus rolled along the winding country lane, where the hedgerows grew so high that the fields on either side were nearly totally obscured. Here and there, the roof of a house was visible behind the high green rows, and several times Olivia glimpsed wide meadows where cattle and sheep grazed contentedly. This was the England she remembered best, the England of winding lanes and drooping Queen Anne's lace, of yellow cowslips that peeked out from unexpected places, and bridges of ancient stone arching over slow-moving rivers that flowed as steadily as the ages. She and her father had visited what felt like nearly every country churchyard, dovecote, and ruined abbey in all of Britain.

She thought of her father with an unexpected pang. Although their relationship had often been complicated by his unyielding interests, and his inability to understand his daughter's own passions, she knew he'd loved her in his own detached way. This trip had shown her just how much of his knowledge she'd absorbed. Ever since they landed, Alison had been saying over and over again how lucky Olivia had been. And when Olivia had responded that as a teenager, she'd been lonely and bored most of the time, Alison had retorted that as a teenager, she'd been lonely and bored, too—in New Jersey. Olivia smiled to herself. The fact that they were both only children was one thing that had brought her and Alison so close. Even though Alison herself had been an only child, the O'Neills were a loud and boisterous clan who'd welcomed the stray chick with open arms. When Olivia was younger, she'd thought her father had only allowed her to stay with Alison's family to keep her out of his way. Now she was beginning to realize that perhaps he had not only been bewildered by her very presence in his life, but wholly incapable of understanding that his only child had not shared the passion that consumed his life.

Consumed it literally, she thought, her face turned to the glass. He'd died suddenly right after Thanksgiving, slipping and falling on a patch of ice as he'd hurried into the university library, eager to retrieve a book that had come in for him. His death had come just when he had nearly finished his research. With a little sigh, she laid her head against the high back of the seat and shut her eyes. The stuffy air and rhythmic jouncing of the bus were making her sleepy. Beside her, she knew Alison drowsed as well. This trip had been a good idea, she thought as she drifted closer toward sleep. Alison, in her own wise way, had somehow known just what Olivia needed to do in order to lay the last of her ghosts to rest.

All too soon the bus jerked to a stop. Olivia took a deep breath, opened her eyes, and looked around. Alison's head drooped against the back of her seat, and she was breathing deeply and slowly. Uh-oh, thought Olivia. Waking Alison from a nap was always next to impossible. She looked around to see Mary Higgins hauling herself to her feet, clipboard in hand, whistle poised between her lips, as the babble of the passengers increased steadily in volume. The bus doors pulled open with a sound like a loud belch. Olivia peered past Alison's head and saw a sprawling mansion of peach-colored brick, which appeared to incorporate the architectural styles of nearly half a dozen centuries. She saw a Georgian bay window cut into a wall of blackened oak half-timbering beneath a gabled Tudor roof with twisted chimney pots, and what could only be a Victorian Gothic addition, with a glass garden room and long doors of stained glass opening out onto a pseudo-Renaissance terrace. For all its incongruity, however, the house seemed to nestle into a dip in a low hill. The leaded diamond-paned windows that overlooked the courtyard were framed with ancient ivy.

Mary raised her free hand and gave two short bursts from her whistle. "Ladies! Ladies and gentlemen!"

Olivia glanced at Alison, who was totally oblivious.

"Now, do not—and I must repeat—do not forget your special spectacles!" She waved hers in the air. "The eclipse is now just eighty-two minutes away. Once we've exited from the bus, we'll proceed into the dressing areas, which are part of the original stables. Gentlemen, your area is on the right. Ladies, you may follow me to the left." She eased her considerable bulk from between the narrow seats, and Olivia tapped her arm.

"Excuse me, Mary?"

"Yes, dear?"

"My friend—she's awfully tired, and, well, it's sometimes difficult to wake her when she falls asleep like this. Can we catch up?"

Mary peered at Alison. "Oh, my." She looked so blank, Olivia nearly laughed. This must be the one contingency she was totally unprepared for. "But of course, my dear. Do try to hurry. Our tour begins in"—here she peered over her bifocals at her wristwatch—"in just fifteen minutes. You see that doesn't really give us very much time at all."

"We'll be as quick as we can."

"All right, then, everyone!" Mary gave another short chirp from her whistle and marched down the aisle toward the doors. "Follow me!"

Olivia waited until the bus was empty. Gently she

nudged Alison. "Allie?" Predictably there was no response. "Allie?" She shook her a little harder and, this
time, was rewarded by a slight smile.

"Mmmm," sighed Alison.

"Hey, come on, Sleeping Beauty. You have to wake
up. We're here."

"Okay," Alison breathed, nestling even closer into the
seat cushion.

"Allie! Wake up! Now!" Olivia tugged at Alison's arm,
and she bolted upright, knocking her head against the
back rim of the seat.

"Ow!" Alison rubbed the back of her head. "What's up,
Liv?"

"You are, finally. We both fell asleep on our way over
here. But we're here now—and you have to hurry. You've
got to change into your costume and catch up to everyone
else. The tour starts in less than fifteen minutes."

"Oh . . ." Alison yawned and ran one hand through her
short curls. She stretched her long arms over her head.
"Okay, I'm up."

Olivia got to her feet and struggled into the narrow
aisle. "Come on. This will be fun."

"I'm coming, I'm coming." Alison unfolded her tall
frame from the cramped seat.

Olivia grabbed both of their purses and started down
the aisle. She smiled at the bus driver, who was lounging
by the side of the bus, smoking. "Which way?"

"That way, miss." He took a long drag from the ciga-
rette and pointed in the direction of two low stone buildings. Olivia paused, looking around, as she waited for
Alison to catch up.

The curious blend of styles, ancient and new, was not
unpleasing, she thought. Talcott Forest rose, stately and
formidable, over the high stone walls that bounded the
converted stables. The roofs of other outbuildings were
just visible above the ivy-covered walls. There was a
sense of peace here, as well as a sense of sterility, and
inexplicably, Olivia felt sad. It was all so clean, so

stripped of any evidence that lives had actually been lived here for centuries. Something had been lost here, she realized, something cannibalized and exploited, something that her father had appreciated in a way that had always escaped her, and that he had spent his life in search of. She looked down at the worn cobblestones at her feet. The silent stones bore no testimony, but she wondered what kinds of men had tramped over them, what horses had worn them down. Had Cromwell himself marched across their uneven surface, or had the feet of the immortal Gloriana glided over them? And all the ordinary people—the foot soldiers, the milkmaids, the grooms and stable boys—her thoughts trailed off in another direction. The people who lived here today—the landlords and shopkeepers and tour guides—so many must be the descendants of those very same people.

She remembered how her father had often stood staring up at the great medieval keeps, or how he sometimes muttered to himself as he traced his way through the ruins of some old fortress. Was this what her father had seen when he'd looked at those churches and castles and towers— the past leap into life? She'd tagged along, occasionally stumbling over half-buried stones, usually bored in the way that teenagers and older children are often bored by their parents' interests. If he had thought to make her a historian, he was sorely disappointed. But something must have stuck, she thought. The plays of Shakespeare and Marlowe and Jonson had drawn her to the theater.

"Hey, which way?" Alison's voice interrupted her reverie.

"You go that way." Olivia pointed. "And I go this way. I'll catch up with you in"—she checked her watch—"say about an hour. Beware of tourists bearing cameras."

"Thanks for reminding me. Have fun." With a wave, Alison strolled off yawning.

Olivia made her way to the main office, where an ancient air conditioner loudly blasted cold air in all directions.

"Can I help you, miss?" asked a woman wearing a pink Fair Isle sweater around her shoulders. She sat behind a battered desk.

"I'm Olivia Lindsley. I telephoned yesterday—"

"Oh, yes, of course. The American professor." She peered over her bifocals at Olivia, looking her up and down, and, self-consciously, Olivia smoothed her jeans with one hand while she clutched her notes closer with the other. "I hope you don't mind my saying, but you seem a bit young, dear."

"Professor Lindsley was my father," Olivia answered. "I'm—I was his research assistant."

"I see." The woman raised one eyebrow as if to suggest she did anything but, and rose to her feet. "Well, come this way, Miss Lindsley. Lord Talcott left word that you were to be provided with whatever materials you requested. I'm Doris Parmell. I'm in charge of the archives."

She led Olivia down a short corridor and into a small, well-lit room that, unlike the main office, was obviously climate-controlled. It reminded Olivia of the rooms where precious manuscripts were kept in libraries. Which, she realized with a start, was exactly what it was, on a smaller scale. "Now, I believe you were specifically interested in the family around the turn of the sixteenth century? I've taken the liberty of searching out everything we have on the family during that period. It's all there." She pointed to several leather-bound books of obvious age, wrapped in special cloths.

"Thank you," Olivia said. She placed her notes on the table. "There seems to be a fair amount here."

"If you tell me what you're looking for specifically, I might be able to help you pinpoint it. I understand you're here for the revel as well?"

"Well, my friend is. She came along for the ride, so to speak, and we thought that might be a fun way to while away the time."

"Of course."

"Specifically, I'm looking for an Olivia, Lady Talcott—she would have probably been about—well, my age in the mid-1590s or so."

"Nicholas Talcott was the master of Talcott Forest during that period, and—" Doris smiled. "Come to think of it, I believe his wife was named Olivia. Didn't you say that was your name?"

"Just a coincidence."

"Ah, well. Right over here." With an efficient bustle, Doris opened the book lying on top of the stack. "I think you will find the information you're looking for here. But Olivia Talcott was very obscure, surely. Why the interest?"

"As I explained to Lord Talcott, my father believed that Lady Talcott may have been Shakespeare's Dark Lady. You've heard about the cache of letters discovered a few years ago? Well, as part of that find, there were a number of letters written to Shakespeare from a woman who signed herself Olivia, Lady Talcott. There've been several candidates, but it's taken quite a while to track them all down. And actually my father, right before his death, felt that this Lady Talcott—if certain things add up—might well be the Dark Lady. But there's a certain mystery surrounding her. My father wasn't ever able to discover exactly who she was."

"Hmm," mused Doris. "How interesting. I hope you find what you're looking for, Miss Lindsley. I'll be right down the hall. Do call if you need any assistance." With another chilly smile, she left Olivia alone.

Olivia settled into the straight-backed chair with a little sigh and a fervent prayer that this might be the answer to her father's lifework at last.

An hour later, Olivia carefully shut the last of the ancient chronicles and rewrapped them in their special casings. She pushed herself away from the table, stretched, and gathered up her notes. She'd certainly learned a fair amount of interesting tidbits about the family. The maze, for example, had been built by one of the younger Talcott brothers in 1585. He'd apparently died suddenly the following year, shortly before his older brother had married her elusive namesake. Like so many avenues of inquiry into the past, this one only yielded another mystery, as tantalizing as the one for which she'd come to find an answer.

She walked slowly back to the front office.

"Find what you need?" Doris asked.

Olivia shrugged. "Can you tell me anything about Olivia Talcott? Where she was from? I see she married Lord Nicholas in 1587, but before that she seems to come out of nowhere. There's no family name for her, I don't see any record of a dowry—"

Doris spread her hands. "You're more than welcome to come again. I can't say I've made a very thorough search through the old records—I know the family tree fairly well, and so I recognized the name. But for those kinds of details . . ."

"Are there any other records?"

"Not that I know. But I can check with Lord Talcott when he returns from Paris tomorrow. He may know of some ancillary records—church records and so on—that I'm not aware of. Would you like me to take the name of your hotel in London, and perhaps give you a ring?"

"That would be very helpful, thanks," said Olivia as she jotted down the number on a card. "I have a funny feeling this may be the lady. But it's odd how sketchy the information on her is. Are there any portraits of her in the main part of the house?"

"No, there aren't." Doris shook her head. "There's one that's thought to be Lord Nicholas, I believe. But quite a few of them were lost during the Civil War. They were taken out with many of the family treasures, and many were never recovered."

"I'll have to be sure to look for the one of Lord Nicholas," Olivia said, glancing at her watch. "I guess I should go change into my costume for the revel. Can you tell me how to get to the changing area from here?"

"Oh, yes. It's very easy."

After another promise to call her in London, Olivia said
good-bye to Doris Parmell and made her way through the
long corridors to the changing rooms in the converted
stables. Another woman in a blue smock directed her to
a locker where a blue satin dress and a flowered wreath
hung from a wooden hanger. The costume was cleverly
arranged to look more authentic than it actually was—a
white lace ruff helped conceal a zipper, and the farthingale
was actually a large hoop sewn to the skirt, rather than a
separate article of clothing. Olivia had just finished pulling the dress over her head when she was startled to see
Alison, wearing a green satin gown, hurry into the room,
glancing over her shoulder as though she was afraid someone was following her. "Allie?"

"Oh, thank God, Liv. Are you finished? Do you need
some help?"

"No, I think I can manage. But you look like you're
running away. What's the matter?"

"I am running away. From that dreadful Jim Hicks."
Alison gave a mock shudder. "I don't know why I'm such
a nerd magnet. You look great. I look like a green satin
Titanic."

"Oh, you do not." Olivia laughed as she placed the
wreath on her head. "Where's yours?"

"My wreath? I already look ridiculous enough, thank
you. Come on. Let's go see if the coast is clear. They
were heading for the maze when I slipped away. Now that
you're back you can run interference for me."

"You think my notes will be all right here?" Olivia
looked around dubiously.

"Everyone left their purses here. The lockers lock.
See?" She held up her wrist, from which dangled a little
key on bright elastic. "We're going to miss the eclipse."

"That wouldn't be the first thing we've missed."

"Everyone at home's probably amazed we made the
flight."

"And won't they be surprised when we actually make it home."

"Yeah, well, we haven't done that yet. Let's not make any assumptions." Alison led the way to the door. "So did you find what you were looking for?"

Olivia adjusted her bodice. "Well, yes and no. I found out some interesting stuff. For example, did you know that Lord Nicholas Talcott left specific directions in his will in 1624 that under no circumstances was the maze ever to be torn down? Isn't that strange? And he married an Olivia in 1587—which makes the timing perfect for her being the Dark Lady. But there are hardly any details about her that I can find. I might have to come back day after tomorrow. Will you mind?"

"Only if I have to wear this thing again. I can find something to keep myself busy in London. But you think this could be the one?"

"I think I'm pretty close—" Olivia broke off as Alison placed her finger to her lips. "What's wrong?"

"I want to make sure that guy's not waiting out here. I thought he might follow me all the way to the ladies' room. I guess he gave up," Alison said after peering around the deserted gardens. "The maze is this way."

"Then, come, my dear lady Alison. Let us make haste to the revel!"

Alison led the way into a wide stone courtyard. She looked up at the sky, which was thick with grayish white clouds. Imperceptibly, the sky seemed to darken. "I think it's starting. We should hurry." Picking up their skirts, they shuffled as quickly as the billowing fabric would allow.

"So much for dignity," Olivia said as they scurried past the wide herb beds. All around them the gardens, some open, some bordered with high hedges, lay in some formal arrangement. "This is magnificent."

"If you think this is a sight, wait until you see Mrs. Higgins."

Choking back giggles, they passed an open rose garden,

arranged around a fountain, and another herb garden, this one laid out in concentric rings. High stalks of lavender scented the humid air.

"There's the maze." Alison nodded in the direction of a high hedge. "I think the coast is clear."

Practically scampering to keep up with Alison's longer strides, Olivia gathered her skirts. The costume was undeniably authentically uncomfortable in the heat. They must spend a fortune on dry-cleaning the sweat stains out, she thought as they stepped between the tall hedgerows. Box yews rose all around them and, straight in front, another row of hedges made a corridor that led off in both directions. "You sure they're in here?"

"Mrs. Higgins said we'd view the eclipse from the center." Alison paused and frowned again. "I think I hear them."

Olivia cocked her head, trying to listen closely with Alison. "I think you're right. This way!"

Down the narrow corridor between the high rows the two friends went, pausing at the opening. "This way?"

"No, this way," Olivia said, wishing she could remember what her father had told her about hedges and mazes. "Didn't Mrs. Higgins say something about this maze? It didn't sound that complicated—just keep turning in one direction and eventually you come—" They came to a dead stop. Hedges rose on all three sides. "Damn."

"Maybe we should've turned in the other direction." Alison winked.

Olivia laughed. If there was one thing she loved about her friend, it was her ability to always see the funny side of any situation. "Obviously."

"Come on."

Up and down the maze they walked, peering back and forth, straining to hear the voices, which seemed maddeningly elusive. The sky darkened even more, and Alison looked up. "Wow, look, Liv—it's the eclipse. Did you bring your funny glasses?"

"I think I left mine in the office."

"I left mine on the bus, or maybe back in the locker room."

As if in unspoken agreement, they slowed their pace as the clouded sky grew even grayer. The thick air stilled and, despite the darkened sky, the heat grew almost unbearably oppressive. Olivia felt waves of dizziness come over her, and she took a deep breath. She glanced at Alison's face and saw that her friend was pale. "Are you okay?"

"Yeah," she answered unconvincingly, "just a little queasy for some reason. Maybe I'm hungry."

"I feel strange, too," Olivia said. She took a deep breath. "How long is this supposed to last?"

"Just a couple minutes." Alison started to glance up, remembered the repeated warnings not to look at the sun, and looked down. "Let's go."

Olivia reached for Alison's arm as another wave of nausea rolled over her. "It's been more than a couple minutes." She glanced down at her watch, then remembered she'd left it in the locker room. The light began to brighten, and then, inexplicably, the sky darkened once more. "That's really weird," she murmured. "I don't think that's supposed to happen."

"There's something really weird about this maze," said Alison. "How long have we been in here?"

Before Olivia could reply, the whole scene seemed to shift in and out of focus. She took one step forward and stumbled, as though she'd tripped. She looked over her shoulder at the ground behind them, as the light began to strengthen at last, and saw nothing lying across the path. "Now that's really strange. I could've sworn—"

"Look—there's the entrance." Alison pointed.

"How—how could we have been that close—" Olivia broke off as they stepped out from between the high hedges.

"I don't know," Alison answered. "That was creepy. Thank heavens we're out of there. I thought for sure they'd have to send in a search party. Hey, where's that music coming from?" She raised her head and pointed. "Look—that wasn't there before."

A large buff-colored tent was pitched on a slight rise. Bright pennants of all shades of blue and yellow and russet flew from high stakes. The music—a high-pitched piping that began and ended in fitful starts as though someone was practicing—was definitely coming from that direction. The smell of cooking meat wafted past on the breeze. Olivia sniffed appreciatively. "Mm. That makes my mouth water."

Alison sniffed deeply, smiled, then gagged. "But, my God, get a whiff of that!" She made a face in the opposite direction. "What on earth—?"

Just then a young man in his middle to late twenties rounded a corner. He was dressed in authentically theatrical clothes, noted Olivia. In fact, the authentic side won out over the theatrical side, as she noted sweat stains under the arms of his doublet. His whole appearance seemed a bit grimy, as though his costume hadn't been cleaned thoroughly in some time. He was muttering to himself as he approached. "Excuse me!" she said.

He looked up with a startled expression, as though the two women were the last people he expected to see standing next to the entrance of the maze. An odd expression crossed his face, and Olivia continued: "Can you tell us how to reach our group? We got separated and we haven't been able—" She broke off as the young man's face drained of color.

His mouth dropped open, his eyes grew wide, and his face blanched. "By our Lady, it worked!" He stammered, just before he toppled over in a dead faint.

Chapter 2

ALISON BOLTED to his side, with Olivia, shocked and completely dismayed, close at her heels. She knelt beside Alison, who was feeling for his pulse, and loosened the ties that held the grayish-white ruff in place around his neck. "What do you suppose is wrong with him?"

"I don't know—he's not warm or anything . . . color's okay—except for being so pale—here, he's coming around. Must be the heat."

The young man's eyes fluttered open, and Olivia could see they were a shade of light brown, flecked with gold, almost the color of sherry. They widened the moment he glimpsed the two of them leaning over him. His mouth opened, and a little sound escaped.

"You'll be okay," Alison was saying. "Just lie there and take it easy. That costume's probably too hot for this weather. How about we get this top thing off?" She reached for the lacings of his doublet, and the man's mouth dropped open even further, revealing strong, even, white teeth.

"Mistress, what do you do?" He pushed her hand away with a horrified look and struggled to sit up and move away.

"I'm just trying to make you more comfortable. You've got to be sweltering in that get-up. Come on, take the top thing off."

"I will not!" The young man sat up and backed away, glancing at Olivia.

"We're only trying to help," she said. "Have you fainted like this before?"

A dazed look came over his face and he looked from one to the other, utter disbelief warring with something that could only be curiosity. "Your manner—your speech—you—both of you—you—" He broke off, his mouth hanging open in a way that made Olivia want to giggle despite his obvious distress.

Alison threw up her hands in disgust. "Here all we're trying to do is help you and all you can say is that we talk funny? Sorry that we're just a couple of lowly tourists trying to help. Is there a doctor on the staff here? A nurse? There's got to be someone around—look, Liv, you stay with Prince Charming here and I'll go see if I can find one of the guides. God only knows where our group has got to by now." She'd started to rise, brushing off the green satin of her gown, when the young man grabbed her wrist with an even more horrified look and pulled her back down.

"No!" he cried. "You mustn't go anywhere. No, you must not." He was looking from one to the other, and his breathing was coming in short, ragged gasps.

"Take it easy," said Olivia. "You're going to hyper-ventilate."

He slowly turned to look at her, eyes wide and frantic. "Hy-per-ven-ti-late?" He made another little sound, and shook his head slowly, turning back to stare at Alison. He shook his head again, clearly bewildered by the word. "Pray, mistress, we never do that—ever. Now, just, just—just wait." He raised both his hands, and held them up. "Good ladies, we'll just pause here and think. Yes, we'll just think a moment."

"About what?" demanded Alison. "Think about what?

We have to find someone to take care of you—you may have heat stroke or something. It's god-awful hot out here." She tugged at the neckline of her costume, and the young man's eyes widened once more in shocked horror.

"I prithee, madam, do not do that again!" He raised his hands to his face and stumbled to his feet. "The queen's grace will have you dismissed as a doxy, and, and that contraption you wear on your wrist—pray, hide it, for nothing like it yet exists."

"Huh?" Alison held up the yellow elastic band on her wrist. "This?"

"We'll all be burned at the stake for witchcraft, mistresses—Nicholas will see us all burned at the stake!"

"Burned at the stake?" Olivia stood up, brushing the loose grass from her own gown. "Look, you don't have to stay in character. We're only trying to help. I'm sure you won't get into any trouble. It's really hot today, and with all this humidity, and those clothes . . ." She reached out and plucked at his thick sleeve, and the young man jerked his arm away with a little gasp.

He shut his eyes and put one hand to his forehead. He bent his head, and Olivia noticed that his hair was nearly the same sherry color as his eyes, and that the nape of his neck was white. Clearly this was one actor who wasn't concerned with the pursuit of the perfect tan. "Let me think, mistresses. Let me think." He drew a few deep breaths and, turning away, visibly seemed to calm himself. When he turned back to face them, he seemed to have his emotions almost under control. "Tell me," he said, speaking with great deliberation, "tell me where you think you are."

Olivia exchanged glances with Alison. Alison lifted one eyebrow, as if to say: Let's play along. Olivia shrugged. "We're at Talcott Forest, just outside of Sevenoaks, Kent. In England."

"Ah." He nodded and stroked his chin. "Good. Now, tell me what year you think it is."

Olivia's eyes widened but Alison cocked her head.

"What in God's name are you talking about? It's 1999, of course. What year do you think it is?"

The young man swallowed hard, glanced up, and muttered, "Blessed Jesu." Then he said, "It's the year of grace fifteen eighty-seven, mistress. And Her Glorious Majesty, Elizabeth, has reigned over our fair country for nearly thirty years."

Alison rolled her eyes and made an impatient gesture. "Oh, come on, give it a rest. Look, let's just find someone who can tell us where the group has got to. I'm getting really hungry. I'll be the next one to faint if we don't get something to eat soon."

Instantly, the young man seemed solicitous. "You're hungry, mistress? Ah, that's good. Yes, that is good. I'll take you to the house and, uh, have a tray sent up to you both. And you'll be able to eat, while I—" He broke off and looked distressed once more. "Never mind that now. Just come with me, and I'll see you have plenty to eat." He reached to take her arm, but Alison stepped back, jerking her elbow out of his reach.

"Just what are you talking about? We don't want a tray. We're not going into the house. We have to find our group. We're supposed to be at the revel. There is a revel here, right?"

At that, the young man's face drained of color, and for a moment Olivia thought he might faint again. "Yes," he whispered faintly. "There is most undeniably a revel to be held here this day. Please, I beg you, good mistresses." He turned to Olivia with a look of supplication on his face. "I beg you come with me. There's more here than you know."

Something about the tone in the young man's voice rang true. There was an urgency that warned of real danger in his words and in his manner. Clearly he was very frightened. "Alison," Olivia said slowly, her gaze not leaving the young man's face, "I think—I think there is something going on here."

"Damn right there is, and we're missing all of it because this dolt won't—"

"I assure you I am not a dolt, mistress." The young man drew his slender body straighter with an injured air, and Olivia was amused to see that he towered even over Alison.

Olivia held up her hand, biting her underlip. She ran her eyes up and down his body, taking in every detail of his clothing. He was wearing a russet doublet made of wool and, beneath it, a linen shirt that looked as though it had never seen a proper wash. But it was his hose that made her stare. Instead of the nylon dance tights she was used to seeing actors and reenactors wear, these were thick, clearly handmade, and, although reasonably fitted, didn't cling to his legs with the same ease or flawlessness of fit. His shoes were blunt-toed and flat. She cocked her head, trying to assess what was odd about them, and realized suddenly that they could be worn on either foot. Not until the early seventeenth century had right and left shoes come into use. She swallowed hard as the evidence before her eyes began to mount into a conclusion so outrageous and absurd her mind reeled. "No, Alison—Alison, there's—there's something definitely—not right—" Her heart began to pound, and her breath caught in her throat. For a moment, she thought she might be the one to faint next. She drew herself up and, in what she hoped was the proper Elizabethan manner, asked, "Good sir, will you honor us with your name?"

He looked momentarily taken aback, but responded, with a little bow, "Geoffrey Talcott, at your service, mistress. And may I have the honor of knowing yours?"

"I'm Olivia Lindsley, and this is my friend Alison O'Neill. We're from"—she hesitated, wondering how he would react—"a country called the United States of America."

He stifled a short gasp. "America?" He glanced around with a wild expression in his eyes, and Olivia had the distinct impression that he thought he might be dreaming.

She practically expected him to pinch himself, but he only turned to look at both of them and forced a smile. "America? There's nothing there but a land of savages and—" He shook his head and broke off. "We'll talk more later. We *must* talk more later. But *now,* and I beg your forgiveness, ladies, you *must* come with me. We don't have any time right now—" He broke off again and glanced over his shoulder in both directions. Clearly he was afraid they would be seen. He beckoned. Olivia glanced at Alison, who shrugged, although the suspicion in her eyes never faltered. The women gathered their skirts and started off.

"Why aren't you taking us over there—" Alison began, pointing toward the tent, but broke off as they rounded the other side of the maze and the house came into view. "Oh, my God, the house," she whispered.

Olivia felt as though the air had been punched from her lungs. Geoffrey clutched her elbow harder as she sagged involuntarily. "I'm okay," she said, taking a deep breath. "Really. I'm fine." But the house that rose before them was very different from the one they had just left, a few scant moments ago. Talcott Forest in 1587 was smaller, without the Georgian touches and Victorian additions. The house had originally been built in the shape of an H, like so many other Tudor manor houses, and the brick was still relatively new. Ivy grew around the base of the walls, and the later terraces were notably absent, but clusters of great trees crowded close about the walls, trees that didn't exist in the twentieth century. Suddenly, in some cool, detached corner of her mind, Olivia understood why the house was called Talcott "Forest."

"What happened to the house?" Alison was whispering. Her face was as pale as the back of Geoffrey's neck.

"Don't you see, Alison?" Olivia said softly. "He's not playing a part. He's telling us the truth. He *is* Geoffrey Talcott, and this *is* fifteen eighty-seven. We've gone back in time."

"That's impossible," Alison snapped.

Olivia looked up at Geoffrey. Something about his manner—apologetic, startled but not disbelieving—and the words he'd used when he first saw them step out of the maze all seemed to indicate that, shocked as he might be, the notion of time travel wasn't quite as unbelievable to him as *they* thought it to be. "Is it?" she asked, with an accusing stare.

He cleared his throat and coughed, looking sheepish. "Well, mistresses, no, actually it isn't."

"What do you mean, it isn't?" Alison's hands were on her hips, and Olivia noticed that she was so tall, she practically looked Geoffrey in the eyes, something that the poor man obviously found disconcerting.

"Well, what I mean is, I did think—I—for the longest time—you see, the idea has intrigued me—and so I made a study and it seemed—the more I studied—it could be possible, and, well . . ." He hesitated once again, scraping his toe against the graveled ground.

"Well, what?" demanded Alison. "I've never heard of anyone traveling through time. Even now—even then—even in our century," she sputtered. "No one's ever done it."

"There are more things in heaven and earth, Horatio," quoted Olivia, speaking more softly still, "than are dreamt of in your philosophy."

Alison rolled her eyes. "What on earth are you talking about, Liv? You know it's impossible!"

Olivia drew a deep breath and slowly surveyed their surroundings. "Yes, I've always thought it had to be impossible. But"—she nodded first at Geoffrey and then at the house—"look around you, Allie. I think we're in the sixteenth century. I mean—smell!" She took a deep breath and beneath the odors of roasting meats and newly mown grass, a deep stench filled her nostrils.

Geoffrey looked apologetic. "I'm sorry, that's the middens. In the summer it's practically impossible to keep them smelling sweet—I guess you don't have that problem where you come from?"

"No!" said Alison. Her arms were still folded across her chest. "No, we certainly don't. So can you explain how we got here?" There was a distinctly schoolmarmish tone to her voice, and the steely gaze she fixed on him was calculated to cower the toughest kid from the meanest city streets.

"Well," Geoffrey began, looking even more uncomfortable than ever, "I suppose it is my fault."

"Your fault! You brought us back in time? Why? Why would you want to do such a thing? And how on earth did you do it?"

"Yes, what did you do?" asked Olivia, overcome with an almost academic curiosity. This was one for MIT.

"I built the labyrinth. You see"—he ran a hand through his mop of unruly curls and waved the other toward the massive hedges—"I've had this theory—about time. And I've done a lot of reading at university, you see, and studied a great deal with Dr. Dee—"

"Who?" asked Alison.

Geoffrey looked faintly shocked and Olivia answered smoothly, "He was Queen Elizabeth's physician and astrologer. He was revered as a man of very great and esoteric learning. Though I suppose at this point in some places, he still is," she finished with a wry smile.

"Exactly," said Geoffrey. "You are very learned, too, I see, mistress. Has no one yet built a time portal in your time?"

"No!" declared Alison. "No one's even tried such a thing. It's impossible!"

"Do we really know that, Allie?" Olivia shook her head as she gazed from the manor house to the clusters of trees to the high hedge behind them. "Do you really think it's the sort of thing we'd be told about, if the government or anyone else were experimenting with such a thing? Look at all the TV shows there've been about time travel. Everyone's considered it. And just because we don't know about it, why wouldn't it be possible that someone's done it?" She glanced up at Geoffrey, who was listening to this exchange with a confused look on his face. "Obviously, someone has."

Alison took a deep breath. "All right. I'll concede that maybe it's possible, and all right, I guess it can be done. But now what? How do we go back? Reverse the way we came? Walk backward through the labyrinth?"

Both women turned to Geoffrey, who flushed. "Well, mistresses." He paused. He sighed. "The truth of it is, I'm not quite sure. I—I must confess I don't know how it worked to bring you here. My intent was to go forward in time, not backward. And—and I never gave it any thought." He looked down at his shoe with the same sheepish look. "It, uh, it really didn't occur to me that I might bring someone back."

"Good God." Alison groaned as she rolled her eyes. "Spare me from mad science run amok. How did you think you were going to get back? Or didn't it ever occur to you that you might want to? Didn't you ever think that maybe you wouldn't like the future? Or not understand it? Or not want to stay?"

Geoffrey looked momentarily confused by this verbal onslaught. He opened his mouth, but almost instantaneously, his expression changed to one of alarm. "Oh, by our Lady," he whispered, his face blanching paler than it had when he'd fainted. "It's Nicholas."

"Who?" asked Alison, looking as confused as Geoffrey had just a moment ago, but Olivia drew herself up and automatically smoothed the blue satin skirt, her attention drawn to the tall, dark man in the center of the crowd who approached with an arrogant set of his shoulders. He was much too young to be Geoffrey's father, but in this time and place, thought Olivia, her judgment could be very wrong. His hair was dark and clipped close about his head in the Elizabethan manner, but it curled in soft ringlets about his ears, and on his forehead. He bore a strong resemblance to Geoffrey, but his coloring was more intense, as was the expression he was wearing when he saw

Geoffrey and the two women. He looked five or six years older than Geoffrey.

His clothing was far more ornate than Geoffrey's, for he wore a bright blue doublet shot through with silver threads that sparkled in the sun, and scarlet hose. His Venetian breeches were alternating panels of blue and scarlet. Olivia was momentarily dazzled by a style of masculine dress that was as brilliant as a peacock's display. He was not alone, Olivia noted, which was doubtless the cause of Geoffrey's immediate alarm. He was surrounded by at least thirty people, mostly men clothed in the same ornate elegance. Beside him, her hand on his arm, walked a white-faced woman wearing a curly, dark red wig and dressed in an elaborate gown of cloth of gold and black silk, ornately embellished with pearls. Her face, despite its masklike makeup, was animated; her lips moved as they walked. Everyone who followed was listening with rapt attention, and Nicholas's head was bowed down respectfully.

She could be only one person, thought Olivia as a shiver ran up her spine. To borrow from Mary Higgins, thought Olivia, here was the immortal Gloriana herself, on the arm of their own, albeit unknowing, host. Think fast, she told herself. "Alison, mind what you say and hide that key thing," Olivia said softly, speaking through clenched teeth. Beside her, Geoffrey was audibly breathing hard and looked as though he might faint again.

"Liv, who is—" Alison broke off as the party approached, but slipped the yellow elastic band off her wrist and hid it in her clenched palm.

"It's the Queen," Olivia replied, feeling her own face flush and then pale. "We have to be careful. Watch and do what I do."

And then there was no more time for words, for the entire party was upon them, and Geoffrey was bowing low, a polished courtly bow that was in some way subtly different from the theatrical bows Olivia was used to seeing, but there was no time to consider in just what way, for she, too, was sinking into a low curtsy that brought her nearly to the ground, and Alison, Olivia saw out of the corner of her eye, was imitating Olivia with a grace that made her suddenly grateful that her friend was such an accomplished athlete.

"And this, my lord, we assume is your brother, Geoffrey," a female voice, surprisingly low and lyrical, but commanding, spoke from just above Olivia's head, and her heart fluttered in her chest. There could be no doubt from the tone who was speaking. "A scholar of some repute, I trow? Dr. Dee has mentioned him to me in passing, my lord. You must be very proud."

Geoffrey gently raised both women to their feet as he himself straightened, and Olivia met the bright-eyed scrutiny of one of the most formidable women in all of history. "Geoffrey Talcott, at your service, Your Majesty. It is an honor this poor scholar never hoped to have."

"You speak as prettily as your brother, sirrah. I see whatever else you lack, it isn't want of manner." Elizabeth nodded approvingly, her gaze lingering on Geoffrey's shoulders. Olivia felt almost embarrassed by the frank, assessing stare. She hadn't expected such bold scrutiny from someone her father had revered almost as a goddess. She stole a glance at the courtiers who crowded around Elizabeth. Nearly all of them were male, and most were uncommonly good-looking. Elizabeth might well be the Virgin Queen, but she certainly had an eye for a handsome young man. No wonder she smiled up at Nicholas Talcott with such coquettish charm. "And who are his companions, my lord?" continued the Queen, turning a far less favorable look upon first Olivia and then Alison.

Nicholas himself looked puzzled as he opened his mouth to speak, but Geoffrey cut in, answering with a smoother lie than Olivia would have thought him capable of fabricating. "Cousins, Your Majesty, but newly arrived from the North."

Elizabeth raised one questioning eyebrow and looked the women over carefully, assessing their clothing with a jaundiced and well-practiced eye. "Indeed, Master Tal-cott?" It was obvious that her brain was working furi-ously, doubtlessly assessing the attire that was in actual fact nothing but a semblance of proper Elizabethan dress. Beside her, Nicholas's dark brows were gathered in one thunderous line across his face. He knows something's up, thought Olivia. If he knows anything at all about Geof-frey's theories, he has a good idea where we've come from. Nicholas had opened his mouth once more to speak, when Olivia, taking a deep breath, interrupted him.

"Distant cousins, Your Majesty," she said, aping Geof-frey's accent as best she could. She stepped forward and sank once more into a curtsy that she hoped was authentic. "My name is Olivia Lindsley and this is my sister, Alison. We are deeply honored to meet you."

"A forward chit," murmured Elizabeth. "Are you, now, girl? Stand up and let me look at you. Such clothing as yours I've never seen outside a mummers' show."

Olivia rose slowly, forcing her face to stay smooth. She was aware of undercurrents running through the crowd. Lindsley was a Scottish name, and it had raised a stir amongst the courtiers, who were crowding ever closer. She raised her eyes to the Queen's. Elizabeth gave her a smooth-faced stare, and then, with the abrupt change in manner chronicled by the contemporary accounts Olivia had read, dismissed her. "She looks thin and sallow, as one must when bred in the North. What say you, Lord Nicholas? The air of southern England is healthier, no doubt, and produces far more beautiful women."

"Your Majesty is, as usual, quite correct," Nicholas re-plied. This time his thunderous look went right to his brother, who smiled weakly in response. "And my brother"—he gave the word an ominous emphasis that Olivia didn't think boded well for any extended wel-come—"was about to take our two"—here he gave Geof-frey another baleful stare—"*guests* inside and show them to their lodgings. They must be wearied by their journey."

"What do they here?" put in one of the courtiers. He

was a burly man, big chested and bulky, dressed nearly as fantastically as the Queen, in green embellished with tiny gems that sparkled in the sunlight. His gray hair was clipped close to his head, but the lower half of his face was hidden by a full gray beard. His legs were slender in the tight-fitting hose, but his paunch hung over his sword belt, from which dangled an elaborately decorated scabbard. He gripped the hilt of his sword and leaned over the Queen with a certain proprietary air.

"My sweet Robin, do you think assassins hide in women's clothing these days?" Elizabeth chided. She tapped Nicholas's arm and tossed her head coquettishly. "Have you any more relations hiding about, my lord? My lord of Leicester will be poking about beneath the beds and twixt the stairs 'til he uncovers all your secrets."

Nicholas's face was murderous, and Geoffrey made a little choking sound that might have been a word that stuck in his throat. Olivia knew at once that the speaker was none other than Robert Dudley, the Earl of Leicester, Elizabeth's favorite since girlhood and the one man in England who'd come closest to marrying the Queen. The silence stretched out ominously, and Olivia, glancing at both brothers in turn, realized neither was capable of answering. There was much tension here, she thought. With a bright smile and an aim to defuse the mounting stress, she said, "We—we but thought to sing Your Majesty a song—a song to welcome you to Talcott Forest. We were about to take our places when you came upon us—we were somewhat startled by your arrival."

"Ah." Elizabeth smiled. "How clever of you, my lord." She raked the women once again with the same intense gaze, but smiled up at Nicholas, as though the explanation satisfied. Nicholas returned the Queen's smile with an uncomfortable one of his own that bordered on a grimace. "Have we so discomfited you, then, that the song is out of the question? Or will you sing it for us now, maiden?"

Olivia gulped, thinking quickly. "As Your Majesty wishes." She glanced at Alison, who was staring at her

with a shocked look. "Just, um, follow along, Alison—
and Geoffrey, you know your part?" She prayed that the
much-vaunted Elizabethan ability to harmonize was one
that had been encultured in Geoffrey. She drew a deep
breath, hoped that Shakespeare had borrowed from pop-
ular culture, and launched into the first song that came
into her head.

"Sigh, no more, ladies, sigh no more; men were
    deceivers, ever,
One foot on land and one on shore, to one thing
    constant, never.
Then sigh not so, but let them go, and be ye blithe
    and bonny,
Forgetting all your cares and woe with a hey,
    nonny, nonny!"

Alison hummed, a little off-key, but Geoffrey managed
to produce a smooth harmony that blended all three voices
into one melodious whole.

Elizabeth looked first a bit taken aback, but smiled graciously as the song came to an end. "So you'd bid me
have no care for men, would you, mistress?" she asked
as the song ended. She clapped her hands with a sly grin
at both Nicholas and Leicester. "Well done, wench.
You're a saucy thing, and you have an able voice. Take
this, with our gratitude." From her belt she removed two
white gloves, lavishly embroidered with pearls, and
handed one to Alison, who looked startled, and the other
to Olivia, who immediately sank into a deep curtsy. Geoffrey bowed, pulling Alison down beside him.

"You are a most gracious majesty," murmured Geoffrey.

Elizabeth smiled appreciatively as both Olivia and Alison murmured thanks. Olivia dared a peek at Nicholas.
He was standing stock-still, his expression still thunderous
and not at all mollified by the Queen's fortunate reception
of the song. "We're on our way to the pavilion, Geoffrey,"

Nicholas said through clenched teeth. "Will you join us as soon as you've seen to our guests?"

"In a moment," Geoffrey replied. "Mistress Alison felt a trifle unwell."

Olivia, watching the Queen beneath lowered lashes, saw Elizabeth raise one eyebrow and step back instinctively. " 'Tis just the heat, Your Majesty," she murmured. "My sister and I aren't used to this weather."

Elizabeth looked relieved. "Who could be? This air is frightfully close." She tapped Nicholas's arm. "Lead on, Lord Talcott. 'Tis best that none of us dither any longer in the hot sun. Let us away into the shade."

Nicholas bowed smoothly, an elegant, courtly bow that was at once so natural and so polished, it put Geoffrey's to shame. There were more actors than she could count who would give an arm to be able to move that gracefully. She noticed that he walked with the same easy grace, and that the lines of his shoulders beneath the embroidered doublet were broad, and tapered to a narrow waist and slim hips that even the puffed Venetian breeches could not hide. No wonder Elizabeth leaned upon his arm, glancing up at him as flirtatiously as a girl, despite her age, which in this year had to be at least fifty or fifty-five, thought Olivia, calculating rapidly. She sank into a deep curtsy as Nicholas led the Queen and her party past. She dared another peek through her lashes, and noticed another man following closely at the Queen's heels, one who seemed out of place among all the gaudily dressed courtiers. He was a tall, spare man, dressed in unadorned and unrelieved black, and his expression was stern and completely at variance with the laughing courtiers. In contrast to this man, Leicester, the Queen's sweet Robin, reminded her of an aging football player—a big man softening to fat after years of indulgent living—and he scowled at Nicholas as the Queen's laughter rose above the rest in response to some jest.

Beside her, she could feel Geoffrey trembling as the Queen's retinue went past. They rose, and Geoffrey, tak-

ing both their arms, led them firmly in the direction of
the house, moving quickly past the curious glances of the
courtiers. "Come with me, mistresses. Quickly."

Without any more conversation, he led them into the
house. Olivia scarcely had time to absorb the furnishings
of the high-ceilinged hall, but noticed that a huge fireplace
dominated one end of the room, and that two other fireplaces, both so high a tall man could stand inside them
flanked both sides. The floor was covered with long
reeds—rushes, thought Olivia—and from the rushes rose
a woodsy, herbal scent. She noticed lavender heads strewn
among the rushes. A raised dais at the opposite end of the
room from the fireplace was placed in front of an ornately
worked screen. Without pausing, Geoffrey led them behind the screen and indicated a staircase that led from the
hall to the floor above. Olivia noticed a sort of balcony
that overhung the hall. The musicians' gallery, she
thought, but all within the hall was quiet. The feast, the
revel—whatever they called it—was obviously being held
outside.

"Come." He gestured, indicating that the women should
climb the stairs. Alison looked dubious, but obeyed. They
followed Geoffrey down a short passageway, past two
doors on either side, and then paused as he pushed open
a third door. "In here."

The two women stepped past him into an Elizabethan
bedroom. A huge bed with heavily carved posts and head-
board dominated the entire room. The wood was dark, but
not nearly as black as similar furnishings Olivia had often
seen in museums and restored houses. It was hung with
embroidered hangings of red wool. They looked, thought
Olivia, stepping closer, as her curiosity got the better of
her, as though they'd seen better days. A table and two
chairs stood next to a relatively small, diamond-paned
window. The floor was bare, and the floorboards, though
clean, were worn smooth. The walls were white, as bare
as the floors, and the ceiling was relatively low.

"You must both wait here," Geoffrey said, indicating the chairs. "I'll return as soon as—"

"Wait!" cried Alison. "What do you mean, wait here? For how long? We can't wait here—we have to get back to our own time. Where are you going?"

Geoffrey glanced from one to the other with an apologetic look. "I'm afraid that's not possible, mistress." He glanced over his shoulder, and, shutting the door behind him, stepped into the room. "You must understand that the Queen's visit is a great honor, and one that my brother has most devoutly sought." He looked frustrated for a moment, and then spoke rapidly, in a low voice, as though he were afraid the very walls might overhear and report their conversation. "You should know, mistresses, that the fortunes of my family have suffered much since King Harry decided he knew better than the Pope of Rome how best an Englishman should worship God. We Talcotts have always been Catholics: loyal to the King, but loyal also to the Pope, and ever mindful of the Lord's injunction to render unto Caesar that which is Caesar's and to God that which is God's. But those are sometimes dangerous sentiments, even now, under our Gracious Majesty. She can blow hot and cold, and Nicholas, who desperately hopes to restore the fortunes of our family—"

"Then why not convert to the new religion?" interrupted Alison. "What difference can it make?"

Geoffrey looked a trifle shocked, but recovered quickly with a wry grin. "I see you come from a far more practical age than ours, mistress. Nicholas thinks much as you do, and has, in fact, gone over to the new religion, but allegiances, and the perception of allegiances—even to an outworn creed—die hard in ours. We Talcotts are seen as Catholic because our father and grandfather before him were Catholic. I am not so sure what difference it makes, either, but in the meantime, until he proves his loyalty to the Queen, such a thing as your appearance in this time and place—" He broke off, and his mouth was grim. Suddenly he looked very old, and Olivia realized that the stresses of the sixteenth century were every bit as acute as those of the modern age. "We could be burned for witchcraft, if it were suspected who you are," he finished.

"We'll stay out of sight," Olivia said quickly.

"Thank you." He looked at Alison. "I'm sorry for any trouble I may have caused you, mistress. Such was never my intent. But unless you can tell me that lives hang in the balance in your time, I'm afraid my brother's needs must take precedence over yours." Without waiting for a response, he bowed out of the room, firmly shutting the door as he went.

"Well, that's just great." Alison strode over to the door and opened it, peering out into the hall. "At least he didn't lock us in here. This is the room that's supposed to be haunted, according to the tour guide."

Olivia let out a loud sigh and sank down into one of the chairs. It felt stiff and cold and alien, and she shifted her weight, trying to find a comfortable spot.

"What are we going to do?" Alison asked, turning back to face Olivia. She closed the door carefully. "How long do you think this revel is going to last?"

Olivia shrugged. "At least 'til dark. It doesn't sound as if the Queen is staying here—she just came for dinner."

"Oh, that's even more great." Alison rolled her eyes. "And what time was the bus leaving?"

"I think we were supposed to be back in London by eleven, so I guess the group would leave around nine."

"Nine o'clock." Alison shook her head. "What time do you suppose it is now?"

There was a long silence. Finally Olivia met her friend's eyes. "I don't think it matters."

Alison strode over to the other chair and sat down. "What—what do you mean?" For the first time, Olivia heard the little catch in her friend's throat that meant that she was upset.

She drew a deep breath. "I don't think it matters what time it is right now." She spoke very gently. "I'm afraid it might not be quite so easy to get home."

Alison bent her head, and the short fall of her strawberry-blond curls hid her face. For a long moment, she was silent. Finally, her shoulders heaved as she drew a deep breath. "What are we going to do?"

Olivia shrugged. She leaned over and patted Alison's shoulder. "It'll be okay. We'll find a way to get back—somehow. If it worked one way, it's got to be able to work the other. It's a pattern—it can't be that difficult to reverse it. It's just that while we're here—" She broke off and bit her lip, trying desperately to remember all she knew about the middle years of the reign of Elizabeth I. But at the moment, it was all a jumbled mess—of new religions and usurping Tudors and imprisoned Scottish queens. But Shakespeare had begun to write his great plays, and Marlowe and Jonson—She raised her head with a start. Somewhere in this time, a man named William Shakespeare had just made his way from a little town in Warwickshire to London. His greatest works probably weren't even glimmers in the writer's eye. Had he even appeared in London yet, or was he still in Stratford? For one minute, she tried to remember, and then dismissed all thoughts of Shakespeare, London, and the Globe Theater. She really was every bit as undisciplined and unfocused as her father used to say. Deliberately, she forced herself to think about the matter at hand.

Alison was watching her. "What do you mean, while we're here?"

Olivia sighed. "This is a very difficult time in Elizabeth's reign. Mary, Queen of Scots, had become a focal point for anti-Elizabethan and anti-Protestant sentiment—there's evidence of plots and treason—all aimed to get Mary on the throne of England and restore Catholicism as the true religion. If this is fifteen eighty-seven—let's say for the sake of argument, it's August fifteen eighty-seven—Mary was executed in February of this year. But even after Mary died—which was something Elizabeth eventually had to order because of the threat to her own life—Spain vowed retaliation, which was really just an excuse to plan an invasion of England. Remember the Spanish Armada?"

Alison nodded slowly.

"I imagine in the shipyards of Spain, even as we sit here, the ships are being built." A little shiver rippled down her spine. What would her father have given to spend even five minutes in this time and place? A wave of sadness came over her as she realized that whatever knowledge she'd managed to acquire from him was going to have enormous importance until they could return.

"But, but," Alison was saying, "but what about our families? If we don't get back soon—" She broke off and dropped her eyes. The only family Olivia had left was a seventy-seven-year-old aunt in a nursing home in New Jersey. Following her last stroke, the woman didn't even recognize her niece. Except for Alison and her own family, Olivia was truly alone. "I'm sorry, Liv, you know what I mean. My family's going to be just as worried about you. Mom's probably going to think it was all my fault. She's always saying I get you into trouble. And what about our friends? Our jobs? What about poor Mrs. Higgins? She's probably all in a tizzy by now at least. She must be frantic."

Olivia gave another deep sigh and, rising, walked to the window. Her ersatz costume swished around her legs. She peered out, but could see little through the leafy green branches of the great trees that hugged the walls of the manor. She strained her ears and, faintly, through the thick leaded glass, thought she could hear the sound of music— of high-pitched piping and the deeper drone of something that sounded like a bagpipe. "I can't imagine what they'll do. And yeah, I agree. Your mom's going to give new meaning to the word *upset*. I wouldn't want to be whoever she's going to talk to from the travel agency."

"How long do you think this will take?"

"Hopefully, if the Queen is only staying for dinner they'll be gone before it gets dark. And then maybe after that we can try—or first thing tomorrow."

"Tomorrow?" Alison squeaked. "Sleep here?"

Olivia looked at the huge bed. "I think there's room enough for two."

"It's not that, Liv." Alison got to her feet and began to pace restlessly. "That older brother gave me the creeps, the way he was looking at us, but especially at you, and the younger one—that Geoffrey—I guess every century has its nerds. And this room gives me the creeps."

"Well, it's probably not haunted yet," Olivia said lightly, trying to inject some humor. "Most likely any ghosts haven't even been born."

"I'm not talking about a ghost!" Alison threw herself into one of the chairs. She picked up the glove the Queen had given her and spread it on the table. "And what about this thing? What are we supposed to do with it?"

"This is actually a very valuable gift." Olivia sank down into the opposite chair and smoothed both gloves out side by side. "Look at the workmanship on the beading—and feel the quality of the leather? Things must be looking up for Lord Nicholas," she murmured as she picked up one of the gloves and peered at it closely. The white leather was soft and supple. Each stitch was tiny and precisely placed. The back of each glove was embroidered with intricate knots and beadwork, lavishly worked with pearls. "Look at this," she murmured as she ran a fingertip over the exquisite stitches. "Can you believe how beautifully it's done? I mean, it seems weird to us, Allie, but this is actually worth a very great deal now. This gift means—"

"Good grief, Liv, stop mooning over that—that artifact and let's think about—"

Suddenly the door opened. Both women jumped to their feet. Framed by the dark wood, Lord Nicholas Talcott stepped into the room, his broad shoulders rigid, his chiseled mouth tight. "You—Mistress Lindsay—come with me."

Olivia exchanged glances with Alison. "My name is

Lindsley, Lord Nicholas. And where do you expect me to go?"

"The Queen commands your presence." He glanced over his shoulder, took another step into the room, and pulled the door shut. He clenched and unclenched his hands with suppressed tension and, fleetingly, Olivia was frightened. The man was like a coiled spring, every fiber of his being held in uneasy check. "Come here and let me look at you."

Startled, the women exchanged another glance, and Olivia had the uncomfortable feeling she was being scrutinized with the same detachment as the man might give to the once-over of a mare.

"Come here." He made an impatient gesture. "Her Majesty is not the most patient of women these days, and your dress is—most odd." He seemed to understand exactly who they were, however, and Olivia surmised he must've seized a few private words with his brother. You had to give him credit, she thought. For someone who'd never even heard of Einstein, he was taking the idea of time travel with remarkable aplomb. Or maybe it was simply his survival instincts. He was clearly determined to make the best of the situation at the moment.

Olivia edged forward a couple of steps. Alison held her ground, and Olivia noticed that Alison was nearly as tall as Nicholas. Beside the two of them, she felt unexpectedly dwarfed. *Thank God Alison is here,* she thought suddenly as his eyes raked over her. She pulled herself to her full height of five feet, three inches, and squared her shoulders as his gaze lingered on her bosom. "Well, sir?"

It was his turn to look startled. "Mistress?"

"Am I to your liking? Do I satisfy?" She hoped she sounded more authentic than she looked.

"Your costume is outlandish, mistress. Were it not for the fact that my brother has been spinning a tale even more outrageous than the truth for Her Majesty's entertainment, I've no doubt we'd all be clapped in irons by now."

"Then why not let her just stay here?" put in Alison. "I don't want to go out there any more than you want us to. Surely it's safer if we both stay put."

He gave Alison a look that bordered on disgust. "Do you not understand, mistress? The Queen commands her presence. And no one gainsays the Queen's commands."

"Well, just tell her Olivia's indisposed or something. Tell her she's sick."

At that he shook his head and made an impatient gesture. "Good God, mistress, if you do not understand what you have been brought to, by God's grace, hold your tongue."

"We're not in Kansas anymore, Dorothy," murmured Olivia. She reached for Alison's hand and gave it a reassuring squeeze. "And when in Rome . . ."

". . . Do as the Romans do?" Alison finished.

Nicholas listened to this exchange with a furrowed brow. "Our lives hang in the balance, mistresses. You, mistress"—here he paused and his intense blue eyes fastened on Olivia—"have managed to captivate our Queen. And thus she wishes another song. I hope you have one ready."

Olivia drew a quick breath, searching through her remembered repertoire of Elizabethan and Jacobean music. "I can sing another, if Her Majesty wishes."

"Her Majesty does assuredly so desire, mistress. Believe me, if I thought there was a way to keep you from her presence, I would've employed it." He put his hands on his hips, and Olivia could not help but notice how the doublet and hose emphasized the slimness of his waist and the breadth of his shoulders. And the codpiece . . . She dropped her eyes, feeling a telltale warmth rise in her face. It appeared to be merely decorative. She glanced at Alison from beneath her lowered lashes. She wasn't sure how much her friend knew about sixteenth-century clothing, but this would be good for a giggle later. And God knew they'd need to find some way to break the tension. Alison's cheeks were pale, but her mouth was pinched

tight, and her brows were drawn together in the way that
told Olivia her friend had reached her limit. Nicholas took
another long look at both of them and finally shook his
head. "There's no time to find you anything else to wear.
Those clothes—she's remarked three times about the colors—" He shut his eyes and Olivia had the distinct impression that his head ached. Suddenly she felt sorry for
him. This mess was not of his making. "Come along
now."

He opened the door and stepped aside, allowing her to
precede him from the room. In the hall, he took her firmly
by the arm and led her back down the stairs, out of the
house, and back into the gardens, muttering instructions
all the while.

Finally, just as the top of the tent—or the pavilion, or
whatever they called it—came into view, Olivia paused.
"Lord Nicholas," she began.

"What is it?" He tapped his foot impatiently.

She raised her chin once more and stared right into his
eyes, trying to ignore the fact that they were the bluest
eyes she'd ever seen. "My friend and I—we want you to
know that this wasn't our idea. We certainly had no intention of crashing—of intruding into your party or your
life, and we apologize if our presence here creates any
awkwardness for you. We are both aware of how tenuous
your situation—and ours—is at the moment. And we are
not quite the doddering bumpkins you apparently think us
to be. We understand, sir, that lives hang in the balance
here. And we will certainly do our best to follow the necessary cues in order to bring this off to our mutual satisfaction."

Nicholas's face softened an infinitesimal amount. He
raised his head and looked at the colored flags flying from
the corners of the pavilion and at the great red and gold
crest that announced Elizabeth's presence. "If we all yet
live by dawn tomorrow, mistress, I will be well satisfied."

Olivia raised her chin and squared her shoulders with
an assurance she didn't feel, hoping to defuse the tension.

Elizabeth was no fool. If they didn't act as naturally as possible, she would sense that something was afoot. She forced herself to meet his eyes with a smile and, momentarily, the stern look he wore softened. Well, she thought, hadn't she always wanted to be an actress? This was going to be the greatest performance of her fledgling career. "Then lead on, Lord Nicholas. Even in my time, Her Majesty is known as the most impatient of women."

Chapter 3

OLIVIA'S HEART POUNDED in her chest, and she found herself clutching Nicholas's arm with a grip like a vise. A few of the faces that turned to look at them as they rounded the corner into view of the pavilion seemed friendly—some men raised their goblets as Nicholas passed, and smiled or bowed, and one or two even offered cheerful jests or toasts to his health. But most of the courtiers only stared silently as they went by, and Olivia sensed Nicholas's anxiety rise to an even higher level. So much depended upon both their performances, she reflected. She forced herself to smile and nod graciously to even the most suspiciously hostile of faces, as though she, too, were to the manor born and had every right to be here, on the arm of this admittedly good-looking hunk of a guy, who happened to be an English lord to boot. They reached the open space before Elizabeth's dais, and sank into low obeisances. Olivia looked up to see the dour-faced Puritan in Elizabeth's train staring at her, his expression one of disgust mixed with something that in another man she would have thought blatant desire. She suppressed a shudder and fixed her eyes on Elizabeth, who was watching her with a bright, dark-eyed stare.

Olivia met the Queen's gaze squarely, knowing instinctively that Elizabeth would recognize any kind of prevarication or dissembling.

"Welladay, mistress," Elizabeth was saying, tapping her fan against the arm of her chair, "your song pleased me greatly. Can you give us another?"

Olivia drew a deep breath. "It would be my very great pleasure, Your Majesty." Nicholas had withdrawn to the side, where he stood watching with folded arms. She glanced in his direction. His expression was wary. Here goes nothing, she thought. With a deep breath, she launched into one of her favorite songs from *Twelfth Night*.

> *"Oh, mistress mine, where are you roaming?*
> *Oh, stay and hear, your true love's coming,*
> *Who can sing both high and low.*
> *Seek no further, pretty sweeting, journey's end in*
>   *lovers' meeting—*
> *Every wise man's son doth know.*
> *In delay there lies no plenty,*
> *Then come kiss me, sweet-and-twenty,*
> *Youth's a stuff 'twill not endure."*

As she began the second verse, she was startled to hear other voices chiming in, picking out harmonies and embellishing the top notes with trills and little vibratos. Her gaze darted among the crowd of courtiers, most of whom joined in the singing enthusiastically. The song went on and on, with Elizabeth herself joining in, her voice a surprisingly strong contralto, rich and sure. As the song ended, Olivia dared a peek at the sour old Puritan whose eyes seemed to bore through the flimsy fabric of her costume. She felt a hot flush creep up her neck, and she shifted her gaze to Dudley, burly and balding. He was sitting next to the Queen on the opposite side from the Puritan, watching Olivia with amiable interest. He winked and she automatically smiled back as all the voices faded into silence. She glanced at Nicholas, who had not moved.

The Queen smiled and applauded enthusiastically, and the entire company followed suit. Olivia remembered that Elizabeth was known for her gracious reception of all the entertainments offered for her pleasure on her visits to her subjects, and she sank into another curtsy as the Queen spoke. "A pleasant, if melancholy, tune, maiden, but well sung."

Olivia rose, wondering how long she would be required to stay before the Queen, but Nicholas was there, stepping beside her, bowing with that same polished grace even as he said, "If Your Gracious Majesty will allow, Mistress Lindsley will retire. She is yet fatigued from the journey, and her sister is unwell."

Elizabeth smiled fleetingly and raised her hand in dismissal, her attention diverted by Leicester, who leaned upon her arm and whispered something in her ear that made her laugh. Olivia saw the Queen glance at the sober Puritan and laugh again, but the meaning of the byplay was lost, as Nicholas once more took her arm and escorted her from the pavilion.

When they were safely out of earshot, he said gruffly, "Thank God you pleased Her Majesty well enough. Now stay out of sight, until either my brother or I come for you."

Olivia looked up at him in disbelief. She'd saved both of them with that performance, and he couldn't even offer so much as a simple thank-you? She didn't speak as he strode into the house, his long strides practically forcing her to scamper just to keep up. He marched her into the house and up the steps. At the door to the room he paused. "Remember, stay here and don't leave this room."

Olivia raised her chin. "You forget, Lord Nicholas, that neither my friend nor I am any happier than you are that we find ourselves here."

Nicholas shook his head and looked over his shoulder, as though he feared someone listened. "My brother is a heedless fool who thinks only of his own interests. Give me your word you will not leave this room."

Olivia met his eyes fearlessly. "You have my word. There is no need to lock us in."

Nicholas hesitated, clearly torn. "Very well, mistress. I will trust your good sense not to risk your own lives." He pushed the door open and waited for her to walk through. Without another word, he pulled it shut behind her, and she heard his footsteps echo down the stairs.

Nicholas breathed a sigh of relief as he pounded down the stairs. His footsteps echoed in the silent hall. Thanks be to the God who'd made them all that the one woman, at least, had the presence of mind to understand his need. Which was more than that fool of a brother did. He'd known exactly what had happened the moment he'd seen the two women standing beside the maze, dressed in their bizarre clothing, Geoffrey beside them with a sheepish look all over his face. It was bad enough that Geoffrey and his eccentricities, as Nicholas preferred to name them, should ever put them in danger of the Tower or worse. Fortunately, with the execution of Queen Mary of Scotland, Elizabeth seemed to have lost her taste for punishing Papists. But nothing would save them from a charge of witchcraft—and Geoffrey would be hard pressed to explain how the two women had appeared if he were ever dragged into a court, ecclesiastical or otherwise. He ran a hand through his dark hair and tugged his doublet into place. Just a few more hours and the Queen and her retinue would be gone. And then he would have to deal with the women and his brother. Pray that the maze was as effective in reverse, and the two women could be returned to wherever they happened to come from. Without warning, a vision of Olivia's face rose before him, her expression the soft and earnest one she'd worn to sing before the Queen. Then it rapidly changed to become the determined look she'd had when she confronted him about their unexpected appearance. Fleetingly, he wondered what it would be like to talk to her about her time, and then he instantly dismissed such a dangerous thought. The less he knew about the whole appalling episode the better. And as soon as it was safe to do so, he'd have Geoffrey dismantle that damnable maze. God only knew who—or what—might come stumbling out of it next.

A soft cough from the side of the room startled Nicholas out of his reverie. He glanced around to see a simply dressed man sitting on one of the long benches that lined the walls of the hall. With a start he recognized the man as Master Christopher Warren, someone he'd assumed was one of Elizabeth's gentlemen pensioners, the male equivalent of a lady-in-waiting. But the man was dressed nearly as plainly as the Puritan Sir John Makepiece. The thought of Sir John brought an unpleasant taste to Nicholas's mouth, and he forced the image of the man out of his head even as he walked slowly over to the man, who clearly waited for him. "May I help you, sir?" Nicholas asked, puzzled as to why the man would have followed him into the house, and cold all over at the thought that perhaps he'd noticed the suspicious behavior of Geoffrey and the two women.

"I wondered if we might have a word, my lord." Master Warren smiled, and Nicholas noticed that his lips merely folded, and that the expression did not reach his eyes.

"An you will, sir. Master Warren, isn't it? Is there something you require?"

"Not I, my lord, but the Queen."

Nicholas frowned, genuinely perplexed. "The Queen is well served, I trust. She seems quite pleased."

"Ah, by the feast, yes, of course. Your hospitality has pleased her greatly, and your choice of entertainment is most—most charmingly unconventional. But that's not what I meant, my lord. There are other matters—matters in which it's come to our attention that you might have an interest."

"What sort of matters?" Nicholas asked.

"You know of the work of Sir Francis Walsingham?"

Nicholas's lip nearly twisted in a grimace, but he forced

himself to keep his face smooth. A chill ran down his spine. There had been talk that the Babington plot and the executions that had followed it had been a concoction of Walsingham's ferocious determination to see Mary of Scotland dead. Any member of any Catholic family, no matter how loosely connected to the Roman faith, knew of Walsingham and his fanatical hatred of Catholics. "Who doesn't?"

"We know how hard you've worked to establish yourself as a loyal subject of Her Majesty."

Nicholas began to frown at the implication that he'd been under scrutiny and just as quickly forced the expression off his face. "Then you know of my implicit and absolute allegiance."

Warren spread his hands. "Your valor with Lord Leicester in the Low Countries was remarked upon far and wide. And thus we turn to you, in hope that you will perform another service for Her Majesty, such as can only be performed by a man of courage and discretion."

This time Nicholas did frown. There was something about the man that made him wary, something about the flat look in his dark eyes that made Nicholas's blood run cold. "What sort of service?"

"Please, my lord. Will you sit?" With a broad sweep of his hand, Warren indicated the empty space beside him on the bench.

I'd sooner sit beside a snake, thought Nicholas, then instantly suppressed the feeling. Walsingham's crew might be fanatical, but he knew that the Queen and Cecil, her secretary, trusted them implicitly. If he had merited the favorable notice of Sir Francis, it could only be a positive thing. "What can I do for you, sir?"

"We have reason to believe that the King of Spain continues in his plots against our most gracious Majesty. An agent of the Spanish government has been intercepted in London—an Englishman, I might add. He was to meet a member of the Spanish government in Calais and receive the plans for an invasion of England. But we have him in our custody now. Still, we would like to have the plans. So—"

"You would want me to masquerade as this Englishman and go to Calais?"

Warren smiled. "You understand perfectly, I see."

"Who is this English traitor?"

"A man of no consequence any longer, I assure you. But you will travel under his name to disguise your true identity. You bear a certain resemblance to this man, you see. That's why I have been instructed to come to you."

Nicholas stared into the empty hearth, his mind racing furiously. "I will think on it."

Warren's expression did not change. "An you will, my lord. But think on it quickly, I pray you. Time grows short, and all who endeavor to keep our shores free of the Spanish threat will be amply rewarded."

"I've not refused."

"I leave for London at dawn. I had hoped to return to my master with an affirmative response."

Nicholas took a deep breath, considering. There was no reason why he shouldn't agree. Except, perhaps, Geoffrey and his damnable interests. The thought of the two women waiting in the upstairs bedchamber flashed through his mind. If Walsingham had any suspicion . . . "I'll do it." He turned back to face Warren and met the man's inscrutable eyes.

"Excellent," Warren replied. He got to his feet. "My master will be well pleased, and your efforts on Her Majesty's behalf will be well rewarded, I assure you."

Nicholas rose as well. "Then if you'll excuse me, Master Warren, I must return to my guests. Are you coming?"

Warren smiled again, another smile that didn't reach his eyes. "I'm just on my way to the jakes, my lord. I'll be there in a trice."

Nicholas nodded. He inclined his head in a brief bow and left the hall, fighting the urge to turn back, and wondering why he felt as though Warren watched him like a hawk poised to kill.

• • •

Olivia let out a deep breath as Nicholas's footsteps faded out of earshot. Her shoulders sagged with suppressed tension as Alison turned from the window. "Liv! Are you okay? What happened?"

Olivia shrugged. "I sang another song. One from *Twelfth Night,* this time. I hope I haven't caused some disruption in the time-space continuum."

"What are you talking about?" Alison was looking at her as if she'd suddenly grown an extra head. "What time-space continuum?"

"You know." Olivia grinned. "The one they're always talking about on TV—*Quantum Leap, Star Trek,* that sort of thing. Whenever anyone goes into the past, there's always concern about whether or not they're going to change the future by their presence in the past."

"Good grief, Liv." Alison rolled her eyes and sank down into her chair. "Don't you think that's the least of our worries right now? How soon do you think we can try to go back?"

Olivia shook her head. "I guess if Elizabeth and the court are gone by tonight, there's no reason we couldn't try once everything quiets down. But it's a huge undertaking out there—you should see all the people."

"I can smell the food." Alison looked longingly out the window.

"Nicholas said he'd send something up to us." Olivia crossed the room and sat down opposite Alison.

Just as she did so, there was a knock at the door. "Enter."

A sheepish Geoffrey ducked his head beneath the lintel and pushed the door open with his foot. In his hands he carried a basket covered with a linen napkin. "My apologies, mistresses. I know you, Mistress Alison, said you were hungry before. I had no way to slip away 'til now. I hope the food is to your liking." He placed the basket on the table with a little bow.

The fragrance of freshly baked bread and roasted meat

rose from the basket, and Alison pushed the napkin aside.

"There's everything you need in there, I think." Geoffrey looked from one to the other with supplication, and
clearly seemed torn between a desire to stay and talk and
the knowledge that Nicholas demanded his presence with
their guests.

"We'll be okay," Alison said.

"We'll be fine," Olivia put in, seeing confusion cross
his face at the strange word.

"Okay?" He repeated. "It means—fine?"

"Yeah," said Alison, "it's a general sort of all-purpose
word. It gets used a lot."

"Ah." He nodded, digesting the information. "I see.
Okay." He smiled. "Okay." He nodded at the food. "This
is—okay?"

Alison laughed, and Olivia was glad to see her friend
relax. "Right. The food's okay, but you better get back to
your brother, because I have the feeling you won't be
okay if you don't."

"Ah." He returned her smile. "Right." He crossed to the
door, reached for the doorknob, and turned back to the
women. "I'll be back as soon as I can. And you'll see,
everything will be—okay." He shut the door behind him.

Alison turned to Olivia. "For a nerd, he's kinda cute."

Olivia rolled her eyes. "This is hardly the time to notice. What'd he bring us?"

Alison removed the napkin. "Hmm. Here's what looks
like bread—wow—whole grain, huh?"

She handed Olivia what looked like a large dinner roll.
"Actually," said Olivia thoughtfully, turning the crusty
loaf in her hands, "this is probably the equivalent of our
most refined white bread. What else?"

"A nice cheese . . . a flask of something . . . here's some
cherries . . . and, well, I guess this must be the equivalent
of take-out burgers, huh?" She held up a haunch of what
smelled like beef on an earthenware platter. "Here's more
napkins, and plates, and two cups, and knives. Hmm, no
forks or spoons." She placed the items on the table.

"Forks weren't in widespread use yet," Olivia said. "And I guess there's nothing here that requires a spoon. Let's eat, shall we?"

For a few minutes, the women were silent, munching the crusty bread, the mild cheese, and the roasted meat. The food, although somewhat bland, had an undeniably fresh taste to it, which defied Olivia's attempts to describe it.

"It's good, isn't it?" asked Alison between bites, as if reading her thoughts. "Better than I thought it would be, anyway."

"Yes." Olivia nodded. "Salt would help, but otherwise, it's not bad at all."

"Meat kind of tastes barbecued, don't you think?"

"Well, it was roasted on a spit over an open flame. I guess it is barbecued." Olivia shrugged and they went on eating.

Finally Alison wiped her mouth and fingers. "Liv? What if we can't get back?"

Olivia met her friend's eyes reluctantly. The same thought had occurred to her more than once, but she'd managed to suppress it, pushing it down into the dark recess where she kept all the thoughts she'd rather not confront. "We haven't even tried yet, Allie."

"I was thinking the whole time you were gone . . ." Alison turned her head away from Olivia, but from the little catch in her voice, Olivia could tell she was upset. "What if we just can't get back? What if we're stuck here?"

"Oh, Allie." Olivia set aside her napkin, rose, and put her arm around her friend's shoulders. "It'll be okay. You'll see. We'll get back. I know we will."

Alison took a deep breath. "I'm not so sure, Liv. And it's one thing for you—you know so much about the history, and you're an actress. You'll be able to figure out what to do. But me—I'm a walking liability every time I open my mouth! You at least have an idea of the lingo— me, I'd sound like a puffed-up snob if I tried to talk that way. If we can't get back, I'm screwed."

"Allie, it's going to be okay. I'm sure of it. Look, if it
worked once, it's bound to work again."

"But if it's really as simple as building a maze, why
isn't it done all the time? Why aren't there people popping
in and out of the past every day?"

"Well," Olivia said slowly, trying to think of something
that would allay her friend's fears, "who says it isn't that
simple? We just don't know, Allie. Do you really think
the governments would want to encourage this sort of
thing? Or let the public know about it?" She retreated to
her chair and picked up her napkin. "Come on, let's try
to remember exactly how it happened. And, um, while
we're at it, why don't you pour us some of whatever's in
that flask? We might as well experience as much of the
past as we can while we're here."

"A word if you will, my lord." Sir John Makepiece
stepped out from the side of the pavilion just as Nicholas
signaled for the musicians to begin their final round of
dance music. The middle of the pavilion was crowded
with dancers, and Elizabeth herself was leading, energet-
ically dancing with a red-faced, sweating Leicester, who
was practically jogging in time at her side.

Nicholas allowed himself to be led a little way apart.
"Sir John?"

"Your two—guests," began Sir John, his thin mouth
pursed tight. "I was quite surprised to see them."

"No more so than I," answered Nicholas, with complete
honesty. Damn Geoffrey and his single-minded passion.

"Indigent cousins, I assume?"

"Ah, well . . ." Nicholas hesitated. It would never do
for the man he was considering as a future father-in-law
to think that extraneous relations burdened the Talcotts.
"Not exactly. Unexpected, as you say, but not indigent."

"Good." Sir John gave him a tight-lipped smile and
turned away.

"Sir John," Nicholas began. "I was expecting to meet
with you on the morrow to discuss your daughter's hand."

An odd expression crossed the knight's face. "If you wish, my lord."

"Is it something you no longer wish to entertain?"

"My daughter is young yet, my lord, being but fifteen and somewhat flighty. But we can talk on't, tomorrow." Abruptly he turned and walked quickly away, leaving Nicholas wondering what could have brought about the knight's change of heart. Geoffrey, he thought. Geoffrey and those damnable women. Involuntarily, Olivia Lindsley's face flashed before him—the smooth oval upturned, the way her dark eyes had flashed with fire, her sweet voice raised in song. She was nothing like Patience Makepiece, whose pale looks and skinny frame were like a watered-down version of Sir John. Not exactly the sort of wife he'd envisioned for himself, but the promise of a healthy dowry and her father's inheritance were exactly the sort of infusions the Talcott fortunes desperately needed. Especially after this, he thought, hands on his hips, surveying the dancing crowd. Elizabeth's red head bobbed enthusiastically as she romped through a country dance with yet another courtier—a younger one, this time, who looked as though he was better at keeping up with the Queen than Leicester was. Leicester had returned to his seat, where he was quaffing large gulps of wine. He'd been a good friend to Nicholas. Perhaps he could advise on whether or not an alliance with Sir John's family was judicious.

Night had fallen by the time Geoffrey came back for them. A soft knock on the door roused Olivia from a fitful sleep. Beside her, Alison lay oblivious under the sheet, curled up on her side, wearing only her underwear. Her discarded costume was folded across one of the chairs. Olivia sat up and paused, trying to remember where she was. Then a long sliver of moonlight falling through the leaded panes of the window made her remember. The past. Fifteen eighty-seven. Talcott Forest. Olivia slid to the floor, grabbing a blanket from the bed and wrapping it around herself. "I'm coming!" she whispered loudly.

She opened the door and peered out. Geoffrey Talcott stood in the hall, wearing only his shirt, and hose. He held a flickering candle. "Do I disturb you, mistress?" He glanced away, his eyes avoiding hers, and Olivia realized that in her blanket and underwear, she was probably in a much more undressed state than Geoffrey was used to seeing.

"We fell asleep," she replied. "It's been a stressful day."

He looked momentarily confused, and then he recovered. "To be sure, mistress, full of"—he hesitated over the awkward usage—"stress. For all of us. Can you rouse Mistress Alison? I would like to try to send you back through the maze—the torches are lit in the park for the Queen's visit, and I vow it's still as broad a light as day out there."

Olivia glanced over her shoulder. "Sure. I mean, of course. Will you wait?"

"I am madam's most humble servant," he said, without a trace of insincerity.

Olivia shut the door. She quickly pulled her costume back on and jostled Alison awake. "Come on," she said, fumbling with the zipper of her gown. "Geoffrey's here. It's time for us to go back."

At that Alison bolted upright, instantly alert. "Thank God." She hauled herself out of bed as Olivia handed her the costume. "Thanks." In a few short minutes, they were both dressed and presentable. "Let's go!"

Olivia turned to look at the room. "Good-bye, sixteenth-century," she murmured.

Together, the three made their way down the staircase and out of the house, into the nearly silent park. Servants still scurried amid the gardens, carrying baskets of refuse, linens, and other supplies. High torches cast a flickering yellow light, and Olivia was reminded of a production of *A Midsummer Night's Dream* she and her father had attended in an open-air theater one summer. At the entrance to the maze, they paused.

"Now what?" asked Alison.

Geoffrey looked a bit worried, Olivia thought.

He glanced around and held out the candle. "Hold this, please?" He reached into his leather doublet and withdrew a folded parchment. He unfolded the thick parchment, and in the gleam of the torchlight, Olivia saw a map or plan of the maze, drawn in thick strokes of black ink. Arrows ran various directions, clockwise and counterclockwise, and here and there, certain arrows were crossed out and others, pointing different directions, were substituted. Oh dear, thought Olivia. This doesn't seem very clear.

"All right." Geoffrey handed Olivia the map. "This is the entrance, here, and this, well—" He broke off, frowning. "Yes, I think that's what I meant—yes, that's it. You make sure you turn to the left—"

"Are you sure about this?" demanded Alison. Her face in the candlelight was tired and drawn, but her eyes were alert, and her shoulders were rigid with tension.

Geoffrey hesitated. "As sure—as certain as I can be of anything in these matters, mistress." His forehead was creased with a frown, and his mouth was thin with worry, Olivia thought. Suddenly she was much less certain that they would be able to go back.

"Can we take that with us?" She asked, more as a way to break the tension she could feel emanating from both Alison and Geoffrey like a signal.

"Well . . ." He hesitated once more, then thrust the paper at Olivia. "Here you are. Take it. And Godspeed."

"Come on, Liv." Alison tightened her hold on the candle and stepped into the maze. The candlelight wavered dangerously.

"Farewell, Master Talcott," said Olivia. She clutched the parchment, still warm from his body, and stepped into the maze after Alison. The candle flickered in the darkness, throwing up huge shadows on either side of the hedges. Holding the map of the maze between them, and keeping the candle high, the two managed to find their way through the darkness. Carefully, following the arrows first in one direction, and then another, they rounded corners and stepped through archways, twisting and turning, doubling back and forth. Finally, the candle was nearly gone. They reached the final arch.

"Thank God," breathed Alison. She took a giant step through the dark arch, into the darkness beyond. Olivia, following with the candle and the map, heard her groan.

"What's wrong?" She began, hurrying to catch up. She nearly walked into Alison's back, and realized immediately why Alison stood stock-still, her shoulders slumped in dejection.

Smoking torches still burned against the night sky, and the odors of roasting meat and raw sewage blew past them on the wind. Beneath a tree, slumped against the trunk, Geoffrey Talcott snored in happy oblivion.

"Oh, no," murmured Olivia, as the full implication hit her.

" 'Oh, no' is right," said Alison, her voice heavy with despair. "I knew it. I just knew it. We're stuck here, and I don't think we're ever going back."

Chapter 4

OLIVIA LOOKED UP. In the dark sky, millions of stars—more stars than she thought she'd ever seen in one place—twinkled like crystals strewn across black velvet. It's still the same sky, she thought . . . or was it? Hadn't the constellations changed at some point? Momentarily she wracked her brain for the answer, and then dismissed such inconsequential thoughts. You're behaving like Dad, she scolded herself. This isn't an exercise in academic inquiry.

"What are we going to do?" Alison moaned. There was more than a catch in her friend's throat. Olivia looked up and saw a tear sparkle on her friend's cheek in the dim light. Alison sniffed and wiped it away, even as Olivia reached for her hand.

"I don't know, Allie. We'll think of something. Don't worry. We have to try and stay calm."

With a deep breath, Alison visibly forced herself to relax. "Okay." She sniffed again. "Okay, I'm calm. Now what?"

Olivia looked around then shrugged. "Well, it looks as if we're both spending the night. So I suppose we wake up Master Geoffrey over there, and make him find us something to sleep in. If I never see this blasted costume again, it will be too soon."

At that Alison giggled. She sounded just a little hysterical, but Olivia was glad she could laugh at any part of the situation at all. "I was thinking the very same thing." She strode over to Geoffrey, leaned down, and shook his shoulder. "Hey!"

"Hm?" Geoffrey muttered and smiled in his sleep.

"Hey, Master Geoffrey, wake up!" Alison shook him again, harder this time, but Geoffrey only smiled and snored.

"He's as hard to wake up as you are, Allie," Olivia said. She bent down on the other side and spoke loudly. "Geoffrey Talcott! Wake up!" She gave his shoulder a shake that was practically a blow.

"Hm?" With a start, Geoffrey bolted awake, hitting his head against the trunk of the tree. "Oh!"

"Sorry," Olivia murmured.

"Hi," Alison said.

"Who—?" Momentarily Geoffrey looked confused, and then memory dawned. "Mis—but what—why didn't you— I thought you went through the maze."

"We did go through the maze," Alison said. "It didn't work this time."

"Oh." Slowly Geoffrey straightened. "Oh, dear." He sighed and got to his feet. "I was afraid of that."

Alison threw an exasperated look at Olivia. "Why didn't you warn us?"

Geoffrey gave each of them an apologetic look in turn. "Well . . ."

"I think he was afraid to, Alison." Olivia sighed. "Look, it's too late to do anything about it now. We'll go back to the house and get some sleep. Surely tomorrow, when everyone's rested, would be a better time to try again. Okay?"

Alison drew a deep breath. "I guess that's the only plan that makes sense right now. How about it, Sir Galahad?"

Geoffrey scratched his head. "Of—of course. Nicholas will—"

"I don't want to hear about Nicholas," Alison snapped. "He can just deal with it."

"We're both tired," Olivia added, almost apologetically. Trying as the situation was—unbelievable as the situation was, she corrected herself—she felt sorry for Geoffrey. He'd clearly stumbled into something he barely understood. Was it really any different from some of the things twentieth-century scientists had been known to do?

"Come with me, mistresses." Geoffrey led the way, his shoulders slumped with dejection. He brought them back into the house, where a few candles burned in sconces set high in the walls, but otherwise all was still. He paused at the base of the steps, took one of the candles from a sconce, and used it to light their way up the darkened staircase. At the door of the bedchamber where they'd been before, he paused. "I'll send a maid to attend you, mistresses." He handed Alison the candle. For a moment, he looked as though he wanted to stay something more, hesitated, then turned on his heel and fled down the steps, leaving the women alone in the dark and quiet house.

A fitful flicker beneath the closed door of Nicholas's study told him that his brother was still awake. Geoffrey paused before the thick oak door, squared his shoulders, and knocked.

"Enter!" Nicholas barely glanced up from the thick ledger book spread open on his desk. "All in all, a fine revel, I'd say, wouldn't you?" He smiled a little and went on scratching numbers.

"Very fine," Geoffrey said, feeling for all the world as he used to when he was very small and was forced to answer to their father for whatever most recent scrape he'd found himself in.

"Those two women are gone?"

"Well . . ."

At that, Nicholas looked up and set down the quill. "Well, what?"

"It, uh, it—the maze—it didn't do what I hoped it would do this time, Nicholas. I—I couldn't send them back. They're upstairs and I sent old Janet to wait on them."

Nicholas gasped softly, as though he'd been punched. "What?"

"I—I don't quite know how it happened in the first place, Nicholas—you know I've been working day and night—"

"Damn it, Geoffrey!" Nicholas slapped the surface of the desk with his open palm, and the whole massive piece of furniture shuddered. "What will it take to make you give up these daft dabblings? I've spent the whole of my adult life trying to restore our family's fortunes, and you've spent the whole of yours endangering what's left. Are you truly mad? Or simply blind?" He ran his hand through his hair, pushed his chair away from the desk, and stalked to the window. A full moon shone down on the August night and, outside, the land lay quiet under the stars.

"W-well, Nicholas, I fully intend to send them back as soon as I—"

"Figure out how?" Nicholas turned back to glare at his brother. "In God's good world, Geoffrey, I do not understand the way you think. Father should've made you join the priesthood—sent you to France when he'd had the chance. Now see what you've brought upon us." He turned back to the window, shaking his head.

"I—I don't think it will take forever—" Geoffrey began again, but Nicholas cut him off with an impatient wave.

"You don't think at all. If you spent two minutes thinking about the reality of our situation, you'd realize that all the time you spend dreaming such nonsense is more dangerous than if you took a dagger and threatened the Queen herself. Sweet Christ, if you did that, you'd be the only one who'd pay for your madness. You wouldn't bring ruin down about both of us."

"I haven't exactly ruined anything, Nicholas. Be fair."

"Fair? Do you think when they come to burn you as a warlock, the court that convicts you will be fair? Do you think the Queen's Grace will be fair when she divvies up Talcott Forest? Geoffrey, you—you—" Shaking his head in frustration, Nicholas pressed his lips together in a thin line.

"I'll work on the problem as soon as—"

"As soon as you leave this room, do you hear me? I want them gone—gone by the time I return from Calais."

"Calais? You're going to Calais?"

"Aye. At least one of us had better keep an eye to the direction the wind blows. I've been approached by one Master Christopher Warren—an agent in Walsingham's network."

Geoffrey frowned. "Nicholas, are you sure you ought to do this?"

"You of all people think to question my judgment?"

"Well . . ." Geoffrey hesitated. He frowned, thinking furiously. The name Warren was ringing a very unpleasant bell in his mind. He scratched his chin. "Who is this Master Warren?"

"He's one of Walsingham's men. I know what you're thinking, Geoffrey," Nicholas said, dismissing the troubled look on his brother's face with a wave. "Walsingham's been no friend to Catholics—or to former Catholics. But I think I've proved myself to be a loyal subject of Her Majesty—"

"No one could doubt that. So why involve yourself in one of his schemes?"

"What makes you think it's a scheme? An agent of the King of Spain has been arrested in London—they've asked me to go to Calais and keep the appointment this man would've made." Nicholas looked over his shoulder at the window, as though someone might be listening. "It involves the plans of an invasion of England."

"An invasion?" Geoffrey shook his head. "I don't like the sound of this, Nicholas—perhaps we should talk about this tomorrow, when we both aren't so tired—"

"You're the last person to concern yourself with such matters." Nicholas cut him off. "You have your own tangled coil to sort out. And by Her Royal Majesty's grace, you damned well better sort it out, and then that damnable maze is coming down if I have to tear it out with my own hands. If you want to dabble in such unnatural arts, you'll have to find another place to do it. I won't have you risking everything I've worked for, do you understand?"

Geoffrey drew a deep breath. A wave of exhaustion washed over him, and his shoulders slumped. "I understand, Nicholas."

"Good." Nicholas pulled out his chair and sank down at his desk once more. He picked up the quill and looked up at Geoffrey expectantly. "Is there anything else?"

"No, Nicholas."

"Good night, Geoffrey." He dipped the quill in his inkpot and began to write, the tip scratching over the thick parchment the only sound in the quiet room.

Geoffrey hesitated. There was so much he wanted to say to his brother, so much he wanted to try to explain. He understood why Nicholas was so angry, but couldn't his brother understand what an amazing thing he'd accomplished? And wasn't Nicholas the least bit curious? How could he not seize the opportunity to talk to people from a time even their great-great-grandchildren would never live to see? He looked at Nicholas's dark head bent over his ledger. His brother's back was straight, but he leaned against his left hand as he wrote. Nicholas was as worn out as he. Geoffrey took another deep breath. He walked quietly to the door, pulled it open, and glanced back. Nicholas was rubbing his eyes; the quill drooped in his hand. "Good night, Nicholas," he said softly as he gently closed the door.

•   •   •

Beneath the midnight moon, a dark shape emerged from the shadow of the oak trees that lined the long drive, as the clatter of hooves announced the arrival of Sir John Makepiece. "Well, Master Warren?"

"Thank you for meeting me like this, Sir John." The other man's voice was soft in the night air.

"I like this not, Master Warren—this sneaking about betweentimes. Honest men are long abed, and so should we be."

"No one agrees with you more, Sir John, but Her Majesty intends to leave for Hampton Court early on the morrow, and I must be away to London at dawn. I had no other time."

"As you say, Master Warren. What's your news?"

"It was as I suspected. He intends to leave for Calais within the week. I trust your plans are made?"

"Aye, I've passage booked from Dover three days from now. He mentioned my daughter's hand once more—I intend to meet with him on the morrow and address it."

"The question of your daughter's hand . . ." In the dark, Warren leaned closer in his own saddle, despite the fact that in the dark night, Sir John's face was nothing but a pale smudge against a black backdrop.

"Have no fear. I'll not say yea or nay until this business is concluded. It's not one to my liking, Master Warren. The more I think on't—"

"Her Majesty will be most grateful for your service," interrupted Warren smoothly. "And will reward that service in a manner most fitting, I assure you."

"And there's the question of those two doxies he's suddenly related to—seems most suspicious to me, the whole business does."

Suddenly Warren had an idea that would damn Nicholas in Sir John's eyes for all time. He smiled to himself. The plan merely required a bit of tweaking. "Well, what do you expect from one who serves neither God nor the Queen?"

In the brief silence, Sir John's horse stamped at the

ground, as though anxious to return to its stall. "I expect this matter to be concluded in as expeditious a manner as possible, Master Warren."

"And it shall be, Sir John. Once Talcott is apprehended with the plans . . ."

The knight gave the reins an impatient tug, and the horse knickered and wheeled around. "I'll do my part, as I gave my Christian word, Master Warren. But there's to be no more midnight meetings. If such business cannot stand the clear light of the Lord's own day, I'll have no more truck with it."

Warren watched the knight gallop off down the tree-lined, moonlit drive. It was as well that Sir John's role in the main part of this was ultimately peripheral at most. He glanced up at the round white moon. He'd see Talcott convicted beneath the light of the Lord's own day indeed, he thought. And burn beneath a noonday sun.

Chapter 5

"THIS MATTER MUST be concluded as quickly as possible." Nicholas stood with crossed arms beside the empty hearth in the cluttered tower room that served as Geoffrey's "study," although, thought Olivia as she looked around, it was hard to tell exactly what it was he studied. It seemed to be some arcane combination of alchemy, astrology, and mathematics, for the floor was littered with parchments covered with long algebraic formulas, and the long tables were covered with an assortment of the oddest instruments. The astrolabe and the compass were really the only two she recognized at once. Her fingers itched to prowl through the whole untidy mass, touching for herself the accouterments of the infancy of science. Next to her, in a pair of Geoffrey's hose and with one of his long linen shirts belted at her waist, Alison stretched her long legs. She'd flatly refused to wear any of the dusty dresses Janet had proffered that morning. Not that Olivia blamed her. The clothing that had belonged to Nicholas and Geoffrey's mother dated back at least thirty years or more, and although they'd been carefully stored in chests lined with cedar, and strewn with lavender, they were indisputably musty. And old Lady

Talcott had been much shorter than Alison and stouter than Olivia. Olivia pulled her own shirt closer. It was one of Nicholas's—and beneath the scent of sun-bleached linen, the fabric held the scent of something that was a tantalizing blend of horses and masculine sweat and soap, something which could only be him. It made her uncomfortable to be wearing an item of his clothing, while he was standing there glowering at them all. But there'd been nothing else for them to wear—the scullery maids were the only women in the Talcotts' bachelor household who might wear clothing that would come close to fitting them, and even Nicholas had not considered their garments suitable. When Geoffrey had approached him to give up one of his shirts and a pair of hose for Olivia, he'd merely shaken his head in disgust. But he'd handed over the clothes. Apparently, their scandalous dress—or lack thereof—was something he was prepared to overlook, so long as they kept to Geoffrey's study and their own bedroom as much as possible.

"We all agree that you two must be sent back to your own time as soon as possible." Geoffrey sighed. He ran his fingers through his hair, which at this point stuck up in all directions. It would've been comical if the situation weren't so grim.

"Well, what do you intend to do about it?"

"The trouble is—" Geoffrey broke off. Once more Olivia felt sorry for him. He made a helpless little gesture. "I'll check through my calculations. Perhaps the angle of the sun . . ." He sifted through a series of parchments, mouthing formulas. "The answer has to be here somewhere."

Nicholas shot him a look of pure exasperation and opened his mouth to speak, but he was interrupted by a knock upon the door. "See who it is."

Geoffrey leapt to his feet and opened the door just a crack. He spoke a few words to whomever stood on the other side, then turned back to Nicholas, shutting the door once more as he did so. "A gentleman to see you. Master Christopher Warren."

Nicholas looked surprised. "I'd better see him. You do what you can. I'll be back." With a muttered oath, Nicholas left the room, shaking his head.

Geoffrey sighed when his brother was gone. "He's really not like this usually. It's just he's—"

"Upset," finished Alison. "Well, we're all upset." She got to her feet, sorting restlessly through the parchments. "What is all this, anyway? Is there any way we could help you make sense of this?"

Geoffrey looked faintly shocked. "In truth, mistress, I doubt—"

Alison narrowed her eyes and pursed her lips. "This looks like algebra. Or some weird sort of advanced calculus." She shook her head. "Your brother's upset, you're upset, we're all upset. What we have to do is stop being upset and think. Nothing else is going to get us out of here and back home."

Geoffrey narrowed his eyes and picked up the parchment Alison had dropped. "You—you understand these calculations, mistress?"

She shrugged. "Well, I don't understand the specific equations without working through them—but, yes, I understand the math. I even got an A in statistics in grad school."

Geoffrey looked mystified. He scratched his chin. "Would you—would you be able to help me, then? Review my work?"

Alison shrugged again. "Of course. Don't ask Livvie, though. She's hopeless at math." She looked over her shoulder at Olivia and winked.

From her place beside the window, Olivia grinned ruefully in agreement. "Right, Don't count on my help there." She looked out the window, from which she could just see the tops of the hedgerows that formed the maze, and, from this height, she could discern something of the intrinsic pattern. "But maybe—maybe I could retrace our steps through the maze, try to figure out where it was exactly we got back, and work backward from there. Remember, Allie, there was that weird feeling of tripping over something at one point, but the path was perfectly clear?"

Geoffrey nodded. "That's worth trying. And there is something else—something I hesitate to mention to Nicholas, but it may be the easiest and the most expeditious way of solving the problem."

"And what's that?" asked Alison, looking up from the calculations on the parchments.

"Dr. Dee, John Dee—I mentioned him yesterday—he was my tutor at Oxford, and we've corresponded frequently over the past few years. He knows of my, my experiments and he's offered advice—given me suggestions—he may have some ideas. I'll send a letter to him posthaste, and ask for his help."

Olivia exchanged a glance with Alison. "So, in other words, Geoffrey," Olivia began slowly, "what you're really saying is that it isn't going to be quite as easy as you thought to send us back. You don't think you can do it today—"

"Or tomorrow, or the day after," Alison finished. She got up and stalked out of the room, shutting the door behind her with a slam.

Geoffrey looked helplessly at Olivia. "Mistress Olivia, I'm sorry."

Olivia shrugged. "I know you're sorry, Geoffrey. But Alison's frightened. She needs to return to our time, and our lives before. She has so much waiting for her there."

Geoffrey cocked his head and met her eyes with his soft brown ones. "And you don't?"

Olivia hesitated. "It's different for me," she answered slowly. His brown eyes were alight with unasked questions, and Olivia suddenly felt uncomfortable. There were too many things she'd rather not discuss—such as why she felt so much at home in this time and place. Was it all the history she'd learned? Her unrealized ambition to act? Her father's belief that history was something to be experienced, not learned? Whatever it was, it was definitely making her feel odd. "I'd better see to Alison."

He gave her an awkward bow, and she left the room, still wondering why she felt so much more at home than she had ever felt before.

"What do you mean, I won't suit?" Nicholas leaned forward with a puzzled frown. "But surely—just yesterday—"

Warren spread his hands helplessly. A soft breeze blew in from the open window, and he glanced pointedly at it, as though he feared someone lurked, listening, beneath. "Yesterday I was not aware of all the details, shall we say."

"Details?" Nicholas gestured with an impatient hand. "What details? You said I bore a resemblance—"

"And that's true enough, my lord. But what you must understand is that we've learned that the man who's to meet the Spanish agent is expected to travel with his wife. The Spanish agent will be looking for a married couple. And you, my lord, have no wife. At least, none you've acknowledged publicly." He bent his lips in a semblance of a smile, and Nicholas felt a sliver of unease. Geoffrey had seemed uncomfortable about Warren for some reason. Had he said why?

"A wife?"

"Aye. A wife." Master Warren leaned back in his chair and sipped the goblet of wine.

Nicholas got to his feet and paced to the window. "And what if I could produce a wife? Or yet the semblance of one?"

Warren raised one eyebrow. "A semblance of a wife, my lord? What do you mean?"

Nicholas paused, thinking furiously. There might be a way to turn Geoffrey's mistake into an advantage. He raised his eyes to the ceiling. The two women upstairs—at least one of them could come with him. The whole journey—to Calais and back to Talcott Forest—would take less than a week, if the winds and weather were favorable.

No more than two at most if they were not. He stroked his chin. "My, uh, my cousins. I believe you saw them yesterday—when they sang for the Queen? What if it were possible that one of them could—"

"Masquerade as your wife, my lord?" Warren leaned back and shrugged. "Think you one of the ladies would be willing?"

Nicholas smiled grimly. The lady would have no choice, he thought. The taller one had such strange mannerisms she would never pass, but the other—the one who sang—she had a prayer. Momentarily Olivia's face rose before him, and he wondered what it would be like to kiss those full, rosy lips. With more effort than he wanted to admit, he dismissed the thought. After all, the two of them owed him something, if only for appearing at the most inopportune time imaginable. Geoffrey had better not object, either. "I see no reason why not," he replied smoothly. "The fortunes of all the Talcotts are linked, are they not? It would be in my cousins' best interests, I would think."

Master Warren raised his goblet once again, this time in a toast. "Then I shall inform my master that you are, indeed, the perfect man for this task, my lord. And may I be the first to congratulate you upon your most propitious union?"

But even as Nicholas raised his own goblet in an answering gesture, he had the unpleasant thought that Warren's eyes really were as black and as flat as a snake's.

"You want one of them to do what? Nicholas, now who's mad?" Geoffrey stared at his brother in disbelief.

"I'm not mad at all. You created this wretched mess and here's a way to turn it into our advantage. And I'm not talking about the tall one—Alison, right? I mean Olivia. She charmed the Queen herself rightly enough. She can do the same for the Spanish agent."

"By our most blessed Lady." Geoffrey slapped his forehead with the palm of his hand and turned away, shaking his head and muttering. "What if I send them back first? You would rather be rid of them as soon as possible, wouldn't you?" There was a questioning note in Geoffrey's voice that told Nicholas that his brother seriously thought he might be mad.

"Of course I'd rather be rid of them. But tell me, how promising it is that you'll be able to send them back by the time I leave for Calais?"

"When do you leave?"

"Four days hence."

Geoffrey bit his lip. He glanced at the parchments, now arranged in neat piles on the table, and the astrolabe, which he'd begun to use once more. "I—I am not sure," he finally admitted. "I may have to write to Dr. Dee."

"Dee? The Queen's own physician? In truth, Geoffrey—"

"The Queen's own astrologer and a very learned man. There's no one else in all of England who can possibly help me untangle this coil save Dee. And he's discreet. He'd say nothing to anyone, lest he find himself without a head, as well."

Nicholas narrowed his eyes. "And where is Dr. Dee?"

"At Oxford, last I heard. I intend to send a letter to him today."

"Then, Geoffrey, there's plenty of time. You won't hear back from Dee in the time it will take me to arrive in Calais, conclude this business in London, and return. It will all be finished in a fortnight. And then you and Dr. Dee can send our two guests back to their own time, our fortunes will be restored, and all will work out happily. Surely you see the wisdom?"

"I like this not. Can't you see how difficult it is for both of them? How different this is from anything they know?"

Nicholas waved an impatient hand. "That's as may be. But the dark one—Olivia—she fit in well enough to please the Queen herself. Let her come with me. You and the tall one—Alison—you can stay here and work with Dr. Dee."

"Nicholas, I beg you—"

"As I've begged you to cease your endless dabbling into things best left alone?" Nicholas shook his head. "Not this time, little brother. This time one of your experiments may actually have some use for both of us. And I intend to take every advantage."

"What if she won't do it?"

"We'll have to convince her she must do it."

"How? These women aren't like the ones you and I know. They aren't like any other women we've ever met, or could meet. Can't you see how different they are, in outlook and in temperament? They'll not be ruled by any man."

Nicholas hesitated, then grinned. "Ah, Geoffrey, you've spent too much time with your pens and parchments. No woman is ever ruled by a man. But very often, there are ways to convince them to do as they'd be bid."

"How?"

"Make her believe it's her idea, of course."

"And just how will you do that?"

Nicholas adjusted his doublet and straightened his shoulders. "Leave the managing of Mistress Olivia to me." Geoffrey rose to his feet and started for the door.

"Where are you going?"

"To find Mistress Olivia and tell her you wish to talk to her. Shall I tell her to come here?"

"No, I'll wait for her in the garden. We'll walk a bit."

"I thought you wanted them to stay out of sight."

"Ah, but this is a matter best broached beneath the open sky. And besides, women love flowers. Even Her Majesty remarked upon the beauty of our gardens."

Geoffrey shook his head in disbelief. "You may well think I'm mad, Nicholas. I only wanted to transcend time. You want to transcend a woman's mind. You're not only as mad as I am, you're more of a dreamer than I ever expected, as well." With another little shake of his head, Geoffrey was gone.

He was waiting for her beneath the trees that lined the path that led to the maze. Olivia's heart beat faster when she caught sight of him. He wore only the simplest of clothing—shirt and hose and a plain leather doublet—but the rough clothing could not disguise the lean contours of his body, nor the width of his shoulders. His face was half in the shadow and half in the light, and the stark planes of his high cheekbones and his slim, straight nose gave him the appearance of a Renaissance prince. Which, she thought wryly as she approached, in some ways he was. She smoothed her own shirt, consciously forcing her face into a semblance of composure. He looked up as her feet crunched on the gravel.

"Mistress Olivia." He bowed, more formally than he ever had before to her, and Olivia's heart gave a little leap.

Stop that, she scolded herself. Yes, he looks like a Medici prince, but you've got nothing in common with him. You barely speak the same language. "Lord Nicholas," she murmured in return. "Geoffrey said you needed to speak to me? About something important?"

"Yes," he said, looking suddenly as uncomfortable as she felt, "it is a matter of very great import, and—" He broke off, and suddenly Olivia saw the resemblance between the two brothers. In the shadowy light, he looked much younger, younger even than Geoffrey.

"What is it?" She cocked her head, genuinely puzzled.

"Will you walk with me?" He indicated the path.

She nodded and they fell into step together. She was aware that he consciously matched his longer strides to hers, yet there was a certain hesitancy about him that surprised her. When a few minutes had passed in silence, she said, "What do you want to say to me, Lord Nicholas?"

"I—I—you must forgive me, mistress. I am not usually so awkward or at a loss for words."

"This situation is awkward, to say the least."

"Aye, at the least." He gave a short laugh that sounded nervous. "There's no way to ask you this but directly. The truth be told, Mistress Olivia, I need your help."

She stopped in the middle of the path and turned to face him. They were in the full sunshine now, and the light revealed the blue-black highlights in his hair, and the way the little hairs curling on his chest peeked through the open collar of his shirt, but his eyes were still dark, shadowed pools. "My help? How in the world could I help you?"

Nicholas sighed. "It is not easy to explain, especially to someone who isn't of this time." He shook his head and seemed once more at a loss. "But you . . . I noticed at once you see more comfortable than your sister—your friend, I suppose she is—and you did please the Queen greatly. And so I come to you to ask you for a favor. A very great favor."

Olivia stared up at him, completely puzzled. "Well, what is it? As we'd say in the future, spit it out!" She laughed softly, trying to ease his tension.

A ghost of a smile lifted his lips, and he glanced back at the house. "Come, let's walk a pace. I think better when I walk." He made as if to start off again, but this time it was Olivia's turn to stare at him. "Yes, mistress? I said something which sounded odd to your ears?"

"No." She shook her head, waving her hand, seeking to regain her composure. "Not at all. But that's what my father used to say. My father was a great scholar, you see, and he was most fascinated by this period of history."

"Ah." He raised one brow and gave her a long, searching look. "Then perhaps you will understand." He held out his hand. "Please come."

She placed her hand timidly in his. His smooth, strong palm closed firmly around hers, and he turned it, pulling her closer, so that it appeared they strolled arm in arm down the long, curved path. "It begins with my father—mine and Geoffrey's. He was a good man—if somewhat misguided at times. He believed in the teachings of the Church of Rome with all his heart, and he meant to be a good man. But like so many good men, he was led astray by his own passionate beliefs. He stood strong under Protestant Edward, the present Queen's brother—who died young. But under Mary—under Catholic Mary—his beliefs took on the tinge of the fanatic. He'd struggled so long, I suppose." Nicholas paused, and she could feel the deep sigh he suppressed run through the length of his body. "At any rate, he did not endear himself to those who are now currently in power. And thus his fortunes suffered greatly. He died greatly impoverished, lucky to have anything at all to leave to me." He paused again, looking around. "This house you see—it is nearly all that's left of a patrimony once as great as any in England. I have worked all my adult life—for the last fifteen years—to restore what I can of my family's fortunes. I fought with Leicester in the Low Countries, spent time at court, courted the favor of any who could help me. And now, at last, I think I have an opportunity to prove my loyalty once and for all to the Queen and all her court. And so I need your help."

"But what can I do? You yourself said our very presence here was a danger—and I agree with you. Knowing what I know about this time and place, I can't imagine—"

"I want you to pretend to be my wife." He blurted out the words.

"What?" She stared up at him in amazement, doubting she had heard the words correctly.

"I must go to Calais in four days' time. There, I am to meet with an agent of the King of Spain and intercept plans for the invasion of England. But this agent is expecting a married man, a man supposedly on pilgrimage with his wife, and thus—"

"You want me to go with you to Calais and pretend to be your wife."

"Aye."

There was a long silence. Finally she said, "But what

about Geoffrey? Alison? What if Geoffrey is able—"

"To send you back?" Nicholas shook his head. "Aye, mistress, and I suppose it's possible Geoffrey could build us a machine to fly us to Calais, but I doubt it's likely in four days' time."

"Isn't there anyone else?"

"Quite simply, no. There's no one who's as disinterested in the outcome as you—no one I could trust in the way your very disinterest makes possible. I could hire a whore, but that would hardly serve. And what lady do you think would travel with a man who was not really her husband?"

Olivia frowned. "Are you suggesting I'm a woman of low morals, sir?"

Nicholas opened his mouth as if to speak, then hesitated. "Forgive me, mistress," he said after an awkward pause. "That's not what I meant to imply." He drew a deep breath and his shoulders heaved. He looked around desperately, as though seeking the words, and Olivia felt sorry for him.

"I know that isn't what you meant," she said softly. She placed her hand on his arm. He looked down at her, a surprised expression on his face. "Come, let's walk and tell me more."

They started off again, and as they walked, Nicholas shook his head. "In truth, mistress, perhaps you should tell me if you find my request outside the bounds of anything you would consider proper. I see that I've neglected to consider your feelings. Forgive me."

It was Olivia's turn to look up at him with surprise. A feeling of sympathy swept over her, a desire to help this man in any way she could. What was it about him that made her feel such deep sympathy for his plight? Was it merely that he was someone out of the past her father had made so real that she felt as though she knew Nicholas and his brother already? Or was it something more, something that transcended time and history and all the years that lay between them? "It's very plain to see that you have a lot on your mind."

"On my mind?" he repeated, turning the unfamiliar idiom over on his tongue. He smiled suddenly, as understanding lit his eyes, and she saw that without the habitual expression of care, he appeared much younger. "Very well put, mistress. Indeed, I have a lot on my mind. And I know I've been a less than gracious host to both you and your friend." He drew another deep breath and paused on the path, dragging the toe of his boot in the gravel in a gesture nearly identical to Geoffrey's. The brothers were a lot alike, Olivia realized with a start. Both pursued their passions with a single-minded intensity.

"What is the world like in your time?"

For a moment, Olivia was surprised by his sudden question. She cocked her head, thinking how to describe the world on the eve of the twenty-first century to a man from a world still lit only by fire. "It—it's very different, in some ways. And in some ways, still remarkably similar."

"What do you mean?" His eyes were locked on hers, and the intensity of his expression took her breath away. She deliberately tried not to think about how good-looking he was, with the faintest haze of beard darkening the cleft in his chin, and the strong cords in his throat where the lacings of his shirt gaped open. Suddenly, she was very aware that the hose exposed the shape of her legs in a manner to which he could hardly be accustomed.

"Well," she hesitated, searching for words. "People haven't changed much. Not at all, really. There're still wars—over the same things, even. People are still fighting over religion and land and money—the names have all changed, but you'd recognize a lot. The world seems a lot smaller than it must to you—we can go places much more quickly because we have machines to travel in."

"Can you fly?"

She laughed. "Well, not personally—no one's grown wings, yet. But yes, there are machines called airplanes that fly—all the way around the world, some of them. I came to England from America on a plane."

"But the language you speak—it's the same as mine, no? Or close enough that we understand each other."

"English has spread all over the world. I doubt there's a country left that hasn't absorbed English words into its native tongue. It's funny, but the English language is probably England's greatest gift to the ages."

He stroked his chin. "And does this all"—he waved his hand—"does this all seem strange to you?"

She gazed around. Behind them, the great house rose from the sheltering branches of the great trees. In the distance, she saw the softly rolling hills, green with the summer's bounty, the long, even rows of crops in variegated rows of green and buff and brown. The gardens lay around them, the low stone walls guarding neatly laid-out beds of vegetables, herbs, and flowering shrubs. "In some ways, yes. But I have something of an advantage, I guess you could call it. My father was a historian. A scholar— he studied history—and his favorite period was Tudor England, especially the years under Elizabeth. I was his research assistant until just a few months ago."

"What happened?"

"He died. It was an accident, quite sudden. He slipped on a patch of ice, hit his head, and died. No one expected anything like it to happen—he was very healthy, and just about to publish his greatest and most consuming work. That's why I came to England from America, you see. I came to finish my father's work." She paused briefly and then went on. "My mother died when I was born. There was nothing else I needed to do."

Suddenly he took her by the arms. "Then you do understand. I see that you do. That's what I want to do, you see—finish my father's work. He was loyal to the King all his life—he just never understood why old King Harry turned away from the one true Church. And when Queen Mary came to the throne, he thought that at last England would return to the true religion, and he did all he could to ensure it, but . . ."

"He bet on the wrong horse," Olivia finished softly.

"In truth, mistress, truer words were never spoken. He died a broken man, nearly penniless. All you see here is the result of my work, since I was barely sixteen." He hooked his thumbs in his belt and looked around. "I've accomplished much. The Queen's visit here was a most favorable sign. And now—now I have the chance to really serve Her Majesty, to do something which will pave the way to royal favor and reward."

"I see," said Olivia. "And what exactly is it that you have the chance to do?"

Swiftly, Nicholas outlined the plan. "But just this morning, Master Warren arrived unexpectedly and said that they needed someone who had a wife—and, obviously, I have no wife—but I thought . . . I saw how you pleased the Queen, and so I thought—"

"That I might be able to play the part of your wife."

"Yes." He paused briefly. "Would you do that? Could you do that?"

She hesitated, thinking furiously. What would Alison say? Alison was likely to think she'd completely lost her mind. And what about Alison? This whole time period was much less familiar to Alison—would her friend be all right, left here at Talcott Forest? And what about returning? What if Geoffrey discovered the way to get them back to the future? "I—I suppose I could," she began slowly. "But I have to talk to Alison. I can't just leave her here—she's not as familiar with all this as I am. I can't just go off and leave her, especially if she's feeling alone and frightened."

"She'll be safe here. My brother will watch out for her. Nothing will happen to her here."

Olivia took a deep breath and looked around at the peaceful scene. Bees buzzed contentedly in the sunshine, and in the kitchen gardens, two teenage boys weeded on their hands and knees. Somewhere close by, a woman was singing. The whole atmosphere was one of peace and tranquillity. It was hard to believe that civil unrest and religious persecutions simmered beneath the placid surface. "I do not doubt that you would want her to be safe here, and I believe that Geoffrey would do all that he could to protect her from any kind of harm. But you and I both know that circumstances can change on the turn of a dime—a shilling," she corrected herself. "And it seems to me this undertaking, as you describe it, is filled with a certain amount of risk. What if something happens?"

"I wouldn't let anything happen—"

She held up her hand. "I know it wouldn't be your intention. But this is not without danger. And my first loyalty must be to my friend."

"Will you talk to her?"

"Of course."

"And if she agrees, you'll go?"

Olivia hesitated. Privately, she doubted there would be a snowball's chance in hell of Alison agreeing to this scheme. The last thing Alison would agree with was involvement in Elizabethan intrigue. But the more she thought of it . . . "How long would I be gone?"

A smile danced at the corners of his mouth. "I must leave four days hence. I expect to be in Calais no more than a day or two—long enough to make the contact with the Spanish agent. And then we'll return immediately—I'll bring you back here before I go on to London."

"So no more than two or three days?"

"Four or five, I expect. Some of it depends on the seas, you see. The crossing may be delayed if the weather is foul."

Olivia shifted her weight. "I'll talk to Alison. I can make no promises."

A wide grin spread across his face, and he took both her hands in his and brought them impulsively to his lips. "It may be that you've brought me the Queen's own luck, my lady." He pressed her hands together and took one step toward her. For a moment, she thought he meant to kiss her, when a dry cough made them spring apart.

"Do I interrupt, Lord Nicholas?"

Olivia jumped. Sir John Makepiece, dressed in his un-relieved black, stood on the path, gazing pointedly at the couple.

Nicholas recovered, bowing to Sir John. He released Olivia's hand slowly, as though reluctant to let it go. "Good morning, Sir John. My cousin and I were enjoying this beautiful day."

The Puritan raised his eyebrow, and his expression showed quite clearly exactly how he thought they were enjoying it. "Indeed." There was a long pause as he ran his eyes up and down Olivia, taking in her masculine garb. His eyes lingered on her legs, and Olivia fought the urge to cross her arms over her breasts. Suddenly she realized that the shape of her legs through the thick hose undoubtedly constituted a scandalous exposure. "You pre-fer men's clothing to women's, mistress?"

Olivia wet her lips. "My own, my own clothing was ruined in the journey, sir—a careless groom—everything must be laundered." She glanced up at Nicholas, and their eyes met. She read approval and something which could only be gratitude at her ready lie. "If you'll both excuse me, I'll go and see how everything is coming along."

"And how does your sister, mistress?" Sir John's dry voice startled her as she turned on her heel.

"Alison is feeling much better, thank you, sir." She bobbed a little curtsy and withdrew, knowing that both men watched her as she hurried back to the house.

There was another brief silence. Nicholas waited until Oli-via disappeared around the corner of the path, and Sir John's dry cough once more broke through his reverie. "Would you care for some refreshment, Sir John?"

The knight merely gave him a sour look. "I came to discuss my daughter's betrothal, Lord Nicholas, but such doings as a woman dressed in a man's clothes is surely an abomination before the Lord. What sort of household do you keep, sir? My daughter has been raised to do her duty as the Lord instructed, to be a comfort to her husband. But such a sight—Did you perchance forget my visit, as you were no doubt busy entertaining your, ah, cousins?"

"Of course not, Sir John." A pang went through Nicholas as he thought of Sir John's pale, skinny daughter. Patience Makepiece was about as far from the toothsome Olivia as he could imagine. A pity he could only ask her to pretend to be his wife. She was far closer to his idea of what a wife should be.

"I have given the matter some thought," Sir John was saying. "And upon reflection, while I am not yet opposed to the idea, I see that this is not a matter to be rushed. I am not ruling out the possibility of a marriage, you understand, but I cannot know what to think of you, seeing that, that, spectacle just now."

Of course not, you old goat, thought Nicholas, watching the man's thin lips purse as though he'd tasted something sour, *you covet my lands too much.*

"If you must have your leman—"

"My what?" Nicholas burst out. "I beg your pardon, sir!"

"That lady, if such she be, is no more your cousin than I am, Lord Nicholas," the knight said dryly. "But I understand that a man has needs."

Nicholas folded his lips together and drew himself up. He met the knight's eyes with a cool stare that conveyed more clearly than words the gap between their respective ranks. "I find you forward, Sir John. That lady is no more my leman than you are, sir. And I will thank you not to insult her. Her clothing was, as she explained, quite ruined in the journey, and this is a masculine household—I have few comforts to offer a lady as yet. There was nothing among the maids to fit her, and I could not be so cruel as to shut her up till the laundry was done." The idea of marrying Patience Makepiece and thus forging a legal relationship with her overbearing, sanctimonious father was

seeming less and less attractive. Sir John might well be
rich, and Patience's dowry might go a long way toward
restoring the Talcott fortunes, but he'd almost rather
marry Olivia in her borrowed shirt and hose than anyone
related to Sir John in a cloth o' gold. "I'm off to Calais
in a few days. I suggest we meet again a fortnight hence,
and give the matter more reflection. I may not be a suitable match for your daughter."

Anger flickered in the knight's watery eyes. Greed, and
the opportunity to annex the Talcott lands, warred with
clear dislike of the younger man. "As you wish, Lord
Nicholas." Without any more ado, the knight turned on
his heel and stalked back to the house.

Nicholas narrowed his eyes, watching until the knight
was out of sight. Perhaps the Queen's favor would bring
the interest of another heiress, and he could forget he ever
thought of courting skinny Patience Makepiece. The
thought that Sir John might be his father-in-law, and have
the right, through his daughter, to enjoy anything of Talcott Forest, made Nicholas's blood run cold. And somehow, Nicholas knew that there would be no more
conversations regarding a betrothal to Patience Makepiece.

"He wants you to do what?" Alison stared at Olivia, alarm
clear on her face. "How could you even think of it?"

Olivia sighed. "Well . . ."

"You want to do it, don't you? I can see by the look
on your face the whole idea intrigues you."

Olivia shifted uncomfortably. "Well, I won't if you
don't want me to, Allie. I don't want to leave you alone."

Alison made an impatient gesture. "Oh, cut that out.
We've known each other too long, Liv. Look, I can understand why *you'd* want to do it. This whole thing has
to seem like a dream come true for you. And I can tell
that Charming Nicholas thinks you're okay, too. But are
you sure you can pull this off?"

Olivia shrugged. "I guess I really don't know. But think

of the opportunity, Allie. This is a chance my father would've given both arms for."

"But you aren't your father, Liv," Alison said gently.

"Listen, I don't have to do this. If you think you'd rather—"

"Livvie, stop." Alison leaned back against the hard back of the chair and stretched both her long legs out on the other one. She smiled at Olivia. "This isn't about me, and you know it." She waved one hand in the general direction of the door. "Charming Geoffrey's just fine. He's a good sort, and I think I might be able to help him. At least math isn't a complete mystery to me." She winked at Olivia, and Olivia knew she was referring to the fact that Olivia'd had to try three times to pass Algebra I in high school. Only intense tutoring from both Alison and her older cousin had helped in any way. "The real question is, Do you want to? And do you really understand what you're walking into?"

Olivia sighed. She bounced a little on the bed, her legs dangling like a child's from the high mattress, twisting her hands together in her lap. "I—I think I do. I mean, do you know, all the time, what you're getting into, at one of those schools? I mean, when you get involved in breaking up a fight or something, how do you know one of those kids isn't armed?"

"I always assume they're both armed." Alison grinned. "I can see this is the opportunity of a lifetime for you. It's this perfect blend of the history that you know better than the back of your hand and a chance to play a part— but, Livvie, if you get it wrong, what can happen? I don't think Geoffrey was kidding when he was talking about burning at the stake. Do you?"

"No." She met Alison's eyes squarely. "I don't."

"So I guess the question is, Are you willing to risk your life to do this?"

There was a short silence. Finally Olivia drew a deep breath and nodded. "I guess I am."

Alison got to her feet, adjusted her shirt and her hose,

and patted Olivia's shoulder. "Don't guess. Be sure. This is your life we're talking about, and the prospect of an excruciating death."

"But what about you? What if Geoffrey finds a way to send us back?"

Alison laughed. "Afraid I'll get back without you?" she teased. "Look, if it happens that Geoffrey can get us back—well, what do you think I should do?"

"I think you have to go. There wouldn't be any point to just hanging around here waiting for me. If you get the chance to go back first, just tell everyone I decided to stay in England for a few more days. And that's kind of the truth, right? You can tell Mrs. Higgins and the tour company that I went off on my own. Just say something about me being a crazy academic type. You know, a nutty professor. And keep your fingers crossed that Geoffrey can make it work a third time, okay?"

Alison bent slightly and gave her a swift hug. "Oh, Livvie, I want you to be careful. Promise you'll be careful."

"Of course I'll be careful." Unexpectedly, Olivia's eyes filled with tears. Trust Alison to cut to the heart of the matter.

"What about clothes? Where's he going to get all the stuff you're going to need?"

Olivia shrugged. "Beats me. I didn't even ask him about that. I didn't want to encourage him too much, you know."

"From the way he looks at you, I'd say you don't have to encourage him too much at all."

"Oh!" Olivia playfully slapped Alison's arm. "You always say stuff like that."

"Come on." Alison jerked her head in the direction of the door. "I can't wait to hear how Prince Charming intends to pull this one off. Let's go hunt both of them down and tell them we like it here so much we've decided to stay permanently."

Olivia burst out laughing as she slid to the floor. "Oh,

Allie, I think that would give both of them heart failure."

"Humph." Alison rolled her eyes. "If Geoffrey can't figure out how to get us back, he's going to wish that's all he gets."

They dined by candlelight, even though the light lingered long into the summer evening. A soft breeze blew through the open windows of Geoffrey's study, making the flames flicker on the creamy white tapers. Nicholas had said he felt it wisest to keep the two women away from as many of the servants as possible, and he had sent his agent, an older man who normally dined with the brothers, off to Canterbury on some pretext of pressing business before his trip.

Olivia watched silently as Geoffrey and Alison discussed the calculations with great animation. She chewed her food carefully, watching her friend's face. Alison's cheeks were flushed a delicate pink. Geoffrey's eyes sparkled, clearly mesmerized by her nimble mind. There could be no doubt that Geoffrey found her the most entrancing woman he'd ever met. Olivia's gaze shifted, and she happened to meet Nicholas's eyes. He was watching her, eating as silently and as carefully as she.

"Is the food to your liking?"

His words startled her. "Why, yes," she managed to say without dropping her bread. "It's very good."

"You sound surprised."

"We are surprised," said Alison. "In our time we think you all had constant cases of ptomaine poisoning." She laughed.

Nicholas and Geoffrey exchanged confused looks. "Toe-main?" asked Geoffrey.

Alison held up a piece of meat. "Like this meat—the perception in our time is that since you didn't have reliable means to preserve it, it was constantly going bad, and making people sick."

Nicholas wiped his mouth and fingers delicately on his napkin. Both brothers had faultless table manners, Olivia noticed. "It is a problem indeed, mistress—but one that your age has resolved?"

"Oh, yes," answered Alison.

"Tell me," said Geoffrey, leaning closer, his eyes alight with curiosity. "Tell me, how—"

"Forgive me, Geoffrey." Nicholas rose to his feet. "There're matters I must discuss with Mistress Olivia concerning our trip. If you're finished, mistress, will you join me?"

Olivia picked up her napkin and carefully wiped each finger just as he'd done. "Yes. Yes, of course. I'm quite finished."

"You don't mind, Geoffrey?"

"Not at all, not at all." Geoffrey gave an airy wave. "Please, mistress, pray continue. How is this accomplished?"

Before Alison could launch into a description of modern refrigeration methods, Olivia rose to her feet and slipped out of the room with Nicholas. She gave him a wink as she joined him in the hall. "And I beg your pardon, mistress," he said as he offered her his arm. "My brother's constant questions would try the patience of a saint."

She allowed him to lead her down the stairs into the great hall. "I understand his curiosity. He's accomplished something quite amazing, all things considered."

"Hm." For a moment, Nicholas looked grim. "Will you walk with me, mistress?"

She nodded assent, and he led her out of the hall and into the gardens once more. The summer twilight had darkened into a wash of deep purples and violets and pinks across the sky, and the stars were beginning to twinkle over their heads. Without the interference of artificial light, they looked like fairy dust sprinkled over silk. A hush had descended over the gardens, and the night air was warm. Insects chirped steadily, and from the wide beds of flowering shrubs and herbs, a sweet, grassy scent arose, warm and green. Olivia breathed deeply. There was so much here that was truly beautiful—no wonder Nicholas loved his home so much. And unlike the Talcott Forest she'd seen at the end of the twentieth century, this Talcott Forest had a homey, lived-in feeling to it that was totally different from the cold sterility of the future.

"First of all," he said without preamble, "I want to apologize for the way Sir John behaved towards you today. It's my fault—I forgot he was coming, and I suppose it wasn't prudent of me to allow you to walk about in the garden dressed"—he paused and ran his eyes over her— "dressed the way you are."

"What about now, then?" she asked, the hint of a smile playing on her mouth. He was so obviously torn between his desire to play the good host and his discomfort with the whole unbelievable situation. But was it really that? A little pulse beat a rapid tattoo at his neck.

"No one's about now," he replied. "But—Sir John was wrong to speak to you as he did. I want to assure you that despite what you may believe, I do *not* think of you as a woman of loose morals, and neither should anyone else."

"Thank you."

They walked a little further in silence, and then Nicholas said, "He was here to speak to me about a betrothal with his daughter."

"Oh?" She waited.

"Patience."

Olivia waited, and, when he did not continue, asked, "Patience?"

"That's her name. Patience."

"Ah." She wondered, fleetingly, why he was telling her, and why he seemed to struggle so with the words. "Lord Nicholas, please—you need not explain yourself. I understand that Sir John had no idea of the real situation. And I suppose that, given the mores of this time, I *do* appear somewhat—startling."

He laughed, and she was startled to hear how deep and rich his laughter was. "Indeed, mistress. The fact of it is that, Puritan that Sir John might be, he's rich—rich with an only daughter, who, while she may be skinny as her father, and half as toothsome, is yet considered by many to be a great catch." He paused. "You understand me?"

It was her turn to laugh. "Yes, indeed."

"Sir John," he went on, his tone growing serious, "has long desired the Talcott lands—what's left of them," he finished with a bitter twist of his lips. "He offered to buy them some time ago while my father yet was living, and just a few years ago, there was a dispute over the property lines. But now, now that his daughter's come of marriageable age, he's found a new way to acquire the lands—he thinks."

"Will Sir John make trouble for you, since he saw me dressed the way I am?"

Nicholas shrugged. "I doubt it. I find I care little what he thinks in general, and even less what he thinks of you."

"And what will you do? About his daughter? Will he still allow you to marry her?"

Nicholas drew a deep breath. "In truth, mistress, at one point, I found the idea tempting. The prospect of a rich wife is not one to be spurned lightly. But . . ." he hesitated.

"But?" Olivia prompted.

"I do not think after today there will be any more conversations with Sir John."

An odd feeling shivered through her. *What on earth could this mean to you,* she asked herself. *So he's not going to marry some skinny Puritan wench with an insufferable father. What's that to you?* "Is that a good thing, or a bad thing?" she asked, choosing her words with care.

He paused in midstride and swung her around to face him. In the falling dark, his eyes were difficult to see, but his tone of voice was solemn. "If all goes in Calais as I hope it will, mistress, then I'll be able to be a bit more selective when it comes to wives—rich or not."

• • •

The full August moon hung like a round silver coin over the rooftops of London as Christopher Warren slipped into the side door of a large town house. The servant who admitted him wordlessly indicated the stairway with just a nod. Warren silently slipped up the narrow flight of stairs to the heavy oak door on the upper floor.

"Enter," a voice said at his knock.

"My Lord." Warren sank upon one knee before his master. The room was deep in shadow, but for the single pool of yellow light cast by the lone candle on the desk.

Walsingham did not pause in his writing. "Master Warren."

"All is in readiness, my lord."

"You're sure you have the right man?"

"Beyond all shadow of a doubt, my lord."

"Good." Walsingham paused long enough to shake sand across the surface of the parchment. He waited a moment, then emptied the sand into a container on the desk. He folded the parchment, poured a bit of wax on the edge, and sealed it with his ring. "Take this message to my Lord Cecil. Assure him that every precaution's been taken, and that I will personally deliver the plans as soon as we have them from the traitor."

"Lord Cecil knows you'd rather die yourself than let any harm come to Her Majesty," Warren said as he got to his feet. He took the parchment and slipped it into his shirt.

"Of course he does," answered Walsingham, taking up his quill and a fresh sheet of parchment. "It's everyone else who must be reminded." With a pointed look that inexplicably chilled Warren's bones, he turned back to his writing.

The London streets were crowded with people hurrying home in all directions. Warren slipped out of the same side door and joined the general throng of humanity hurrying through the crowded streets. Just before he reached Bishopsgate, he paused as someone jostled his arm. Before he knew it, a pickpocket was taking off down the

street, the precious parchment clutched in his hand. Warren swore beneath his breath and took off after the urchin.
The packet had no value at all—the idiot boy must be
desperate not to realize that he held no treasure. Slipping
and sliding through the muck and filth that filled the
streets, he dashed after the shadowy runaway. The boy
was just about to dash around a corner and down a dark
alley, when a tall shape reached out, grabbed the lad by
the scruff of the neck, and shook him. Warren came running up and joined them.

The man handed Warren the packet, and Warren stared
up into the mild eyes of a tall young man whose face
seemed familiar. "Here you are, sir." His rescuer spoke
with a thick Warwickshire accent.

Warren took in the high forehead, the thick hair
combed neatly back beneath a flat wool cap, the smooth,
clean-shaven face, and judged the man to be about twenty.
He narrowed his eyes. There was something familiar
about this young man, something that rang a bell. He'd
seen this face before, he knew he had. "Thank you," he
said, pocketing the packet securely. "And you—"

He raised his arm to cuff the boy, who still struggled
to get away, but the young man raised his other arm and
blocked Warren's blow. "Now, now, no need for that. He
got nothing for his trouble, did you, lad?" He gave the
boy a little shake and set him free. "Off with you," he
said as the boy took off with the speed of a greased cat.

Warren stared at the younger man. "Why'd you do
that?"

"He didn't get away with anything," answered the
young man, who returned Warren's most formidable glare
with such a good-natured smile Warren wondered if the
young man were simple.

Warren was about to reply when two more young men
rounded the corner. "Will!" the taller one called. "Will
Shakespeare! We've been looking all over for you—Marlowe's announced a new play."

The young man glanced over his shoulder and turned

back to Warren. "A pleasant evening to you, sir." He tugged at his cap and loped away, leaving Warren fuming under his breath and wishing all players consigned to the bottom of the sea.

Chapter 6

THE DAY OF departure dawned fair and promising, after a late-night storm that finally brought relief from the oppressive humidity of the past few days. Olivia woke up next to Alison and lay quietly, listening to Alison's gentle breathing, and wondering what the day would bring. Her traveling costume was laid out on the table and chairs; at the foot of the bed, a small black trunk held the rest of her clothes. She'd been amazed that old Janet, with the aid of three seamstresses commandeered from the closest village, had been able to produce the amount of clothing that they had, in such a short period of time. Of course, the clothes had all been those that had originally belonged to Nicholas's mother, so the major part of the work—the laying out of the patterns and the cutting of the fabrics, as well as most of the sewing—had already been accomplished. But there had been a great deal of fitting and refurbishing, and Olivia had watched in wonder as the four women had turned old Lady Talcott's clothing into three serviceable dresses that fit her perfectly.

Beside her, Alison sighed softly and turned over, snuggling deeper into her pillow. She'd spent the greater part of the last three days closeted in Geoffrey's study, going over his calculations and the layout of the maze. She hadn't seemed any happier to be here, but at least she had something to occupy her time. And the two of them seemed well suited, thought Olivia, in some odd way despite their disparate backgrounds. Geoffrey was intensely interested in everything Alison could tell him about life in the twentieth century, from politics to clothing styles. From what she could tell, the two of them never stopped talking.

A gentle knock on the door startled her. She slid out of bed, reached for the light woolen robe that, like most of their clothing, was a hand-me-down from Nicholas and Geoffrey's mother, and padded to the door, the smooth wooden boards cool beneath her bare feet. "Yes?" She opened the door a crack and saw Janet, with a tray, and two of the younger maids, each with a large bucket of steaming water.

"Breakfast, mistress. And Lord Nicholas thought ye'd like to bathe afore your journey. He ordered up a bath."

A bath, thought Olivia with a sigh. Bless Nicholas. She'd seen at once how labor-intensive it was to bathe. Buckets and buckets of hot water had to be hauled up from the kitchens, and in the five days since they'd appeared in the sixteenth century, the two women had only washed their hair once, and taken sponge baths. She opened the door wider and the maids marched in, followed by Janet and her tray. Behind them, she heard heavy pounding on the stairs.

Janet placed the tray on the table. "That'll be the tub, mistress," she said, nodding toward the door. The words were scarcely out of her mouth when the door flew open and two men, struggling with a large wooden tub, staggered in. Olivia glanced at Alison, who was still sleeping as soundly as ever. Alison would welcome a bath as well.

She stood aside while the men carried in the tub and placed it before the empty hearth. A low wooden screen was next. A procession of maids carried in bucket after bucket of hot water, while Olivia ate her breakfast of coarse brown bread and softened cheese. Finally, Janet added a packet of scented herbs to the steaming water. When the tub was nearly full, she brought in several linen towels and a rough bar of soap and placed them on the table. "The bath's ready, mistress," she said, her round face earnest. If she thought to question the sudden appearance of the two women, she was too utterly loyal to both Talcott brothers to breathe a suspicious word or to ask a potentially unsettling question.

Olivia slipped out of her clothes and stepped into the hot water. The water closed over her shoulders, and she settled back against the wooden tub with a sigh. Suddenly she'd never felt so dirty in all her life. She raised one leg out of the water and surveyed it critically.

From the other side of the screen, she heard Janet gathering up the breakfast tray. "I'll come back in a few minutes to help ye dress, mistress. Is there anything else ye require?"

Olivia hesitated, considering. "Yes," she said, on impulse. "A razor."

"A razor?" Janet peered around the screen, incredulity winning over modesty. "Did I hear ye say ye want a razor?"

"If one's available?" Olivia asked, deciding to brazen out her request. There might be plenty of things she could miss about the twentieth century, but she wasn't going to give up shaving her underarms and legs if at all possible.

Janet nodded, clearly mystified. "I'll—I'll just go see if I can find one from his lordship or Master Geoffrey." The old woman carried the tray out, still wearing a puzzled expression.

Olivia ducked down beneath the water, separating the long strands of her hair with her fingers. She surfaced, reached for the soap, and, working up a satisfactory lather, managed to wash her hair. She rinsed, just in time to see Janet peering around the screen once more, a straight-edged razor in her hand. "Lord Nicholas sent this with his compliments, mistress." Olivia had to bite her lip to keep from laughing at the woman's dubious expression. Loyal as she might be, this was clearly one request she'd never heard.

"Thank you, Janet." Olivia reached for the razor with all the nonchalance she could muster. She closed her fingers cautiously over the blade, and smiled a dismissal at Janet as if she handled straight-edged razors every day of her life. "That's all."

"Ye'll be wanting nothing more, then, mistress?"

"Not at the moment."

"I'll come back to help ye dress, then." With another shake of her head, the older woman was gone.

Olivia took a deep breath and placed the razor carefully on the edge of the tub. She picked up the soap and worked it into a lather beneath her right arm. She gingerly picked up the razor and was about to apply it to her underarm when Alison's voice made her jump.

"Liv! Where on earth did that bath come from?"

She looked up to see Alison peering over the screen, and carefully lowered her arm. "They brought it in while you were sleeping."

"Could I use one of those. Think they'll mind bringing more water up for me?"

"I wouldn't think so—especially since they have the bath all set up. And look—look what I have." Olivia held up the razor.

"That's a razor? You're going to use that to shave your legs? Geez, Liv, that looks more like a murder weapon. Be careful with that thing, huh?"

"I'll try." Gritting her teeth, Olivia gently stroked the sharp edge across her skin, and was gratified to see the short hairs disappear. "Well. It works."

"Just be careful," came Alison's voice from the other side of the screen.

"Don't worry." Working as carefully and as quickly as she could, Olivia managed to shave her legs and her underarms. She washed and rinsed herself all over and stepped out of the tub, reaching for one of the linen towels. She wrapped it around her hair, as Alison handed her the other. "I did it," she said as she wrapped her robe around herself. "No nicks or scrapes. I feel like a new woman."

Alison opened her mouth to reply when a knock at the door forestalled further conversation. "Come in?"

Janet peered around the door. "Mistress Olivia? Are ye finished wi' yer bath, then?"

"Yes," Olivia answered, "and I'm ready to get dressed. Would it be too much trouble to bring up a bath for Mistress Alison?"

"I have the maids heating up the water now, mistress. Lord Nicholas said he thought she'd like a bath, as well."

"My, my," murmured Alison, with a wink at Olivia. "So the handsome prince can be charming, after all."

"He lent me his razor, too," Olivia replied over her shoulder.

"Lord Nicholas's seeing to the horses, mistress. He means to leave wi'in the hour, if you please."

"Then let's dress." Olivia slipped out of her robe and into the linen smock Janet held up. Alison watched as the dressing was accomplished in less time than Olivia expected. Janet, who'd been Lady Talcott's maid, was obviously an expert at dressing a lady of her supposed station.

Over the smock, Janet laced on the bodice, a tightly fitted, sleeveless garment of dark green wool that combined the functions of bra and corset all at once. Next, a padded roll was laced around Olivia's hips. This would provide something close to the fashionable shape created by a hooped farthingale, but without the restrictions of movement that the farthingale would create. Next, two petticoats, one of russet, the other of the same dark green as the bodice, were laced into place. Over the embroidered sleeves of the smock, Janet laced two sleeves of dark green lined with russet, which had been slashed to allow the embroidery on the smock to show through. As a final step, she helped Olivia garter her russet stockings, and lace on ankle-length riding boots of polished black leather. The boots fit a little loosely, having been purchased from a cobbler in a shop in Sevenoaks, the nearest village. But, thought Olivia as she smoothed her petticoats and sat down to allow Janet to braid her still damp hair, they would have to do. Janet placed a white coif around her braids and set a felt hat of dark green, with a russet feather, at a jaunty angle on Olivia's head. She rose and turned to Alison, who'd been watching silently as she'd munched her breakfast bread-and-cheese, sitting cross-legged on the bed.

"Well, what do you think?"

Alison shook her head slowly, still chewing. She swallowed. "Honest to God, Liv, you look—you just look great!" She shot an apologetic glance at Olivia, realizing at once that she sounded much too twentieth century. They had agreed that Alison would try to restrict her speech as much as possible in the presence of anyone other than Nicholas or Geoffrey. She swallowed hard again, and added, much less emphatically, "You look very nice, Liv. Really."

"Thank you." Olivia winked.

"I'll be telling Lord Nicholas ye're ready," said Janet, gathering up the bath things. "Mistress Alison, the girls have started heating up the water for your bath—they'll be up directly to fill it."

Alison smiled and nodded. "Thank you," she said, her manner far more subdued.

Olivia waited until Janet had closed the door, then burst into giggles. "Allie, you'd better watch yourself."

"Thank God I'm not going along on this trip, huh? I'd have poor old Nicholas hung in no time."

"Don't even joke like that," Olivia said. She wrapped her arms around herself and gave a mock shiver. "But really—you think I look okay?"

"Liv, you look like the real thing. You look great. You look just like that picture in the pub. Remember?" Alison wagged her finger. "I'm telling you—that picture was you."

"I'd better go." Olivia leaned over and hugged her friend. "You be good now, you hear?"

"Yes, Mom."

The two friends exchanged a long look, and Olivia knew that both of them realized this could, possibly, be the last time they saw each other. "I'll see you."

"Count on it." Alison winked.

With another quick hug, Olivia left the room, wiping away a surreptitious tear. She was being silly. Of course she'd see Alison again. Of course they'd be together. How could they not? She went down the steps, consciously composing her face.

Nicholas was waiting in the hall, speaking to his agent, Miles Coddington. Both men looked up as she entered the hall. A surprised look crossed Nicholas's face, and it occurred to her that this was the first time he had ever seen her wearing the real accouterments of a woman of his own time, not to mention his mother's recut dress. His ideas of what was attractive were shaped, of course, by the time and place of his upbringing. But her metamorphosis into an Elizabethan lady seemed to have touched some entirely different place in him, for his eyes met hers with a new and deeper light, and his voice, as he addressed her, had a new and richer timbre. "Mistress—" He stopped, paused, smiled, and said, "My lady." He bowed.

Olivia gave a short laugh and curtsied. "My lord." She walked over to the two men. "Master Coddington."

"Mistress Olivia." Miles Coddington was a middle-aged man, in his late forties to midfifties, Olivia judged. It was difficult for her to guess a person's age in this time, because she assumed that people generally aged faster in the past than they did in the future. His broad face and light blue eyes were open and direct. "My lord's told me about your helping him by pretending to be his wife, mistress. He's doing a worthy thing, and bless you for helping him to do it." He tugged his forelock.

"Thank you, Master Coddington." She knew this was someone who could be trusted. Nicholas had explained that Miles Coddington was a veteran of many battles, having served on a number of privateer vessels and, most recently, with Leicester's men in the Low Countries. Nicholas had met him there and been impressed with his gallantry and innate nobility. When the war ended, Miles had been wounded and impoverished. Nicholas had offered him the position of agent at Talcott Forest, and Miles had turned his hand to running the estates with the same efficiency he'd run a privateer ship. A slight limp was the only evidence of his injuries. How much Nicholas had told her about the way of life here, she thought with a start, as she met his dark blue eyes. It was the best history lesson she'd ever received.

Nicholas was looking at her with that new intensity and, unnerved, she momentarily lowered her lashes. "I'm ready."

"So I see." He smiled at her again and took her hand with a sudden casual gesture that seemed so natural she was startled once more by its very easiness. "I agree with you, Miles, on what to do with the lower forty. See that those fences are mended, and hire as many as you need to get the harvest in. It looks as if we're in for a fair spell of weather—I'd like to see as much done by St. Bart's day as you can manage." He turned once more to Olivia. "Shall we be on our way, then, madam?" He smiled a farewell to Miles over her head as he led her away and, for a moment, Olivia had the unnerving feeling that he was treating her exactly as he would were she, in fact, his wife. Her heart beat faster, and a little voice in her mind whispered: *Stop it. You're behaving like a silly adolescent. Where do you think this could lead?* With a sigh, she forced herself to heed the voice of her more sensible side. As they reached the threshold of the house, Nicholas paused and turned to face her.

Her heart once again beat faster, but his words fell like a shock of icy water on her flushed cheeks and fluttering lashes. "Let me look at you." It was said with the same terse disdain he'd used just a few days ago, less than an hour after her arrival with Alison in the sixteenth century. She raised her face slowly and met chill blue. She must've been dreaming, she thought. There was no more interest in Nicholas's gaze than if she'd been the milch cow he'd first made her feel like. "You'll do very well, mistress. I must say, I am impressed at old Janet's efforts. Now, you do remember all I've told about this trip? Our names are Master Stephen Steele, esquire, and his wife, Mistress Katherine Steele. We're on pilgrimage to Notre Dame in Paris, and we receive a message that causes us to turn back to home."

"Why?" She met his eyes with a look of cool determination. She would show him that while she may well be a stranger in a strange land, she was not without wits. He blinked.

"Why what?"

"Whyfore are we on our way to Paris, my lord husband? What boon do we beg? What cure do we seek? Is't an old war wound of yours, sir? Or perhaps something that prevents the growth of your seed in my womb?" She raised her chin and cocked her head, eyes dancing.

A glint of humor made his lips quirk, and momentarily she thought she saw that new look glimmer in his eyes, but whatever flame there was, was immediately dashed. "Point scored, mistress. We'll say . . . an old war wound of mine that makes me incapable of planting a seed in your womb." Another fleeting smile lifted the corner of his mouth. He offered her his arm and pushed open one side of the great doors. Together, they stepped outside onto the broad stone steps that led down to the curving drive. Two horses were saddled and waiting; a third was ridden by the young boy who would serve as Nicholas's squire. Fleetingly, Olivia realized there would be no woman to attend her as Janet had. Who would help her dress? She glanced up at Nicholas in sudden horror. This was no case of maidenly vapors, she thought. There *was* an undeniable attraction between them. And alone, thrown together on a journey, if Nicholas showed any of that charm, what could happen? She suppressed her thoughts with a rueful little sigh. A brief fling, pleasurable as it might be, was hardly what she wanted. It could only lead to hurt and regret.

He lifted her up into the saddle. "You must call me Nicholas until we arrive in Dover," he said gruffly as his hands spanned her tightly laced waist.

She did not reply. She gathered the reins in her gloved hands and sat up straight in the saddle, thanking God that she and Alison had gone through the typical adolescent girl's preoccupation with horses. Both of them had been interested in the beautiful animals long enough to learn to ride proficiently, if not expertly, and once or twice they'd ridden together in Central Park.

The chest that held their clothes was strapped to the back of the boy's saddle. Jack, that was his name, thought Olivia. He touched his forelock in the same gesture of respect Miles had used. His mouth hung slightly open, as though he was amazed beyond words at the sudden appearance of Lord Nicholas's supposed bride.

Nicholas swung into his own saddle. "Let's away, then." There was no sign of Geoffrey, and Olivia wondered if the brothers had had unpleasant words before they'd left.

She gave a last look to the silent windows within the shade of the great trees. "Good-bye, Allie." She whispered a silent prayer that she would see her friend again, then touched her heels to her gelding's sides.

Chapter 7

"ALL FRESH AND clean?" Geoffrey teased as Alison walked in the door of his study.

She sighed, running her fingers through her still damp curls. "You just can't imagine."

"I like to be clean." He put down his astrolabe and crossed his arms over his chest. "We aren't complete barbarians, you know."

"I know you do the best you can. I had no idea a bath could be so much trouble. How do people without servants do it?"

"They don't," he answered. "Or not very often. I guess you get used to bathing all the time, hm?"

"Do you know, there are some days when I take three showers a day?"

"Three?" He blinked.

"Sure. One when I wake up in the morning before work, one after I go to the gym at lunch, and one after I run in the afternoon." She shook her head. "Now that's a lot of hot water."

"Three of these showers—the water runs by itself?"

"Yeah. All you do is turn a tap. That's it. And it's hot

and it's fresh and it's clean—and there's all of it you could ever want."

"What I wouldn't give to see such a wonder." He sighed.

"Well, maybe you should come with us."

"Go with you?" His eyes widened.

"Why not? Think about it. If you can figure something like this out here, now, under these conditions—think about what you could do with all the resources of the twenty-first century. If you'd just hurry up and figure out the way to get us back there, we might even make it in time to celebrate the new millennium. You know, Y2K—the year two thousand and all that."

"I—why, it never occurred to me to go with you!"

"Isn't that what you built the maze for in the first place?"

"Yes, I suppose it was."

"Well, then." She gave his arm a little poke. "Let's get busy there, buddy. If it worked once, it has to be able to work again. And maybe we can figure out a way to sweet-talk Nicholas so he won't destroy it the minute we're all gone. It'd be a real bummer if you didn't like the future and couldn't get back." She winked at him, choking back a laugh at the startled expression on his face.

He picked up the astrolabe and set it down again, turning to the window with a troubled expression.

"Hey, what's wrong? I was only teasing you."

"It's Nicholas. And this whole foolhardy venture of his. I don't like it—the whole thing makes me uneasy, but I can't put my finger on why. I tried to tell him so this morning before he left, but he'd not hear a word I had to say." Geoffrey shook his head and sighed.

"Well, what strikes you as odd about it? It seems reasonable enough to me. Gets him back in the Queen's good graces and all."

Geoffrey sighed again and drummed his fingers on his desk. "It's just—this Master Warren, suddenly appearing out of nowhere. I mean, how does Nicholas even know he works for Walsingham? How can Nicholas be so sure he's even in the Queen's service? It's just too—too—"

"Convenient?"

Their eyes met in sudden understanding. "Yes," he said after a brief pause. "It's too neat. I don't trust this Master Warren, whoever·he is. There was a very nasty incident involving someone named Warren in my father's time. He never spoke of it, but my mother told us both the story after his death. I think it changed him forever."

Alison sat down on a high stool opposite the desk. "I'm listening."

"It was during the reign of Queen Mary—Bloody Mary, they call her now. Did you know that?" When she nodded he shrugged. "So even four hundred years later . . ." He trailed off, then started again after a few moments. "My father was a devout Catholic. His devotion never wavered, even when it was clear it would be safer to sway with the wind. When Mary was finally made Queen, after so many years of suppression, his fervor exploded into something closer to fanaticism. I think even my mother feared him in those years. There was a schoolmaster in the parish—Robert Warren was his name. He had a wife, and several children, and—well, I don't remember him. I wasn't even born. He was accused of heresy, and when an English Bible was found in his home—it was his undoing. Father saw him burned alive at Canterbury."

"Burned?" Alison leaned back, horrified that someone could speak of something so terrible as a distinct reality.

"Aye. It's a thing neither Nicholas nor I am proud of, believe me. It's a chapter best closed, I say. If no one ever burns to death in England again, I say it will be too soon. Surely there can be no crueler death."

"I can't imagine . . ." Alison whispered.

"They don't do such things in your time, I suppose?"

"No—well, cruelty is—there are still terrible people who do terrible things. But in England—and in the United States for that matter—no one is put to death by burning."

"Thank God." He closed his eyes. "Well. That's all there is to the story. When I heard the name Warren, I couldn't help but think of it. I guess Nicholas is too preoccupied with his hopes of restoring our fortunes to remember such a thing."

"Do you blame him?"

"No. It's his purpose as the eldest son and heir to all the family estates. While I, I get to be the eccentric dabbler in the arcane arts."

"We'd better get to it, don't you think? After all, whether or not Nicholas restores the family fortunes, neither Olivia nor I want to be here to enjoy them. How soon do you expect to hear from this teacher of yours—Dr. Dee?"

With a brief laugh, Geoffrey picked up his astrolabe. "With no mishap, I expect my letter to arrive within another day or two. Assuming he writes back within another day or two after that, I expect we'll have a reply by the time Nicholas and Olivia return. And as for you, Mistress Wise-and-Wonderful, be so kind as to check these calculations I did while you were enjoying the comfort of your bath?"

"Whatever you'd like, Master-of-the-Arcane-Arts."

With another shared laugh, the two of them bent over their papers. *Just let Olivia be okay,* prayed Alison to whomever might be listening. An uneasy premonition ran through her mind. She didn't care a fig what happened to Nicholas and his family fortunes. Just as long as she and Olivia made it home to 1999, she'd be happy. After all, was that really so much to ask?

Later, Olivia decided that the best she would ever be able to say about her first sixteenth-century journey was that it was slow. Although she knew intellectually that travel in Elizabethan England was difficult, it was a very different thing to experience it firsthand, especially after knowing the comparative ease of twentieth-century travel. The roads, if such they could be called, were deep, pitted ruts that made her shudder at the thought that one of the horses could be lamed. But the weather was fine—the sun warm across her shoulders and the breeze cool enough to refresh. The countryside was like a picture book come to life: fields gold with summer wheat and green with hay, bustling with peasants dressed in faded blues and browns, who tended sheep or cows or gathered in the harvest.

They stopped for a late lunch beneath a stand of trees that Nicholas said was nearly halfway to Dover.

"What d'ye think, sir?" asked Jack, munching an apple. "Will we come to Dover by night?"

"I expect so," said Nicholas, squinting in the direction of the sun. "The road will open out between here and there. We should be able to make better time." He tore the last bit of meat off a chicken leg and tossed the bone into the brush, then delicately wiped his fingers with his napkin. "Are you quite finished, lady?" Ever since leaving Talcott Forest, he'd addressed her as "my lady," or simply "lady." It was as if, Olivia realized, he was preparing himself to play the part, and she nodded, the hint of a smile on her lips.

"Thank you, yes."

"Do you need to—er"—Nicholas paused and nodded toward a clump of bushes on the far side of the clearing—"refresh yourself?"

Olivia followed his glance and understood. "Ah, yes. A good idea." She got to her feet, gathering and arranging her skirts. And Alison thought chamber pots were awful to use.

They came to Dover just as night was falling over the ancient seaside port. The scent of the ocean filled the air, and the gentle slap of the sea against wharves was a constant soft refrain. Nicholas stopped before a half-timbered inn. "We'll stop here for the night," he said. "Jack, you see to the horses. As soon as you're settled, my lady, I'll book passage on tomorrow's first tide." He swung out of his saddle and led them all through the stone arch, into the courtyard of the inn. A groom came forward to take the horses, and Nicholas reached up to help Olivia down from her saddle. She groaned momentarily, as muscles she'd forgotten she had protested the day's overuse.

"Are you all right?" He frowned down at her.

"Just a little sore. It's been a while since I spent that much time on horseback."

"Ah." He raised an eyebrow and turned away, as if to forestall any further conversation. She smoothed her skirts, and allowed him to lead her into the common room, where the landlord, recognizing at once Nicholas's status by what was probably a combination of dress and bearing, came forward, bowed, and asked what he could offer them. "A room," answered Nicholas, stripping off his gloves. "Two rooms," he amended, looking at Olivia. She lowered her eyes instinctively. She felt him willing her to look up, and she met his gaze. Desire so clearly struggled with control in his eyes, it took her breath away. "Yes. Two rooms," he said again.

"Where do you want me to carry this, m'—sir?" Jack stood in the doorway, the small trunk on his shoulder.

"Follow me," said the landlord, leading them up the steps at the back of the common room. "I have two rooms right beside each other. Share a door, in fact, just so you can—" He started to chuckle, looked over his shoulder at Nicholas's expressionless face, and broke off. "This way."

He led them down a short corridor and paused before a thick oak door. He turned the key in the iron lock. "That's yours, Master Steele." He handed it to Nicholas and, pushing open the door, stood aside to let Nicholas and Olivia pass. "An it please, sir."

Olivia followed Nicholas, looking around at the cozy room. It was neat and very clean, the big bed made with white linen sheets. The scent of fresh, line-dried linen and ocean air filled the chamber. The landlord pushed open a door on the other side of the hearth.

"And in here is the second chamber—with a key in the lock outside the hall door, just like this one."

"Fetch it, Jack," said Nicholas. "This will do," he said to the landlord. He pulled a money pouch from his belt. "What do I owe you?"

"For just tonight, Master Steele?"

"Aye, we're bound for Calais on the morrow."

"Fourpence for each room, an it please you. That includes the stabling of your horses, and room for your squire in the loft above the stable."

Nicholas handed over a shilling. "Send up a bath for my wife, and a maid to attend her. And tell me, where can I book passage? Know you a captain of repute?"

"Aye, my lord, thank you, my lord." The landlord bobbed a bow. "Downstairs now, the captain of the *Merry Harry* is drinking a pint of my best ale."

"Good. Will you tell him Master Steele would speak with him? I'll be down directly." Nicholas turned to Jack when the landlord had gone. "Put the trunk in there"—he nodded toward the second room—"then see to the horses. Here, my dear." He placed the iron key Jack had given him in the palm of her hand. "I'll shut this door when I go down. I'll wait until the maid brings your bath though."

A quizzical look crossed her face. "You can trust me not to say—"

"It isn't that I don't trust you," he interrupted her. His face was hard to read. "There're stories told—of things that can happen. This is a reputable inn and I doubt any of them happen here. But you are in my care and under my protection, and"—he paused, as if searching for a way to finish—"and I would not have anything untoward happen to you."

"Thank you, my lord." Suddenly, she felt very shy.

"You know you needn't call me that." He shook his head. "My name is Nicholas—or Stephen, for now."

"I—I know. I haven't wanted to appear overly forward—" she began, in the very same instant as he said: "It would sound odd if you did not make use of—"

They both broke off and laughed shortly, staring at each

other, and Olivia was acutely aware that they were alone
and that the bed beside them was less than three or four
paces away. *What do you think you're doing?* screamed
the more rational side of her mind.

A sudden knock on the door broke the spell. "Bath to
go in here, sir?"

"Next door." Nicholas did not look away from her.

"Nicholas," she said, hesitantly, almost tasting the
sound of his name, "thank you for the bath, but—why?
Why did you order it? I bathed just this morning."

"You said you were sore from the long ride. I thought
it would feel good and help remove the ache."

"Mistress?" A girl's soft voice interrupted Olivia before
she could speak. "Mistress Steele?"

"Yes?" Olivia said, realizing that this, more than any
other so far, was really the opening scene of the play they
were about to begin. "I'm Mistress Steele." She flashed
Nicholas a bright, reassuring smile and stepped around
him into the part.

The common room was filled with travelers of all degrees
and stations, thought Nicholas as he nursed a pint of ale
beside the fire. In one of the rooms above, Olivia slept,
he hoped, content enough after her bath and dinner. The
long day had tired her out, he hoped, as much for his sake
as for hers. Pray he'd be able to sleep, knowing that she
was just on the other side of the dark oak door. He had
thought her attractive fleetingly, he realized, when he'd
first seen her, and seeing her dressed in his own clothes
had roused undeniable desires. But when he'd seen her
dressed as a lady of his own time, with his mother's
clothes made over to fit her more slender form, he had
been taken aback this morning by her transformation. It
was as if she'd not only donned the clothes of an accomplished lady, but the manner and bearing of one as well.
And yet, there was a touching vulnerability in her dark
eyes that made him want to protect her, keep her safe from
all the dangers he knew all too well lurked at every turn.

Thieves and cutpurses, who would murder them both for their clothing, were the least of them, he mused. He glanced up and was startled to see Christopher Warren slipping out of the room. Their eyes met, and Nicholas knew the man recognized him. He raised his tankard, but Warren was gone, slipping out of the tavern and into the night without so much as a nod. That was odd, thought Nicholas as he settled back into his chair. Or was it? Didn't it make sense for Warren to make sure he was doing his duty as he'd promised? But why not speak to him? Nicholas glanced around at the other patrons. Maybe, he thought suddenly, there were *Spanish* agents about—Spanish agents who would report to their contact in Calais whether or not the Englishman could be trusted. Of course, he thought. That must be it. He settled back in his chair and called for another ale, trying to occupy his mind with thoughts of what he would do with Elizabeth's reward, while all the time thoughts of Olivia snuggled in her bed warred with Geoffrey's nagging warning.

Chapter 8

DESPITE NICHOLAS'S hopes for fair weather, the next day dawned gray and overcast, with a damp wind that whined out of the south, bringing rain in short, vicious squalls. Olivia woke to the sound of rain lashing against the casement window of her room. For a moment she lay still, the coarse linen sheets pulled up to her chin. She rubbed the fabric between her fingers. Coarsely woven as it was, the linen had been washed to soft suppleness by repeated launderings. It smelled of fresh salt air and the sun. She stared up at the ceiling. There were cracks in the plaster above her head, and she could imagine the mice and rats scampering inside the thatch. With a shudder, she forced that thought out of her head. There were some things she'd rather not think about. She sat up in bed, wondering whether or not the rain would delay their journey. Instantly she was chilled by the damp air. She looked at the cold, dark hearth with sudden longing. Would they think her mad if she asked for a fire to take the chill away?

A knock on the adjoining door between the two bedrooms startled her. She climbed out of the high bed, dragging her robe around her shoulders. All her muscles protested. Despite yesterday's warm bath, she was sore in places she'd forgotten she had. She opened the door. Nicholas was fully dressed, and his damp hair and rain-spotted cloak told her he'd most likely been out in the weather.

"There'll be no travel today, lady," he said without greeting. He avoided looking at her.

"What will we do?"

He shrugged. "I've sent for a maid and I've ordered a breakfast for us in the private parlor. If you would care to join me there, you'll find it right off the common room." He broke off, looking distinctly uncomfortable. "Other than that—" He rubbed his chin, and she could see he felt as frustrated as she.

"I'll be happy to join you," she said, as someone tapped briskly on her hall door.

"That must be the maid. I saw her on my way up."

"I'll join you directly, then."

Olivia shut the door and tried not to notice how her hand shook. A day alone with Nicholas—in an inn. She wondered what time it was, but the gray sky prevented her from even guessing how late it was. She opened the door to the same cheery-faced maid who'd waited on her last night.

"G'morrow to ye, mistress," Molly chirped as she entered, dragging in a large bucket filled with steaming water.

Olivia returned the greeting with a smile and a nod. "Good morrow to you, Molly."

"And a cold, miserable day 'tis, in truth. Landlord says ye'll not be traveling today." She bustled to the bed and threw the sheets back. "There—we'll just let that air a bit." She poured half the water into an earthen bowl by the bed, reached beneath the bed, and pulled out the chamber pot. "Y' have a wash, mistress, while I see to this. And then I'll help ye dress—unless of course yer husband—?" She paused, an expectant smile on her face.

"He's a fine one, if ye don't mind me saying so. Man like that gets himself noticed."

Olivia felt herself flush. "Yes," she stammered, mortified by her reaction. "He's quite—quite good-looking. But, no, he, uh, he has affairs of his own to manage—please come back and help. I believe my—my husband is downstairs already."

"An you will, mistress." With a cheery smile, she left the room, shutting the door behind her, leaving Olivia still blushing at the thought of Nicholas helping her dress.

She found Nicholas waiting for her at a table pulled up beside the fire. They were alone in the parlor. He stood up as she entered. "We aren't the only travelers whose plans are delayed by the weather, but apparently we're the only ones who rate the parlor. Tell me, do you play primero?"

Olivia shook her head. "I'm afraid I don't."

"Then perhaps you'll allow me to teach it to you?" he asked as he took his seat opposite from her, across the wide plank table. "It's a way to while away the time. Or perhaps chess? Do you play chess?"

Before she could answer, the landlord bustled in, carrying a large tray on which were a bowl of peaches, a cold haunch of roast meat, and a round loaf of bread. He placed the food before them and stepped back, hands on his hips. "Ale, sir?"

"Aye," said Nicholas, "and cider—hot cider—for the lady." He had noticed that she had not developed a taste for the most common of sixteenth-century drinks. He waited until the landlord had gone. "May I serve you?"

"Please."

She watched while he carved a slice of meat off the haunch and placed it, along with half the bread and a peach, on her plate. "Thank you."

They ate in silence, and Olivia was acutely aware that they were alone, and equally aware of everything in the spare, clean parlor. Every sense she had was alert. The fire snapped and hissed and infused the room with the smoky scent of burning wood. Rain lashed against the tiny panes of the two small windows, which rattled in their frames with the force of the wind. She was preternaturally conscious of the very walls—plain whitewash—and the floor, with its smooth wooden planks, unlike the flagstones in the common room. She was sure she could count every crack, every seam, in the plaster ceiling with its exposed, smoke-blackened beams.

She picked up the peach. It was a heavy velvet ball in her hand—a ripe, golden pink that smelled of the orchard and the sun. She closed her eyes and inhaled, then bit into the flesh. Peach juice, sweet and syrupy and warm, exploded on her tongue. She opened her eyes and met Nicholas's. He was watching her with the same kind of intensity. Who would ever believe this, she wondered. Here she sat, in a sixteenth-century inn, wearing sixteenth-century clothes, eating peaches with an English lord who looked like every woman's fantasy of what an English lord should look like.

This is ridiculous, she scolded herself. *You're behaving like a schoolgirl. Why not just—just enjoy each other?* But another voice intruded, a voice that sounded like her father's, warning her against hurt and regret and to exercise caution in all matters of the heart. This relationship— if such it could be called—could go nowhere. They literally belonged to two different times and places. *Then why,* cried out her less rational side, *why do you feel as though you've known this man forever? As though you understand exactly what he wants? And why does it all seem so simple?* She glanced up. His gaze hadn't moved. To her horror, she felt herself blush. He was looking at her with an odd expression, she realized—a little half-smile that danced at the corners of his mouth, as though he were amused. "Is there—is there anything wrong?"

"No," he said. "It's only—well, I suppose things must be different for you—seldom have I seen a lady tear into a piece of fruit the way you did."

"Oh!" She placed the peach on her plate and picked up her knife, suddenly flustered and embarrassed, remembering that the Elizabethans valued faultless table manners. To Nicholas, her action must've seemed as barbaric as using a chamber-pot did to her.

"No, no," he said, grasping her hand. "Please—I never meant to discomfit you. You continue to amaze me— please, continue eating as you wish. I meant no insult."

She looked from his fingers wrapped around her wrist to his eyes. Instantly he released her hand. "What do you mean, I amaze you?"

He spread his hands and shrugged. "I can scarcely imagine the world which you are from. And do not think, lady, that I believe that I could fit in half so well as you do in this one. I've listened to you and Alison and Geoffrey these last few days, and—" He shook his head. "Trust me. I cannot imagine the life which you have lived." He leaned forward, searching her eyes. "But I have watched you these last few days, as well. And in truth, lady, you— you could have been born into this time and place, so well do you fit. Like a coat true-made to the body of the wearer. Lady, how do you know so much?"

"Well . . ." she began uncertainly. "My father—"

"Yes, yes, you've talked about your father. But what could've prepared you to—to become someone—become someone like—"

"Like you?"

He looked taken aback and then laughed. "Touché, lady. Even that—addressing you so—does not seem odd, or misplaced, in any way. I know you come from a time when all men and women are common, but, surely, there are—"

"It's different," she said softly. "I suppose I should confess."

"Confess?"

"Nothing wrong." She had to suppress a laugh in the face of his sudden obvious doubt. "In my time, as in yours, there are actors—players—"

"There is still theater?"

"Plays of this time are still being performed."

"Indeed."

"Yes. And I, well—the truth of it is that I've always wanted to be an actress. And I've studied—oh, not as much as I'd've liked, but in school, I was always in the plays. I've won medals—awards—for acting. It is my dearest wish to someday act upon the stage—the real stage. The legitimate stage, as it's called." She sat back with a little sigh.

"Ah." The fire hissed even more loudly as a log broke apart. "I see." He stroked his chin. "Even more interesting." They lapsed once more into silence. Uncertainly, Olivia cut a slice of her peach and popped it into her mouth. Juice ran down her chin and she grabbed for her napkin. Her eyes happened to meet Nicholas's and the two of them burst out laughing.

"I don't want you to think I'm a woman of loose morals, you see. I know it's quite unheard-of for a woman to appear on stage."

"Ah." Nicholas waved an airy hand. "Not quite so unheard-of, in some places. But believe me, lady. When I call you that, I mean it. And while you are with me, in the guise of my wife, I will treat you with no less respect and honor as if you were my very own."

A little pulse of heat shivered through her. It seemed to settle in the very pit of her belly and begin a slow, smooth burn. She fumbled with the peach, and he caught her hand in his. "Olivia." He caressed each syllable of her name, drew out each liquid vowel.

She chewed, swallowed, and looked up. "Yes, Nicholas?"

"I . . . have not been the most gracious of hosts. I know that I have been less than hospitable to you and your friend, and—" He broke off and glanced into the fire. "That first day, when you sang for the Queen, you pleased her greatly. I never really thanked you. Please—" He hesitated once more. "Please accept my apology. You did not have to do what you did. I had no right to impose upon you in such a way. And you, you were quite—quite wonderful. Thank you."

"You're very welcome. But I wanted you to know that, to my mind, you've given me a great gift, as well. This, this is quite an opportunity for me, you understand. To see all this—to experience so much . . ." She indicated the room, the food, and the world outside the windows with the sweep of her hand. "And I'm truly grateful, too."

He leaned forward, his eyes alight with interest. "Are you really? Does all this—any of it—matter in your time?"

"It matters a great deal to people like my father." She paused, considering how much to say. "And to me, too."

"Why?"

She met his eyes squarely. "There are things which endure. The plays—that's only one thing. As unbelievable as it may sound to you, there are many things from this time which still matter greatly to many people in my time."

"But tell me which ones matter to you? Which plays do you like best? Maybe I know them, too."

"I'm not sure how much more I should say."

"Why?"

"Well, what if I tell you something, and you decide to do something or not do something, based on what I've told you? What if you went up to London one day, to see a play because I told you it was wonderful, and your horse got lamed, and you got robbed, and you were crippled, and died without ever having a son, and—"

"Then Geoffrey would be my heir. Until I have a son, lady, that's what would happen anyway."

"But don't you understand? You will have a son. You must have a son. In my time, it's known you have a son. And if, because of my presence here, you choose to do something that changes anything that's to come—everything I've ever read or heard about the possibility of time travel always warns of the danger of changing things in the past, because the future may be affected."

"Ah." He raised an eyebrow and nodded. "So I suppose if I go home and tear down my brother's maze, you won't be able to come through?"

"Exactly. Something like that. Perhaps you ought to try it."

Their eyes met and held once more. "And prevent you from coming through?"

"Well, it would uncomplicate things greatly, wouldn't it?"

The corners of his mouth lifted in that quirky little smile she was coming to know. "But then you would not be sitting here with me, on this most dismal day in Dover, waiting to sail with me to Calais, to help me in the restoration of my father's fortunes. So I suppose the question becomes, If I were to prevent you from coming through the maze, how could this be happening now?"

"I—I guess it really couldn't," she stammered, unnerved by his unwavering stare. His eyes were so blue— so damn blue, she thought suddenly, and suddenly she wanted nothing more than to press her mouth against those full, chiseled lips, lips that were carved so beautifully they might have been made of marble.

He picked up her hand, and her fingers twined around his of their own volition. "You intrigue me, Mistress Olivia."

"As you intrigue me, Lord Ni—"

He put his finger to his lips. "Ssh. My name is Stephen, remember? And you're my wife—Katherine—there should be some familiarity between us, for God's sake."

"Sorry." Taken aback by his sudden change of tone, she tried to pull her hand away, but he tightened his grip to prevent her. The pressure of his hand on hers made her heart race.

"Hush. There is no need for sorry." He rose to his feet and, without letting go of her hand, drew her up and out of her chair. Her breath caught in her throat as he leaned over her, and she realized his intent. Her eyes closed of their own volition as his mouth came down on hers.

She was not prepared for the riptide of pleasure that surged through her, a heady wave of heat that raced through her veins like a hot tide. She swayed a little as her bones turned to water, and he wrapped his arms around her, and drew her close. Through the bulky petticoats, she felt the hard pressure of his thighs against hers, and her breasts were crushed against his chest. She moaned beneath his mouth as the kiss deepened. When he finally drew back, she was breathless.

They stared at each other for a long moment. "I should ask your forgiveness," he said at last. "But I'm not at all sorry." She made a small sound in her throat, something that could have been either protest or assent, and he reached out and touched her cheek with the back of two fingers. "You fascinate me in a way no woman ever has before. You are so—so very different, and yet, there's something about you. I look at you and—" He hesitated. "You'll think me as mad as Geoffrey, but, when I look at you, I feel as if I know you."

She nodded, still silent.

"Is it just . . . this whole impossible event? Or is there something more, do you think?" He bent down, before she could answer, and gathered her mouth to his once more.

Olivia shut her eyes tightly, her senses wholly inflamed. Her fingers shook as she reached up and twined her hands in his soft, black curls. He drew back, breaking the kiss, and she opened her eyes with a disappointed little moan. His eyes were blazing pools of azure. "This is madness. Forgive me." He flung himself back into his chair and ran his hands through his hair. "Please—please sit. I'll see if there's a deck of cards—a chessboard, perhaps—and call the maid to clear all this away."

She sank down into her own chair, vaguely disappointed. *What on earth are you thinking,* she scolded herself once more. This was becoming a familiar refrain, she thought wryly. But at least she knew he shared her feelings. The thought of the long day ahead to be spent alone with him made her heart race. She could imagine Alison saying: *Oh, cut that out. You're acting worse than a high school freshman who's been noticed by the captain of the football team.* The rain lashed harder at the window, fierce little pellets of water that sounded as solid as pebbles. She laced her fingers in her lap and forced herself to calm down. The way she was behaving, no one would ever believe that "Master Stephen" had any kind of a war wound at all.

The afternoon passed more quickly than she would've thought possible. A sharp rap on the door startled her just as she was about to place her knight on Nicholas's king's bishop's one.

Nicholas glanced over his shoulder, stretching his long legs before him. "Enter!"

Molly's cheerful face peered around the door. She pushed the door open, carrying an armful of wood. "Master asks if ye'd care for yer dinner, Master Steele?"

Nicholas glanced swiftly at Olivia. "Yes, I think so. But, wait—"

The maid paused in midstep.

"Can you tell me if Captain Percival is in the common room?"

"Nay, sir, he's not been seen all day. Most likely he's down by the docks, looking for some sign that the weather'll break."

Nicholas glanced at the window, and Olivia, following his gaze, realized that the rain had diminished to nothing but a slow drip from the low eaves. "Then perhaps I'll go look for him there." He stood up and turned to Olivia. "And you, my dear? Are you hungry? Or can you wait a bit? I'd like to settle the question of our passage if at all possible before dark."

"Could I—" Olivia fingered the wooden chess piece. "Could I perhaps go with you? I'd be grateful for a chance to stretch my legs."

He looked taken aback, but then smiled, a slow, measuring smile, that spread across his face by degrees. "Most certainly, wife, an that please you. Molly, will you fetch my wife her cloak? The rain seems to have slowed, but it's still damp."

Molly withdrew with a curtsy, and Olivia rose to her feet. "You don't mind if I come along, do you?"

"Not at all. It didn't occur to me you'd like to accompany me—but I must warn you, Captain Jack is . . . he's not exactly familiar to the company of ladies. I'm not sure what you're accustomed to, but from all you've told me today, I somehow doubt you've met too many characters like him."

Olivia rose and gave him a wry grin as she smoothed her skirts. "Of that I have absolutely no doubt at all."

The sky was a wash of grays and pinks and violets as they set out from the inn. A red sun was setting low in the western sky, and the roofs of Dover glistened in the early evening light. The streets were for the most part deserted, and the heavy rains had washed the sewage from the center of the cobbled roads. The shops were shuttered, but the painted signs were a bright contrast to the stone and half-timbered buildings they passed. Smoke rose from the chimneys, carrying with it the scents of cooking food, and the occasional laugh or shout or cry from behind a shuttered window gave a hint of the lives lived within. Three girls dressed like miniature women played a version of hopscotch, while a mixed group of boys and girls ducked behind barrels and ran over stoops in a game Olivia thought could only be tag. The girls' dresses were hiked up to their knees, and their shrieks in the silent evening carried up and down the empty streets. A woman's head popped out of an upper-story window. "Hush up now!" she cried. The children looked up, laughed, and went back to their game, the boys making a great show of deliberately splashing the girls.

"Some things never change," Olivia said as they navigated the narrow streets.

Nicholas smiled, but only said, "I hope the weather clears for tomorrow."

"Red sky at night, sailors' delight," Olivia quoted, nodding at the sunset as they emerged at the end of the street where it ended at the quay.

"You think so?"

"That's how the old saying goes."

They strolled along the quay a little way in silence.

"Olivia—"

"Nicholas—"

They began together and broke off, laughing. "You first," she said.

"No, no, you, I insist."

Olivia smiled and shrugged. "Since you insist. I—I only wanted to say how much I've enjoyed today. You've been very kind and patient with all my—my uncertainties. And I—well, I just wanted to tell you I enjoyed your company."

"As I enjoyed yours, lady. I—" He broke off and would not look at her. They walked on in silence, and finally he said, "I meant no insult this morning. I hope you realize that."

"Lord N—*Master* Stephen," she laughingly corrected herself, "I was not insulted." Their eyes met, and suddenly she felt breathless.

He smiled. "Good." He patted her hand where it rested on his arm, and they continued on in a companionable silence that felt as comfortable as their conversation.

Just as they reached the first of the docks, where the ships rocked on their moorings and the gulls swooped low between the forest of masts and sails, crying out against the darkening sky, he paused and drew back, squinting down the street into the fading light. She heard him draw a sharp breath. "What is it?"

He drew back against the buildings. "Down there—across the street—in front of that tavern. I saw a man go in there just now. . . ."

"Do you know the man?"

"Aye. 'Tis Sir John Makepiece—I would wager my life upon it."

"Is there something odd about his being here?"

Nicholas glanced down at her, then back up the street. "No. No, I suppose not. Sir John *is* a very wealthy man— unlike your humble husband." He bowed with a self-deprecating twist to his mouth, and a wink.

"He's in much favor at court?"

Nicholas shrugged. "I am not certain I would say he's in favor at court. The Queen likes younger people around her—people who can keep up with her and indulge her love of dancing and the hunt. But Sir John, being wealthy, like other wealthy men, is always welcome."

"I see."

They lapsed into silence, and finally Nicholas offered his arm once more. "Come, lady. The hour grows late and I would not be about these streets after dark. The *Merry Harry* rests at anchor just down the quay. Let's be off."

Olivia took his arm and they started off, but she noticed he glanced over his shoulder more than once, and that their business was concluded with more efficiency than she would ever have expected.

They walked back to the inn in silence. The common room was crowded with red-faced men in bleached-out clothing—sailors from the ships. Molly met them in the door and, with a shrug and a nod of her head, indicated the parlor. "Master said to set yer dinner up in there, Master Steele. 'Tis overcrowded in here for your goodwife."

With a nod of thanks, Nicholas navigated their way through the crowded room and pushed open the parlor door. He stood aside to let her pass before him. A table had been laid for them before the fire. Olivia walked into the room, stripping off her gloves, and pushed the hood of her cloak off her face. Flames danced in the hearth. She spread her hands before it, delighting in the heat. She felt him come to stand behind her. She took a quick intake of breath as she felt him slip the cloak off her shoulders.

All day they had pretended to be friends, all day they had successfully tried to put the morning's kiss behind them. But now, in the shadowy room, with the flickering firelight washing across the white walls, she was once again aware of him, of his body, of his scent, of his very self. His hands hesitated on her shoulders for just a split second too long, and she tensed. Then he was gone, the cloak swirling in his arms. He tossed the bulky garment into a chair and indicated the table before the fire with a bow. "Will you sit?"

She gathered her skirts and swept to the table, sinking down into the chair he held out for her. She glanced up at him and saw that his eyes were averted.

"Wine?"

She nodded silently and realized she was clutching the arms of her chair.

"Are you cold? I'll fetch you a shawl—"

"No, no, I'm fine." Her fingers shook a little as they closed around the pewter goblet he held out for her. The scent of the dark red wine filled her nostrils, heady and sweet, reminding her of the way the taste of the peach had inflamed her senses that morning. Or maybe, she thought, glancing at Nicholas, it wasn't the wine or the peach.

"To a successful venture." Nicholas raised his own goblet and touched the rim of it to hers.

Startled, she smiled and drank. The wine flooded her mouth, tangy with the taste of sunshine and the orchard. He only sipped from his and set it down, staring at some point beyond her. "You look troubled, Nicholas."

He shook his head. "I was unsettled to see Sir John here in Dover, that's all. And last night . . . Last night I saw Walsingham's man—Warren—here, in this very inn. He didn't speak to me and I wondered what was afoot."

"You think it was strange, that he didn't speak to you? Maybe he was afraid to give away your identity."

Nicholas sat back in his chair with a shrug and a sigh. "Who knows, lady. What do I know of spy—" He broke off as the door opened with a sharp rap, and Molly peered inside. She was carrying a large tray, on which were what looked like two small chickens in a bed of parsley and other greens.

"Dinner, sir."

They were silent as she served them, and through most of the meal. A few times Olivia looked up to see Nicholas's eyes on her. He averted his gaze each time their eyes met. *This is ridiculous,* she thought. *We're both adults.* She watched him beneath her lashes, as they buried themselves with the tasks of eating. Finally, when the plates were empty but for crumbs and chicken bones, she gently placed her hand on his. He drew a deep breath, even as his fingers twined with hers. "Nicholas," she said softly. "I know this isn't what either of us ever expected. And I know something of your time and how things are done here, but . . ."

"But?" He was listening to her intently.

"I know you want me." She paused and met his blue eyes with a bravado she did not feel. "I want you, too."

"Lady—Olivia—" He broke off visibly flustered. "You must understand how difficult—how strange this seems to me. You aren't like any lady I've ever known either— you are so different from every other woman. I would not insult you, or distress you, or in any way cause you—"

She rose and moved around the table to stand beside him. She placed one finger across his lips. "Not so different from other women." He kissed her fingertip.

"Are you certain you want this?" His eyes met hers. In his gaze she read passion and need and a touching uncertainty.

Here goes nothing, she thought. "Oh, yes."

He stood up and gathered her in his arms, bent his head and kissed her. If this morning's kiss had been gentle, searching, and unsure, this one was hard and hot and demanding. His mouth seized hers hungrily, his tongue exploring hers with a need that left her weak. Her knees seemed to turn to water and his arms instinctively tightened around her as her knees nearly buckled. Her breasts were crushed beneath the layers of clothing, and suddenly she knew she was wearing far too many clothes. "Come," he said at last.

He led her out of the parlor and up the stairs off the common room, where Olivia could hear snatches of ragged singing, which rose and fell beneath shouts for more ale. He slipped his key out of the little pouch he wore at his waist, opened the door, and pushed it open. He looked down at her and hesitated once more. "Are you sure?"

"Yes," she replied, with even more determination.

He grinned. It lit up his face and made him look far more boyish than he usually did. "Then, come. I think we'll need but one room tonight." He allowed her to enter, shut the door behind them, and carefully locked it. He held out his arms and she slipped into them, as easily and as naturally as if she'd belonged there all her life, and he drew her mouth to his once more. One hand worked the pins from her hair, fingers combing through the heavy mass, until it spilled loose over her shoulders and down her back. He gathered the thick dark-brown masses in his hands as she clung to him, her own fingers twined in his short dark curls. They stood together for what seemed like a long time, until at last he raised his head, even as his fingers twined in the lacings of her bodice. "And you'll have no need of a maid tonight, I think."

"That's good," she said, with a grin. "Because I noticed that Molly's terribly busy down there."

"Then we should leave her in peace." He dropped tiny kisses along her cheek, and she closed her eyes as delight rippled through her like a wave. And each successive wave made the heat burning between her legs rise by slow but certain degrees. Piece by piece, he peeled each article of clothing off her, until she stood only in her shift. The floorboards beneath her feet were bare, and she shivered as the chilly air raised gooseflesh on her skin. He picked her up and carried her to the bed, placed her gently beneath the covers, and turned away.

She watched, wide-eyed and breathless, as he stripped his clothes off faster than she would've thought possible and turned to her. She eyed his body, lean and broad-shouldered, the muscles developed from a lifetime of vigorous activity. Her gaze dropped to the hard evidence of his need, and he smiled, even as he slipped beneath the sheets beside her. "Am I made as men in your time, lady?"

"Most of them aren't made half so well," she answered. And then she couldn't speak for a long time, for his mouth was on hers once more, and his hands slipped beneath her shift, pulling the last barrier away, and he rose above her, body poised, the tip of him resting against her own wet and wanting flesh. "Are you sure?" he asked again.

With a groan, she lifted her hips and wrapped her arms around him, pulling him into her. He eased gently into her warm soft depths, and she moaned, writhing beneath him, her body on fire with need. "Never surer," she managed at last.

With a soft chuckle, he thrust deeper, and their bodies matched themselves to each other, as she gave herself up utterly to the timeless cadence of his lovemaking.

Chapter 9

"HE'S SAILING TOMORROW on the *Merry Harry* if the weather holds fair." Christopher Warren leaned back against the grimy whitewashed wall and allowed himself a deep, satisfying drink.

"Aye, or the day after if it doesn't?" Sir John toyed with his own tankard.

"And you understand where to look for him? At the church, St. Mary-by-the-Sea? You have no questions? I leave you tonight for London. From here on, everything relies upon you."

"I do." For a moment, Sir John looked troubled. "It troubles me, Master Warren, to think that a man I almost allowed my daughter to wed would truck with the Spanish—"

"Sh!" Warren held up a warning finger. "The very walls have ears, Sir John. This is not the time to speak so freely. Have no fear, you'll have ample chance to express all your doubts—and your observations—soon enough."

"He's with that loose woman, you say?"

Warren nodded over the rim of his tankard and signaled to the serving maid for another round. "Bold as you please. They're traveling as man and wife."

"Faugh." Sir John looked disgusted. "That's another charge should be brought against him—fornication. I knew that was no cousin of his when I saw her dressed in men's clothes—did I mention that, Master Warren? Such doings—"

"Three times now," Warren said as the maid placed fresh tankards before them.

The knight looked disgruntled. "You may think what you will, Master Warren, but no godly woman parades herself in clothing meant for men. Why, you could see her legs all the way to the thighs. It's an abomination before the Lord." He drained his tankard and pulled the other closer. "And it's struck me as odd, Master Warren, if I do speak plain, that I don't understand why you want Talcott to go all the way across to Calais, and meet up with this Spaniard. Wouldn't it be better to arrest him here?"

The knight's voice carried over the swell of the crowd, and Warren leaned forward, swiftly motioning to keep his voice down. "Caution, Sir John. Not all faces are friendly, even in such a place as this." He glanced around the room, assessing whether or not anyone who might have over-heard could possibly care. No one was looking at the two men, but Warren knew that did not necessarily indicate lack of interest. Inwardly he sighed, and continued, "We need the plans, Sir John. Even if His Catholic Majesty should choose to abandon these particular plans, once he realizes they've fallen into our hands, there are still only a limited number of possibilities. These plans will give us a look into the mind of the King and his most trusted strategists."

"I see." A frown crossed Sir John's face, as though he wanted to ask another question, but thought the better of it. "Well, these are great doings, and I am only a humble country knight."

"Indeed, Sir John, we are all but little cogs caught up in the great wheel of Her Majesty. And, I for one, con-sidered myself blessed to be so."

"To the Queen." Sir John raised his tankard in a toast.

Warren touched the rim of his own tankard to Sir John's. "The Queen." He drank the toast slowly, his eyes darting around the room, over the rim. Was that a French agent he recognized, in the corner by the fire? He downed the contents of his mug in another great swallow. "I'm to bed, Sir John. I will see you here, at Dover, four nights' hence. And may God look kindly on us all."

"An you say so, Master Warren." The knight nodded a good night, then turned back to his tankard, his long thin hands laced around its rough surface. "Good night."

"Yes." Olivia breathed the word in one drawn-out sigh as Nicholas dropped tiny kisses down her inner thigh.

"You like that?" He raised his head and smiled.

"Oh, yes."

"You're so smooth," he whispered, caressing her skin. "You used my razor to shave your body?"

"Do you mind?"

He glanced up with a small grin. "Do I mind?" He slid up the bed to lie beside her and wrapped his arms around her. Their bodies pressed tightly together, legs intertwined. He moved his foot up one of her calves. "Do you think I mind?"

She giggled and reached for his mouth. He kissed her deeply, lips firm and smooth, his tongue probing and insistent. She turned beneath him so that her breasts were crushed against his chest. She felt his hand creep up her side, to cup one breast, thumb pressing gently on the nipple. She sighed again as he drew her bottom lip between his teeth and gently sucked and bit in turn. She ran her hands down his back, acutely aware of the muscles beneath the pale skin, to his buttocks. She pressed against the taut, firm flesh.

"Ah," he whispered, pushing her over onto her back. Her legs spread of their own volition. He reached down, gently twisting one finger in the nest of dark curls between her thighs, and caressing her wet, swollen flesh with the others.

Pleasure, sudden and swift as a flame, arced through her body. She moaned against his mouth. She felt his hard length against her thigh and lifted her hips.

"So eager my lady is." He chuckled softly, nuzzling her ear and her throat. "So wanton."

"And so wanting," she whispered.

"And so sweet," he replied, rolling over to lie squarely in the shallow bowl of her hips. He balanced above her, and she ran her palms over the muscled planes of his chest, caressing his nipples as he had hers. With a groan, he lowered his mouth to hers once more as he buried himself in her flesh. She twined her fingers in his dark curls and moved to meet his thrusts. *This is madness,* the voice of her conscience seemed to say in Alison's voice. *You can only get hurt.* Another stab of pleasure coursed through her, hot and unexpected. She clutched him closer and strained against him. *If this be madness,* the line ran unbidden through her mind, *then let me be mad indeed.* It was her last coherent thought for quite some time.

It was close to dawn when Nicholas roused her once more. "Time to go, my love. We must make the tide."

For a moment, she lay, disoriented, and then the memories of the past night came rushing back. She tried to meet his eyes, and found that she was suddenly shy. "All right," she said. She heard the uncertainty in her own tone.

And so did he, for he turned back to her with a swift, hard kiss. "My only regret of last night, my lady, is that four hundred years and more prevents me from making you, in fact, my wife."

Olivia blinked, even more taken aback than by his initial distance. It seemed too impossible for him to really mean it. "So you doubtless say to all the ladies from the future you meet, sirrah."

He traced one finger down the tip of her nose. "Only the ones who look like you, madam."

She laughed, pushing aside the covers, and swung her bare legs over the side of the bed with a casual air she did not feel. "What time is it? It's still dark."

"Just gone four, according the watch who just went by. The tide is at five, and we must be aboard the *Merry Harry.*" He was watching her closely as she gathered up her things.

"Then I shall go and dress." She gave him a quick smile and fled to the safety of the other room.

The packing was completed in less time than she would've imagined. After a quick breakfast of bread and cheese, washed down by bitter ale, they were on their way to the docks. Outside the sky had brightened, but the streets were still in shadow. Jack led the way slowly, leading the horse, which held their luggage. Olivia clung to Nicholas's arm, trying not to trip on the uneven cobblestones, which were difficult to see in the shadowy light of dawn.

Despite yesterday's rain, the crossing from Dover was accomplished in little time and less trouble. Olivia watched in wide-eyed wonder, feeling like a child on Christmas morning, or an extra in a BBC production. It was one thing to know such things had happened; it was another to watch them being done, without machines, without computers, without the most basic sorts of technology, except those powered by raw brawn and sweat.

The maneuvers of the sailors, who nimbly skipped up and down the rigging with a surefooted grace, who pulled and dragged and hoisted the great sheets of sail that propelled the ship, and who sweated over the oars, cursing between gritted teeth as the huge wooden lengths heaved in and out of the water, kept her staring in unabashed fascination. A few of the men noticed her interest, and either blushed and turned away, or swaggered and exaggerated their movements, showing off their prowess like strutting roosters.

"My lady takes an interest in the sailors?" Nicholas teased. He leaned against the railing beside her.

"It's all so . . ." She paused, looking around. The sky was full of puffy white clouds, and gulls swooped and shrieked between the masts and the rigging. "So real." She breathed the salt air deeply. The tangy aroma was a blend of wet wool and wood, fish and salt.

"It is real," he answered, looking out over the sea. The coast of France was a smudge on the horizon. "It's the only reality I've ever known."

"Did you know that there are scientists in my time who believe that time is simply something our minds have constructed, and that in reality, all time is now. There is only the present, they believe."

He turned to look at her as if he would speak, but seemed to change his mind. Finally he said, "Be careful of what you say, Olivia. When we're alone, it's different. But here—be careful. I mean that only for your safety."

"I understand." She glanced at the water and then back at him. "How am I doing so far?"

He looked puzzled.

"You know—as your wife. Am I meeting all your expectations?"

At that, he picked up her hand and pressed a deep kiss into her palm. He looked at her and laughed. "Believe me, my lady, you've exceeded every expectation, and fulfilled almost every desire."

"Almost?" She frowned.

"All those of last night." He glanced down with a grin. " 'Tis another day. And the inn in Calais is only an hour or two away. We've another day yet before I meet—before I keep my appointment." He reached for her hand again and pressed another kiss into the palm; this time he bit the flesh gently. "Another day to explore the sights of Calais. And another night to explore—"

"Each other?" She raised her chin and smiled.

"Exactly, my lady." This time he stroked he fingers gently, and Olivia knew his touch was a promise, unspoken, but understood.

• • •

"So what do you think?" Alison pushed the last of the parchments at Geoffrey. She ran her fingers through her hair, heedless of the ink stains on her fingers. One left a pale gray smudge across her forehead.

Geoffrey smiled at the smudge, picked up the parchments, and slowly scanned each equation. "I think . . ." He hesitated, then continued, "I think we're missing something, but I can't quite put my finger on what it is."

"You think Dr. Dee will be able to figure it out?"

He met her eyes squarely. "I believe so, Alison."

"You hope so."

He chuckled. "You're very good at getting right to the meat of the matter, aren't you?"

She nodded. "Occupational hazard, I guess."

At that he looked puzzled, and she hastened to explain, "I've told you about my job. When you deal with the kind of problems I deal with, it helps me to be able to cut through all the crap the kids throw at you. The great majority of them aren't bad kids—it's just they've had to deal with a lot in their lives. They tend to treat everyone the way they've been treated. And in a lot of cases, that isn't so nice."

"Ah." He sat back and folded his arms across his chest. "These problems are caused by the drugs you've told me about?"

"Well, drugs, and parents who aren't much more than kids themselves, and streets where a kid who's caught wearing the wrong colors can get killed—oh, it just goes on and on. There's no one reason. And all the reasons are connected, somehow."

"And this is your work?"

"I do what I can. There's a lot of frustration, but the rewards can be incredible. I had one kid, she was thirteen. Her mother was addicted to crack cocaine. It was so sad. But, you know, she's a great kid. She went to live with her aunt, and by the end of the school year, her mom was back in rehab. She seemed pretty cheerful the last time I talked to her, but scared about the summer. They complain about school but it gives them structure."

Geoffrey frowned a little, toying with the edge of the parchment. "But what about—forgive me if I seem forward—but what about a husband? Is not your father concerned? Isn't there someone—?"

Alison shrugged. "Oh, I get plenty of dates. But so far, I haven't really found anyone I like enough to want to marry." She grinned at him.

"But—but your parents?" He looked shocked and completely lost. "Have they not worked to find you a suitable mate? Or at least presented one or two for you to choose from? If you are busy with your work, perhaps you've not the time, but surely they—"

Alison burst out laughing. "Oh, Geoffrey, it's not like that at all anymore. No one arranges marriages—well, I guess in some places they still do, but not where I come from."

"In truth, mistress?" He was staring at her as if she'd suddenly grown another head. "In truth, where do you find your husbands?"

"Well, all over, I guess. Some people meet at school, some people meet at their jobs. Some people—I don't know. Just happen to be at the right place at the right time?" She grinned at him. "But what about you? Both of you? Two such eligible bachelors? How come some proud papa hasn't scooped either of you up?"

Geoffrey rolled his eyes to the ceiling. "Forgive me, mistress, if I laugh. Eligible bachelors indeed. Look around you. My brother is the lord of an estate that's marginal at best, while I, the younger son, have little but my wits and my mind to make my way in the world. There are no fathers beating down these doors, I assure you."

Alison eyed him, head cocked, eyed dancing. "Then haven't you had your share of tumbles with the village wenches? The daughter of the local squire?"

Geoffrey shook his head, laughing. "A few, mayhap, now and again. But in truth, mistress, any bastard Nicholas or I seeded has yet to exist. Mayhap the Talcott line will end right here."

"Oh, but—" Alison broke off and hastily shook her head. "Never mind. I shouldn't have said that."

"Are you saying the line doesn't end with us?" Geoffrey peered at her downcast face.

She looked up and couldn't help but grin. "Never mind."

"Tell me," he said, his voice gentle and caressing, "surely you've had your share of—?"

"Tumbles in the hay?" She sniffed. "We don't have any hay where I come from, either."

He laughed. "You delight me." He shook his head, still smiling. "Would that I could see your time."

"Well, maybe you can. What's to stop you from following us? Or coming with us?"

Geoffrey frowned. "I suspect that if two came back, two must go forward. And perhaps there's something about two—something that triggered the mechanism of the maze? *I* could never make it work." He paused, and his eyes were as merry as hers. "And I can wager every dubloon in the King of Spain's treasure that Nicholas would no more consent to come with me than the Queen of England herself."

"Hm," Alison said, feigning contemplation. "Then maybe we can work something out with Olivia."

At that he burst out laughing. He reached over, seized her shoulders, and kissed her firmly but gently on the lips. She sat back with a start.

"Do I offend?" His tone was light, but his eyes were intent and serious. The sunlight brought out the gold within the light brown depths.

"Oh," Alison replied, her voice very small, her heart pounding nearly audibly. "No, not at all. In the least."

"Good." He leaned forward again, this time gathering her up and into his arms as he rose. "Because I've been wanting to do this ever since I met you."

•   •   •

The dark-haired priest sketched a benedicte over the head
of the woman who scrabbled at his feet in the dust for
the coin he'd just tossed her and murmured a garbled
Latin blessing as movement on the other side of the street
caught his eye. A man and a woman—a well-born man
and woman by the looks of them—were stepping off a
ship that flew the colors of England. His heart beat a little
faster. This was the third day he'd haunted this very spot,
hoping for a glimpse of such a pair as this. The man was
tall and dark and well-proportioned, the woman, slender
and daintily made. A raw-boned servant followed them
down the dock, a small iron-bound trunk on one shoulder,
a leather pack on the other.

Alphonse Figueroa de Valez, agent of His Majesty
King Philip, squinted in the sunlight and muttered a curse
as he nearly tripped over the beggar, who'd huddled as
close to his legs as possible. He glanced up and down the
street, looking to see if anyone came forward to greet
the pair or if they would simply continue on their way.
The man stopped a passing sailor, spoke, and followed the
sailor's nod in the direction of the Gold Angel. Figueroa
looked both right and left, crossed the street, and followed
the pair up the winding street that led from the quay to
the tavern. Was it possible that here was the Englishman
at last?

He kept his head down, but observed the couple from
a safe distance. The man fit the description well enough,
but the wife—hadn't the description of the wife been of
a frail, sickly woman? This woman appeared healthy, for
her step was as quick and as vigorous as her husband's,
and her face was flushed with a healthy color, even if she
seemed a little too thin for Figueroa's taste. But still, the
timing was correct, and they were heading to the place
where he'd been told to expect Master Steele to stay.

Figueroa stuffed his arms up his wide sleeves and bent
his cowled head. He crept along the street and noticed,
not for the first time, a tall man, dressed all in black except
for a plain starched linen collar, who strolled down the

opposite side of the street. Figueroa eyed the man, another Englishman and a Puritan—here his lips twisted involuntarily at the word—by the looks of him. There was an aspect to the way the man walked that made Figueroa think he was following the couple too. Figueroa allowed himself to pause, ostensibly to throw another blessing on a pair of sailors snoring in the sunlight.

The couple reached the tavern, and Figueroa stifled another curse as a passing wagon flung fifth on his priestly disguise. The couple paused briefly, as though reading the sign, then proceeded into the inn. They left the serving boy shuffling his feet outside. The boy set both burdens down as close to the wall as possible, rolled his shoulders back in a stretch, and yawned. His gaze brushed over Figueroa with complete disinterest, but Figueroa was not deterred. After nearly fifty years of Protestant rule, one could hardly expect the English rabble to have the proper respect for a priest.

This appeared potentially promising. Figueroa looked up, but the tall Puritan was nowhere to be seen. Of course he had not been following the English couple. Such fancies were figments of an overheated brain. He dismissed all extraneous thoughts and visualized the leather case of documents he carried in the secret compartment of his own luggage. He adjusted his cowl over his head and made his way to the inn. The blond boy nodded at him as he passed, and he sketched another blessing in the boy's general direction. He was gratified to see the boy cross himself awkwardly in return. Ah, he thought, perhaps . . . His thoughts trailed away as he stood for a moment just inside the door.

In the deserted common room, he took a seat in the corner near the fire. The hearth was empty on this warm summer afternoon. He huddled in the chair and waited.

He did not wait long. An Englishman's voice, well modulated, but pitched to carry, called out, "Jack! Up here!"

The landlord pounded down the steps, his florid face

flushed, even as the blond boy bolted up the steps, the
trunk on one shoulder, the pack on his back. The landlord
pushed past the boy, bellowing for hot water, and disappeared behind a swinging door directly opposite Figueroa's seat. The boy hauled his burdens up the stairs and
disappeared briefly. A buxom barmaid entered the common room from the same swinging door, which Figueroa
presumed led to the kitchen, dragging two buckets of
steaming water. She staggered up the steps.

From the depths of his cowl, Figueroa watched the activity in silence. Finally the landlord emerged from the
kitchen, wiped beads of sweat off his face, and finally
noticed the cowled friar sitting by the fire.

With only the suggestion of a surprised frown, he
crossed the room and put his hands on his hips. "God's
greetings, Friar."

"Greetings, my son," Figueroa replied, motioning the
same blessing in the air with a bony finger. "I'd rest here
a moment or two, if you'll be willing."

"This is a Catholic house, Friar. Rest and be welcome.
Will you have a cup of ale?"

"*Sí*. Ale." He nodded.

At once the landlord retreated to the bar, withdrew a
clay cup from someplace beneath, and filled it to the brim
with foamy ale. He carried it carefully to the small table
and set it gently before Figueroa. Figueroa sipped and
smiled his thanks. With another bow, and a murmur of
apology, the landlord turned on his heel and disappeared
into the kitchen.

For a long moment there was silence, then the sound
of heavy steps on the floor above, followed by the whisper
of a woman's skirts on the stairs, told him that the two
guests were on their way down once more.

". . . to the ostler and see if we can get horses," the
nobleman was saying to his servant, who preceded both
the noble and his wife down the stairs.

"Aye, sir." The boy pulled his forelock and sped out
of the inn.

"Stephen," the woman said as they emerged into the common room, "should we not go and see . . ."

They were speaking English. Figueroa tightened his grip on the rude clay cup and held his breath. Stephen. Yes, that was the name of the contact. He peered at the two of them from under his cowl, secure in the fact that neither of them had yet noticed him. He frowned again at the woman. All reports of her had been that this waiting woman to Mary, Queen of Scots, had deteriorated greatly when she'd gone into deep mourning upon her mistress's untimely death. Only the pleading of the husband, and the payment of a sizable bribe, had allowed him to take her away. But the woman who stood laughing up at her tall husband, who in turn leaned over to kiss the tip of her nose, looked no more sad or sick than a blushing bride on her wedding night. She looked up at her husband with eager, open eyes and soft, slack mouth, the lips slightly upturned in the smallest smile. For an instant, Figueroa was forced to recall the brief months when he, too, had witnessed firsthand that look on a woman's face, and then to endure the flood of grief that inevitably followed, brought on by the memory of how their sweet short months of wedded bliss had come to a bitter end, when his bride died miscarrying their first and final son. Then he coldly dismissed those thoughts and transformed the grief into hatred for the man who pressed a kiss into the open palm of the woman's hand.

"Come, we must get you outside into the sunshine. You're much too pale and peaked after all those months confined."

At that, Figueroa started upright and tried to peer more intently at the woman. She threw back her head, laughed again, and said, "Indeed, my lord, so glad am I to see the sun after all those months abed."

Hmm, thought Figueroa. Something about that speech didn't quite ring true. She sounded more like a schoolboy aping a phrase than someone speaking genuinely.

"If I'd my way," her husband was answering softly,

"you'd spend more months abed—more months of nights." They exchanged a look that twisted Figueroa's heart and, linking arms, stepped outside into the crowded street.

Figueroa stood up and watched them disappear into the press of human bodies. They were clearly here for a reason. The amount of their luggage suggested they were expecting to make a short trip. The man's name, Stephen, was the same name as that of his contact. He would return and inquire the full name from the landlord shortly. The wife was all blooming roses and dewy petals, and she looked younger than he expected. But she'd been in the service of the Queen of Scotland for only a brief time, he remembered, for the last eighteen months or so of the Queen's captivity. And given her relative attractiveness, and the reported wealth of her husband, it would stand to reason that she'd be one of the few of Mary's servants allowed to leave. The reports of her ill health could have been greatly exaggerated. Figueroa tightened the rough rope belt he wore at his waist and started off. He would return when he was much more presentable.

"Ugh," Olivia grunted, clinging to Nicholas's arm as they picked their way through the offal of the fish market. "Don't they clean the streets?"

"Only when it rains," he answered with a laugh.

She wrinkled her nose. The stench was overpowering in the sun, and the piles of rotting fish refuse threatened her skirts at every turn. She breathed a loud sigh of relief as they waded through the last of the mess and, turning a corner, found themselves in the vegetable market street. The air was much fresher here, and the streets were only littered here and there with piles of dung from the oxen and donkeys used to bring the vegetables to the market stalls. Only littered with piles of dung! She laughed to herself and shook her head.

"What is it?" asked Nicholas as he guided her around one of the larger piles.

"I was just thinking how much better this street is from the last, and how much more preferable manure is to fish guts. And then I was thinking that before—before coming here through the maze—not only have I never reached that conclusion, but I never dreamt of actually having either opportunity or need to reach it." She turned her head to look up at him, squinting a little in the bright sunlight. "Does any of that make sense to you?"

"Yes, I think so, yes." He tightened his hold on her arm, as the cobblestones beneath their feet rose unevenly.

"I mean, I suppose there're places where you can still walk down a street and have to dodge dung or fish guts, but I've never been to one. And in all the places I go, the worst you might see is maybe paper—paper trash, blowing around in the wind."

At that he paused, stock-still. "Paper trash?"

"Yes." She waved one hand airily. "Old newspapers, advertisements, candy wrappers—" She broke off, realizing the implications of what he asked. "You never imagined that, either, did you? A world where paper is so worthless we throw it away without thinking."

"Paper—parchment—it isn't something you throw away unthinking."

"I know." They exchanged another long look of sudden and unexpected communion.

Finally he nodded toward the church spire. "Come, lady. Let's find the meeting place. We'll talk more of these marvels in the privacy of our room." And with another smile, they started off once more.

Chapter 10

A POX UPON these whoresons, thought Sir John, as his elbow was jostled by yet another scurvy Catholic. Mass was just ending, and the steady stream of the faithful was at peak tide. He clutched his money belt closer as the crowd pushed by.

Three times now, he'd come to St. Mary-by-the-Sea just as Mass was ending, on the instructions of Christopher Warren. And three times now, he'd endured this human deluge, and so far there'd been no sign of Talcott, or that whore who traveled with him. He flicked away lint and brushed off the fine dust the passing heels had raised. He was just about to retire to his offices above the fish market when he saw a familiar head pass beneath the privet hedge arch. He shrank back into the protection of his niche beneath a stone arch as Nicholas Talcott, and his companion, walked by.

Now in the costume of a Spanish grandee, Figueroa strolled into the common room of the Gold Angel with studied insolence and demanded the landlord in heavily accented French. The barmaid, eyes wide in alarm, hastened into the kitchen, calling, "Papa, Papa!"

A few minutes later, the fat landlord emerged, a scowl on his red, sweating face.

Figueroa yawned. "The Englishman—Master Stephen Steele? Is he here?"

The landlord looked taken aback. "Who wants to know?" He stuck his chin out over his fat belly.

"My name is Iago Montera de Valez." His alter ego as his own cousin was quite useful much of the time. "I have an appointment with Master Steele, and I was to meet him here."

The landlord appeared mollified by this ready information and spread his hands. "A man by that name came earlier, but he left with his lady. They were eager to explore a church—St. Mary-by-the-Sea."

"And when will they return?"

"To be sure, I've no idea. 'Tis not for me to mark the comings and the goings of my guests. But I reckon they'll be back by dinner—he asked for a meal to be laid for them by the supper hour."

"In the private parlor by their room," volunteered the maid, who'd crept out of the kitchens and now peeked from behind her father's bulk.

"Hush, Aliza!"

Figueroa's eyes flicked over the girl briefly. She was not uncomely. Her light brown hair tumbled from her kerchief in heavy locks, and her eyes were a bright and lively blue. Her face was round and rosy. For a moment he was tempted. His priestly disguise demanded the appearance of chastity, and his masquerade as an itinerant monk made even bathing difficult. His metamorphosis into Iago was a welcome relief. But no, he sighed. He'd dare not risk the father's anger. Better to be done with this business and then return to Spain, where he could indulge his appetites in the privacy of his own estates. "Then tell him I shall call upon him tomorrow, at the appointed hour." He smiled at the girl, who simpered in response, and, tossing his short cloak over one shoulder, turned on his heel and left.

• • •

Nicholas and Olivia genuflected before the altar and rose together, crossing themselves. Nicholas peered around surreptitiously. "I believe this is the place."

"When are you to meet him?" Olivia whispered, looking around. A few people lingered after the service, and a young boy on his hands and knees was laboriously washing the dark red tiles around the altar. The whitewashed walls rose between the narrow windows of stained glass, covered, for the most part, in square stone memorials. The crucifix that rose above the altar was ornately carved, the depiction of Jesus in his final agonies so realistic it bordered on the gruesome. There was a familiar hush about the place, and Olivia was struck by how similar the atmosphere was to all the churches her father had insisted they explore. There really was a certain agelessness about the place that tempted her to examine every nook and cranny. It was only with effort that she turned her attention back to Nicholas, who was speaking so softly, she had to strain to hear him.

"Warren said he—the Spanish agent—would contact me first."

"So that means we just—wait?"

Nicholas shrugged. "So it would seem." A lazy smile lifted the corners of his lips and his eyes met hers. "But surely, my lady, there're ways to pass the time—a new city to see? New worlds to explore?" He'd drawn closer and raised her hand to his mouth, when a discreet cough close by made them jump.

Olivia looked up into the eyes of a black-robed priest, who wagged an admonitory finger at them. But the man's dark eyes danced in his wrinkled face, and a smile revealed toothless gaps. With a gesture he indicated the door, winked, and continued on his way.

Olivia laughed. "I think the good father thinks we should find another place to do our exploring. Would you mind if we took a few minutes and looked around?"

"Not at all." He leaned down a little closer and whispered, "But we'll save our discussions for later."

"Of course."

He offered her his arm, and they walked to the windows. Olivia gazed up at the elaborate stained glass, which depicted the scene from the Crucifixion where St. Veronica wiped the face of Christ. The workmanship was beautiful, the colors, unlike modern stained glass, were rich but muted, the depictions intricately lifelike. They walked slowly up the aisle, Olivia pausing briefly before each window or to read the inscriptions carved into the walls, commemorating parishioners. "I wonder . . ." she murmured, forgetting herself.

"Yes?" Nicholas prompted, since there was no one nearby.

"I was just wondering if this church still exists, and if so, how fascinating it would be to find it, and see how much it's changed." Olivia opened her mouth to say more, but stopped in amazement. A tall man, dressed in severe black, hovered at the entrance of the church, next to one of the supporting pillars. His posture was stiff, but his head was turned in a way that made her think he'd been watching them. "Nicholas," she said, before she remembered to call him Stephen, "isn't that Sir John Makepiece?"

Nicholas looked up. "By our Lady," he swore softly. "As I live and breathe. To think the day would come when yet I'd see Sir John darken the door of a Catholic church—" He broke off, clearly puzzled.

"Do you suppose he's following us?"

"Us? Whatever for?"

"Well, he knows we aren't really married, for one thing. Maybe he intends to have you arrested for fornication, or public immorality, or—"

Nicholas held up one warning finger. "Whatever he's doing here, I don't like it." He looked up and down. "There—there's another door back that way. Let's give him the slip."

He took her arm and, as quickly as was seemly, the

two of them hastened out of the church and into the deserted churchyard. Nicholas looked both ways. "Let's walk down that way a little bit. We'll circle around and make our way back to the inn from the opposite direction. I don't like this at all."

He was silent and clearly troubled all the way back to the inn. Olivia scarcely noticed the sights and smells and sounds all around her, so absorbed was she in keeping up with his long strides. He negotiated the crowds with certain ease, and when they finally arrived back at the Gold Angel, he paused in the innyard and nodded toward the building. "You go inside, my lady. I want to find Jack and ask him if he's noticed Sir John hovering around here at all, and to tell him to be on the watch for him. Although it's likely enough Sir John's business matters might take him to Dover and then Calais, I cannot believe anything beneath God's blue sky would make him darken the door of a Catholic church."

Olivia turned obediently, knowing instinctively that he did not want her to concern herself with these matters, when the landlord hailed them both as he was crossing the yard from the stables. "Master Steele!"

Nicholas turned with the hint of a frown on an otherwise bland face. "Yes, my good host?"

"Your friend has been here looking for you," the man said, his English heavily accented.

The frown deepened between Nicholas's brows. "My friend? Sir John?"

"No, no," answered the landlord, waving an airy hand. "A Spaniard, by the look and sound of him—wait, wait, I remember—" He held up one finger. "Igano—no, that's not right. Iaccomo—no, that's not right, either—"

"Iago." The rosy-cheeked serving maid had come up behind her father, her arms full of a basket filled with laundry. "His name was Iago Montera de Valez. He said he'd see you, sir, at the appointed time tomorrow."

Beside her, Olivia felt Nicholas tense. "Tomorrow," he repeated.

"Yes, sir. I'm quite sure that's what he said." She bobbed a little curtsy and spoke to her father in quick French.

Nicholas turned back to Olivia and indicated the inn. "I'll find Jack later. Tomorrow—it seems so sudden, somehow."

"How did he know you were here?"

"This is where we were to come. He must have been watching for us."

A cold chill shivered all the way down her back to her toes, but she said nothing until they were behind the safety of their locked door. "I'm glad it's to be tomorrow," she said as she watched him slide the bolt across the door. "There's something about this that's beginning to make me very nervous."

"And you've been through every calculation? Checked every angle? Cast the horoscope for each day?" Dr. John Dee peered at both of them over the tops of his rimless spectacles. They were the most bizarre arrangement of glasses Alison had ever seen—two round pieces of glass, held together by thin wire and looped over Dee's ears with pieces of cord. They made his eyes look enormous every time she happened to glance at him. But he'd accepted Geoffrey's story and her own presence with remarkable aplomb, and had immediately plunged into the work with an almost fanatical glee. His long gray-streaked hair was pulled off his face in a wispy tail, but the linen that peeked from below his dark blue academic gown was amazingly fresh and crisp. His dark eyes jumped from Geoffrey to Alison, and he no more seemed to find it odd that Alison should be included in the discussions than she did herself. Geoffrey had said something to the effect that the good doctor's close association with the Queen had doubtless prepared him for someone like Alison. Taken aback at first, Alison realized that Geoffrey's own nearly total acceptance of her as an equal was most unusual as well.

Geoffrey and Alison exchanged glances. "We've been

through every single one of those calculations three times or more. I've checked them twice myself, and Allie's been through them herself at least once. I've not yet cast the horoscopes, but I thought I'd better leave that to you."

"Hmm." Dee stroked his beard and sifted through the parchments, the wide sleeves of his dusty academic gown whispering across the surface of the table. "And you've measured all the angles?"

Geoffrey spread his hands once more. "I've begun. But it's a slow process."

"Perhaps Alison—" he broke off. "Perhaps Mistress Alison could help you."

"We, uh, we've thought it best if she stays out of sight as much as possible."

"Stay out of sight? You don't have the luxury of that kind of time. You need her help." He went back to sifting through the parchments. "Hmm." Dee picked up another parchment and held it very close to his nose. He fumbled in the pocket of his gown and looked up at Alison as he held out what looked like a small silver cylinder. "Breath mint?"

"What?" What she thought he said sounded so improbable she knew she had to have heard wrong.

"Breath mint?" Dee was looking at her over the rims of his spectacles, holding out a silver cylinder that ended in what looked like tattered paper.

Alison cocked her head and peered at it in disbelief. "Those—that looks like—"

"Breath mints," he said again.

"You're from the future too." She sat back and stared at him, while Geoffrey gawked at each of them in turn.

Dee had the grace to look embarrassed. "Well, yes, as a matter of fact, I am."

"But, Dr. Dee," Geoffrey managed, "why didn't you ever tell me?"

"Timing, Geoffrey. In all our discussions, the truth was always there. You just couldn't see it."

Geoffrey started to ask another question, stopped, and shook his head with a stunned expression.

"Forgive me, Geoffrey." Dee took a deep breath and inclined his head with an apologetic expression.

"Where are you from?" asked Alison. "You aren't—you aren't from my time, are you?"

"You are a very observant young woman. How did you know?"

"Your breath mints." She held up the silver cylinder. "There's nothing like this—yet."

"You're right." He stood up, his light woolen robes swinging as he moved. "I'm from another hundred years in your future, Mistress Alison. The maze—the time travel device—has been perfected, and I can go back and forth in time between here and there, if you will, at will. I essentially live a double life, in two time periods."

"It took a hundred years to perfect it?"

"It wasn't the sort of thing anyone really wanted to make a mistake with, you know. It made everyone ever involved with the project extraordinarily cautious—probably as cautious as they should've been on most every other project from the atom bomb to the internal combustion engine, but never mind. On this one, so far at least, only the wisest heads have prevailed. Fortunately."

"And why do you do this? Why are you here?"

"To ensure that the first maze was built." He nodded toward the window, and his eyes met hers. There was a merry twinkle in the dark brown depths, and suddenly Alison thought he resembled Merlin in Walt Disney's cartoon.

"So you can send us back. You know how it works."

"Well." He put his hands on his hips and nodded once. "I have a good idea how it works."

"Just a good idea?"

"It took us a hundred years to perfect it. This"—he jabbed his thumb over his shoulder in the direction of the window—"this maze is as rough and crude as they come—no offense, man. It's built of hedge. Have you any idea of the thousands of nooks and crannies within that hedge? And this is the first time it's ever worked."

"Yeah, why?" asked Alison. "How come it worked for us and not for Geoffrey?"

"There are several reasons. One of them involves mass. The two of you together—you and your friend—reached the critical mass level that is necessary to trigger the primitive mechanism of this maze, if you will. That's not exactly how it works, but it's the clearest illustration I can think to give you. And the other reason is part of the reason I'm here. It only works in reverse. You can go back in time, and then forward, but you can't go forward and then backward."

"Why not?" Alison asked.

"We don't know," Dee answered. "We just don't know."

Alison looked at Geoffrey. "Are you okay?"

"I haven't begun to babble yet." He looked up at her and then at Dee. "All this time . . ."

"Geoffrey, I do hope you can understand why."

"I suppose I can." Geoffrey sat back with folded arms. His initial shock had subsided in a kind of quiet daze. "But now what?"

"Well, we need to determine when the next time the door, so to speak, will open. It's a seesaw sort of thing, constantly in motion. Not that it actually moves—"

"It's all right." Alison interrupted. "You can explain it more to us later. Is there something we can do to help you?"

Dee gazed into space. "Yes," he said finally. "The two of you get out there and begin to measure every possible angle of that maze. Even a slight variation in degree could be the answer. And in the meantime, I'll cast the horoscopes—so to speak. That's not exactly what I'm going to do, but it's what my sixteenth-century alter ego would say. You must give me the exact time of day, young woman, as close to the minute as you can remember—"

He broke off when the look on Alison's face made it clear

what her answer would be. "Ah." He sighed. "Do your best. We'll make it work."

"Well," she said uncertainly, "I can tell you this much. There was an eclipse."

"An eclipse!" He looked up eagerly. "Solar or lunar?"

"Uh, solar, I guess. They told us not to look at the sun." For a moment, she was confused by the sudden demand. "Yes, of course it was a solar eclipse." She glanced at Geoffrey, who avoided meeting her eyes. Inwardly she sighed. Last night had been a mistake, after all, she realized. She watched Geoffrey for a moment as he gathered up the surveying equipment, parchment, and pens, then turned her attention back to Dee. "You didn't know that?"

"No," Dee replied. "I don't because you don't."

"But I do know."

"You know about the eclipse. But you don't know exactly how or why that fits into the equation, so to speak." He paused, clearly searching for how best to explain it. "Can I explain it later?"

Alison gave a short laugh. "I'm sorry. I said that, didn't I?" She glanced over at Geoffrey, who was watching this exchange with an inscrutable expression on his face.

"Will you come with me?" he asked.

"Of course." She glanced at Dr. Dee, but he was absorbed in his ephemeris, a huge book of astrological positions.

When they reached the maze, Geoffrey set the equipment on the grassy path. "I suppose we should start at the beginning."

"Geoffrey," Alison began. He glanced at her over his shoulder. "Can we talk?"

He drew a deep breath and looked at her with a troubled expression. "All right." He nodded over his shoulder. "Shall we walk?"

"Through the maze? Aren't you afraid we might come out in another time?"

He appeared to smile in spite of himself. "Not really," he answered ruefully.

They started off in silence. The sun was warm between the tall green hedges, and the short grass tickled her bare ankles beneath the long skirts. Fortunately, an Elizabethan woman wasn't expected to wear quite so many layers around the house as Olivia wore for traveling. "Listen," she said at last, after several twists and turns had taken them deeper into the maze, out of earshot of any who might linger on the periphery, "about last night—"

"I beg your forgiveness," he burst out. He swung around to face her, and she was startled by his look of agonized contrition. "I'm so sorry—it won't happen again—it must not happen again—I cannot tell you—"

"Geoffrey, why are you so upset?" She stared at him, tempted to take his chin in her hand and force him to look at her. "Don't you think I wanted it to happen, too?"

"Alison, don't talk like that—" He broke off in obvious frustration, turned away, and shook his head. "Nicholas will see me hanged." He swore softly beneath his breath.

"What is it?" she asked softly.

He shook his head again, his back still to her. She could see the tension in his shoulders. "What if there's a child?"

For a moment she was puzzled, and then remembered. No birth control. No messy lotions, no convenient pills. No condoms. She'd been at the beginning of her last packet of pills when they'd arrived in the future. Sooner or later she'd have a period if they stayed much longer. Which opened up a whole other set of problems, but she wasn't going into all that now. "Listen," she said. "It's fine. There's not going to be a child, at least not because of last night. I can promise you that. You're right, you know—we got carried away, and it shouldn't have happened, maybe, but—"

"Maybe? Don't you realize the risk?"

"Of a pregnancy? Sure I do—I do this all the time—" She broke off as he looked shocked. "Not *that*—damn it, Geoffrey. Look, I can see you're really upset about what happened, and I'm terribly sorry that you're so upset, but I'm not going to apologize for wanting what we did. I loved making love with you last night. It was"—she hesitated, then plunged—"wonderful. And I'm not sorry at all." He had turned to face her, and the expression on his face was so nearly comical, she almost laughed aloud. But she read the expression in his light brown eyes, and suddenly she only felt sorry for him. "Why don't you tell me what you're afraid of?"

He drew a deep breath. "I am afraid," he said slowly. "You're right, you know? I'm afraid."

"Of what?"

"Of—of so many things, really." He looked like a little boy, despite the dark haze of beard on his cheeks, and the fact that their eyes were nearly even. "If you can't return, and we continued to—" He broke off. "If there were a child, you'd be ruined here. Unless I married you, and Nicholas—I'm not saying I wouldn't want to do that, but Nicholas—" He broke off again and shook his head. "You just can't imagine."

"Oh, I can imagine, all right." She held out her hand. "Look, Geoffrey. First of all, I *must* go back. Now that Dee's here—well, obviously he knows how it works. There's absolutely no doubt in my mind that Olivia and I are returning to my own time. I don't belong here and we both know that. As far as you marrying me and Nicholas being angry—well, that sort of presumes I would consent to marry you, doesn't it?"

"What choice would you have?"

It was her turn to take a deep breath. "We always have choices, Geoffrey. In my time, there're ways to prevent conception—reliable ways. I'm perfectly safe right now. If I stay here much longer, I won't be, but for right now it's fine. There's really nothing to worry about. Last night doesn't have to happen again. Don't you realize that?"

"Of course I do," he said. He dragged his toe through the grass. "But that's not what I want."

Unbidden, Mick Jagger's raspy voice ran through her

mind. *You can't always get what you want*— With a sigh, she pushed the words away. Geoffrey might be ready for a world of computers, electricity, and flush toilets, but the cynicism of rock and roll was probably still beyond him. "It's not what I want, either" was all she said. She gestured back over her shoulder. "I think we should get to work, don't you?"

"Yes," he said. He took her hand and gave it a slight squeeze before releasing it. "I think so, too."

Chapter 11

HE WAS WAITING beneath the arch where the statue of the Blessed Virgin smiled so serenely down on the rows of lighted candles. The afternoon breeze was cool and blew through the open doors. The candle flames flickered in unison. Olivia tugged at her bodice. The girl, Aliza, was not so accomplished as either the maid, Molly, in Dover, nor old Janet. She made up in good temper what she lacked in experience, though, even if her heavily accented English was doubly difficult for Olivia to understand. Now she tugged at her bodice, and wished she'd had the foresight to ask Nicholas to help her before they'd left the inn. She shifted anxiously on the prie-dieu, her knees aching, despite the bulky petticoats, and tried to twist around as surreptitiously as possible. Nicholas knelt beside her, his hands clasped as though in prayer, eyes closed.

"Eyes front, good wife," he murmured.

Olivia made a little noise of protest but did as he said, settling her bulky skirts more comfortably beneath her knees. She bent her head in what she hoped appeared to be a posture of devout prayer.

Footsteps rang on the stone floor of the little church,

echoing in the empty gloom. Olivia's heart beat faster, and beside her, she felt Nicholas tense. The footsteps came closer, the swift of boot heels on the stone. She kept her eyes lowered to her hands, laced tightly.

A dark-haired monk slipped beside Nicholas and knelt, crossing himself as he lit a candle before the statue. "Master Stephen Steele?"

Nicholas nodded.

"Would you care to see the roses blooming in the churchyard, Master Stephen? I understand you have a strong interest in horticulture."

Nicholas smiled tightly. "Indeed I do, Father. How astute of you to notice."

"The eye of God sees all." The monk crossed himself once more and rose, this time including Olivia in his gaze. She glanced down, just in time to see polished boots beneath his black habit. He linked his hands beneath his wide black sleeves. "And you, Señora Steele. Will you walk with us?"

Olivia rose to her feet, smiling shyly. Her heart pounded so hard she was amazed no one could hear it. She followed the two men out the side door, and into a walled cloister, where vines of late-blooming roses covered the walls so closely that it seemed almost impossible that they could be in the middle of a city.

"We may enjoy a fair measure of privacy here," the Spaniard said.

"You are Don Iago?"

The Spaniard bowed and smiled. "At your service."

"The plans?"

The Spaniard coughed discreetly and placed a hand beside his mouth. "You English are so impetuous. We will discuss the plans, as soon as I've talked to your wife."

Olivia raised her head and exchanged a startled glance with Nicholas, hoping that her face retained its smooth mask. Suddenly, she felt very sure the Spaniard was armed beneath his black clerical garb. She forced herself to smile. "With me, my lord?"

"*Sí*, Señora Steele. My master craves the story as you alone can tell it. Tell me, in as much detail as you desire, of the last days of Queen Mary."

Olivia lowered her eyes, frozen to the spot. Her mouth went dry, and suddenly she understood with awful clarity that Nicholas had been sent, unknowing and unprepared, into a trap. And suddenly she knew, too, that the information he'd been given was woefully incomplete. The English could not have wrung the full truth from the captured spy. Whoever he was, he'd gone to his death sure in the knowledge that the plans would never fall into the wrong hands. But he'd reckoned without one thing—one ultimately improbable thing.

She raised her face and smiled sweetly at the Spaniard. "It will be my pleasure, Don Iago." She indicated a stone bench and sank down. "If you will excuse me?"

"But of course, Señora. Forgive my churlishness—it was but my eagerness to hear your story that makes me so heedless of your comfort."

Nicholas stood as rigid as the stone pillars surrounding the cloister. His face had blanched white when the Spaniard turned to Olivia, and his jaw was clenched. He stared at her with an intensity like a high-beam light.

It's all right, she wanted to cry. *Mary, Queen of Scots, was a passion of mine when I was fourteen.* But all she could do was smile at him over the Spaniard's head, willing him to relax.

The color gradually returned to his cheeks as she began to speak, reciting from memory every shred of fact she could recall of Mary's last months. Several times, the Spaniard asked a question so probing she knew he knew far more than he admitted, but each time, she managed to recall enough detail that he seemed satisfied with her response.

"And on that final morning—it was Mistress Curle who bound the Queen's eyes, no?"

"Jane Kennedy had that honor, my lord." Olivia dared a glance at Nicholas. His shoulders were still tense, but his color was completely normal, and although his eyes were wary, his mouth was no longer a thin white line.

"And noon, I think we heard? High noon—the very stroke of twelve?"

"No. It was about ten o'clock in the morning." She sat back, silent, and folded her hands in her lap.

There was a brief pause. The Spaniard turned to Nicholas. "Your lady-wife tells a remarkable tale, good sir."

"Aye," said Nicholas shortly. His eyes met Olivia's and she knew that he too had realized the trap that had very nearly been sprung.

The Spaniard glanced back at Olivia and gave a brief nod, as if satisfied. "The *Merry Harry* sails again upon the tide tomorrow at noon. I will come to your inn at ten o'clock in the morning to deliver the plans."

"As you say, Don Iago." Nicholas exchanged a quick glance with Olivia. She had no way of knowing if this was what he'd been led to expect, but then, it was very clear that whatever information he'd been given was incomplete—woefully incomplete. Neither of them had expected the questioning on Mary Stuart. A chill went down her spine as she realized that without her presence, Nicholas would never have been able to acquire the plans. And what repercussions did that have on her own present?

With a brief bow, and a sardonic gesture of blessing, the Spaniard disappeared into the church. Nicholas and Olivia waited until the sound of his booted feet had faded out of hearing. There was another long pause, and then Nicholas held out his hand. "Will you come, wife?"

She raised her eyes to his as she rose to her feet. His expression was unreadable. By unspoken agreement, they did not speak until they were safely inside their locked room at the inn. He drew her close the minute he slid the bolt home, and he buried his lips in her hair. "By our blessed Lady and all the saints."

She drew back and smiled up at him, feeling as giddy as if she'd drunk a bottle of champagne. "I did well, I think."

"Well?" He shook his head, amazement plain on his face. "In truth, not one of the players in Lord Leicester's Men is likely to ever give so great a show. How—how is it possible you could know so much?"

"It was luck, Nicholas, believe me. The one way my father and I were absolutely alike is that when something takes our interest, it consumes it utterly, wholly, and completely. I remember the first time I heard the name. Mary, Queen of Scots—it had such a wild, romantic ring. I thought you could smell the moors and the heather in it. I was fourteen." She shook her head a little, remembering. "My father noticed me for the first time. I think it was then he decided having a built-in assistant might not be such a bad thing after all. And he helped me, even. Showed me how to do real historical research—let me use his name and his connections to delve into things even most graduate students never have access to. It was an incredible experience. It brought us closer than we'd ever been before."

"You must miss him."

The statement startled her, and suddenly, she felt not so much giddy as drained. "I do, you know." She gave him a sad little smile. "I don't like to think how much." She backed away and settled down in one of the two straight-backed chairs. This time there had been no question of a second room. She stared into the empty tile hearth. "But he could be so difficult, so exacting. If you didn't find just what he wanted—if you left one stone unturned, or one page unread, somehow he always knew it. And the closer he got to the solution of his mystery, the more obsessive he became. Do you know he had me check every register in England for every Talcott?"

"Were there that many?"

"Talcotts? No. But there're plenty of church registers, believe me." She shook her head. "But it sure came in handy today, hm?"

"Handy." He repeated the word and smiled. "Very handy, indeed." He walked over to her chair and extended his hand. "Would you allow this humble gentleman to express his gratitude for such great learning on the part of so lovely a woman?"

She giggled. "Feel free."

He caught her hand in his and brought it to his lips. "Then come. I'm sure the landlord's pretty daughter will be more than happy to bring us the very best of her father's kitchen, along with the very best of his cellar."

"And then?"

"I promise to bring you the very best of pleasures."

With another giggle, and the briefest of kisses, she allowed him to lead her out of the room.

The late afternoon sun had disappeared behind the hedges, leaving the paths of the maze bathed in shadow. Alison wiped her sleeve across her forehead. She was hot and sticky, and her shift clung to her back. She straightened with a sigh.

Geoffrey made a few more notes on the parchment and glanced up. "I suppose that's as much as we can do for today."

"Do you think any of it will help?"

Geoffrey shrugged. "I wish I could say for a certainty that it will. I wish I knew what triggered the mechanism of the maze to work. It never worked for me."

Alison picked up the compass. The needle swung crazily for a moment, and then settled. "It sure worked for us." She stared moodily at the compass face. The slim needle shivered like a living thing.

"We'll make it work again, I promise."

She nodded slowly. "I just wish Olivia would come back." The air was hot and still within the confines of the maze, but Alison felt cold all over. She shook herself, trying to shake away the feeling.

"What's wrong?"

"I guess maybe I've been thinking about everything you said, and the more I think about it, the more I just wish they'd come back."

He reached for her hand and gave it a gentle, reassuring squeeze. "I didn't mean to worry you."

"I know." She sighed. "You know, one of my grand-mothers was supposed to have something they called 'the sight.' Know what I mean?"

Geoffrey nodded slowly. "It's a dangerous thing to admit, mistress."

Alison shrugged. "In my time they just think you're crazy."

"And do you have this—this sight?"

"I don't think so. But sometimes, I do get these feelings about people. And right now—I just have a really bad feeling about Olivia." She raised her head and met his eyes. In the golden brown depths, she read his shared concern.

"Let's go give these to Dr. Dee. It's nearly time for supper."

"Okay."

What else was there to say, thought Alison, as she helped Geoffrey gather the equipment in silence. What else was there to do?

What else was there to do, thought Sir John, as he peered around the corner of the inn. He'd seen nothing of the monk all morning. Warren must have been wrong. A pox on this whole business. He should have followed his conscience and refused to involve himself with such underhanded doings. Let the Lord punish Talcott for his transgressions—he should've left it none of his concern. But the thought of the Talcott acres intruded, tantalizing as that tempting wench of Talcott's. Unbidden, the shape of her legs in the tight-fitting hose replaced all thoughts of land. Faugh, he thought in disgust. What was he coming to? A day's meditation on the sins of Jezebel would soon cure such lusty intrusions. And a day's meditation he would have, he thought, as soon as he was safely back on English soil, back in the bosom of his family where he, like all God-fearing men, belonged. He should've told

Warren to find another to play his sneaking games. He couldn't wait to wash off the stink of this whole trip.

A sudden movement from the stables made him draw back into the shadows once more. Young Jack, Talcott's servant, crossed the yard and entered the inn, whistling. He soon returned, carrying the small trunk and leather pack. So Talcott was on his way home. He was about to saunter down to the docks, when a richly clad figure on horseback clattering slowly up the crowded street drew his attention. The rider was dressed more gorgeously than any nobleman he'd seen outside of Elizabeth's court. With a shock, as the rider drew closer, Sir John recognized the monk. Instinctively, he drew back as the man approached, straining his ears as he disappeared out of view. The man reined the horse to a stop just outside the inn and tossed the reins to Jack, who caught them with a startled sound.

"Is your master about, boy?"

There was a mumbled assent.

Sir John peeked around the wall. The bulk of the horse blocked his view of all but the man's gartered legs as he strode into the inn. He peered into the leaded window. The smoky glass revealed only the man's gorgeous costume. He swept his hat off his head and shifted his cloak. Across his chest, Sir John saw a flat leather pack strapped into place. That's it, he thought.

The Spaniard spoke to the landlord, who heaved his bulk up the steps. Behind Sir John, a church clock chimed the hour. The Spaniard looked up the steps, as if called, and followed.

Sir John waited. No more than five minutes passed, and the Spaniard was once more out the door and into his saddle. He looked neither right nor left, nor offered any word of thanks to the boy. Sir John drew back once more. He'd wait another few minutes before taking off for the docks. He'd have to persuade his captain by force of arms if necessary, though bribery would probably work, to set sail for Dover immediately. There was no longer any doubt that Warren's word was true. His heart began to pound as his brain began to calculate the value of the Talcott estate.

From the window of the bedroom above, Olivia watched Figueroa disappear down the street. She breathed a deep sigh. "I'm glad that's over."

"Nearly over." Nicholas met her eyes. "I've but to hand these plans to Warren."

"It's certainly been an adventure, hasn't it?"

"It has." He walked over to stand beside her. "Olivia, I—I'm not sure how to thank you. Without you, I—"

"Hush," she said. She placed one finger against his lips. "You'll take the plans on to London?"

"Yes. We'll have one more night in Dover, and then Jack will see you back to Talcott Forest. If you set off at first light, you should be there long before dark tomorrow."

"And when will you come?"

"As quickly as I can. I'd hope to have an audience with the Queen, but . . ."

"But?"

"But I'd rather come home. After all, I—I'd—" He broke off and shifted on his feet.

"Yes?" she prompted gently.

"I'd like to spend the time with you."

She smiled. "Oh, Nicholas."

He opened his arms and pulled her close. "Olivia, I wish I could tell you how I feel, but in truth, I scarcely know. These past days—"

"And nights?" she teased.

"Aye, wench, and nights." He nuzzled her hair as he tightened his arms around her. Abruptly he pulled back to look into her eyes. "I know I shall be sorry to see you leave."

She drew a quick breath. Nothing she'd experienced before had prepared her for these feelings, a blend of discovery and certainty and—and rightness. She averted her face, blinking away tears, as unexpected emotions overwhelmed her. The thought of leaving seemed suddenly impossible. *What on earth can you be thinking,* the rational side of her mind screamed. *You've known this man less than a week—and he's not even from your own century.*

"Olivia?" he was saying, lifting her chin with the tip of his forefinger. "What's wrong?"

She brushed away his hand and turned to the window. How could she begin to answer that? *Everything's wrong,* she wanted to say. *Everything. I'm falling in love with a man who died centuries before I was born, in a place that disappeared long before anything I've ever known.*

"Please," he said. "I can see that you weep. What is it?"

She wiped the tears away with her fingers. "I'm just— just being silly. Being here, in this time, and seeing all of this—I don't know how to explain it. It's like I belong somehow, in some way I can't begin to describe, let alone understand. And then—" she broke off, flustered, not knowing how to continue.

"And then?" he asked.

Her throat thickened. She shook her head.

"Is that all?" he asked softly. "Is it only the places we've seen? The time?" He brushed her cheek with the back of his hand.

"What about you?" she replied.

"Me?"

She turned around and faced him, shoulders squared, chin high. "Does any of this matter to you?"

He stared down at her, his blue eyes dark with some expression she could not read. He glanced away, and then met her eyes once more. "My lady, in the last few days, I have come to"—he hesitated, clearly searching for the word—"to appreciate you in a way I have never imagined appreciating any woman. You are so different, and yet so—so enchanting. I find you quite"—he paused once again and then continued—"extraordinary, and I will miss you sorely when you are gone."

Olivia smiled and looked down at her hands. "I'll miss you, too."

He drew closer and lifted her chin once more. She raised her face and closed her eyes as she realized his intention. Her mouth opened eagerly as his lips came down on hers. For a long moment, they clung to each other, the kiss sweet and deep and tender. When they finally drew away, they smiled at each other, and Olivia was amazed to see that his eyes were wet. She glanced out the window, suddenly disconcerted by his obvious emotion, and noticed with surprise a familiar figure in the street below. "Nicholas, isn't that John Makepiece crossing the square?"

Nicholas followed where she pointed. The tall black hat was as unmistakable as the spare gaunt form. "Aye. So it would seem."

"This is the second time we've seen him here."

Nicholas shrugged. "He has business interests in Calais. 'Tis not so odd as when we saw him in the church."

"But what's he doing here? So close to this inn? Don't you think that's strange?"

"It looks as if he's heading for the docks, sweet. I think it's not as strange as that. Come, you're only overwrought. I promise we'll soon be safe in England. I'll be back from London by the day after tomorrow. And then—" He broke off, bent his head, and kissed her gently on the lips. The kiss deepened, and she held him fast, savoring the hard strength in his arms as he held her closer.

And then, she thought, *the only thing we'll have left to do is say good-bye.*

Chapter 12

T HE WHITE CLIFFS of Dover loomed on the horizon, far sooner than Olivia had thought possible. Or was it only because she didn't want this trip to end, she realized with a start. She looked up at Nicholas, who clung to the rail, his face impassive as he watched the land rise higher and higher out of the sea. The choppy waters of the Channel flung spray in their faces, and the gulls swooped and cried between the masts. She drew a deep breath and let it out in a soft sigh. He said nothing, but his hand closed over hers and covered it on the damp wooden rail. She glanced up at him. His expression had not changed. She was coming to understand that the stern countenance he often wore was nothing but a mask for his true feelings, which were much more complex than the ones possessed by the arrogant, ambitious nobleman she'd first thought him to be. She twined her fingers in his, and was rewarded with an answering pressure.

"Home again," she said.

He nodded, still silent. "What do you think of all this?"

The question took her by surprise. "I think it's quite beautiful," she replied, uncertain of his meaning.

"Not this." He waved an impatient hand. "I meant, what

do you think of *now?* Of the way we live? Of the way things are done?"

She hesitated, searching for the right words, totally taken aback by his query. What could he be thinking? "I think . . . I think that life seems in some ways much more difficult, but in other ways, it's much—" She paused. "Richer. Earthier. More real."

He gave a short laugh. "Perhaps."

"I mean, death is so much more imminent here—at least it seems that way to me. Life seems so much more precarious. But maybe that's not true. Or maybe it's just the way I see it, given what I'm accustomed to."

"And what are you accustomed to?"

He turned to face her. He reached out and twined a stray curl around one finger, smoothing the silky strands beneath his fingers. Desire sparked through her, and she drew a soft breath. He smiled. "Well," she answered, "you know some of the things I've told you about. Vaccinations, indoor plumbing, airplanes."

He traced one finger down the line of her cheek to her jaw. "And this?"

She laughed softly, a little nervously. Everything about him unsettled her, made her want him, need him in a way she'd never imagined, let alone experienced with anyone else. Her emotions were like the ocean, roiling like the waves as the smooth keel of the ship cut through choppy water. "No, there's nothing like this," she managed to stammer as he bent down and gently kissed her mouth.

She drew a deep breath, and closed her eyes, as delight rippled through her all the way to her toes. He drew away almost at once, and she opened her eyes, disappointed. He was smiling at her, and his eyes were dancing. "Such a wanton, wanting wench you are. What will the sailors think?" He raised one eyebrow and jerked his head over his shoulder.

"Why, they'll think I'm in love with my husband." She cocked her head and matched his teasing tone, expecting to see his smile broaden into one of his rare real grins.

But his response puzzled her even more. He turned back to face the sea and gripped the wooden rail with both hands. "Aye," he muttered, so low she had to strain to hear him over the creak of the ship and the slap of the water against the sides. "Indeed, my lady. No doubt."

He was silent the rest of the trip. Olivia stood quietly, avoiding his gaze, trying to wrestle her emotions into some semblance of control. What would Allie say, she wondered. Oh, she could imagine her friend's reaction well enough. You're crazy, Livvie—that's what Allie would say. You need to get back to the future and go on with your life. Your real life, not some silly fantasy.

But this is real life, too, the other part of her insisted. Just as real, actually more real. Except for Allie, what was there to go back to? The thought shocked her. She bit her lip. What was she telling herself? That she didn't want to go back? That she wanted to stay? She was crazy. She snuck a peek at Nicholas. She could practically hear Alison speak. *Yes, he's charming and incredibly good looking and a wonderful lover and you find him absolutely fascinating. But do you really want to die of something a good dose of an antibiotic could cure? How about losing all your teeth? How about never reading a newspaper or a book or a magazine again? How about giving up chocolate?* Olivia sighed, and this time, Nicholas was too lost in his own thoughts to notice. Which was just as well. Talking to him only confused her more and more.

All too soon, it seemed, they reached Dover, and had docked among the rows of ships at the busy seaport. Jack picked up their luggage and Nicholas carefully handed her down the gangplank to the dock, which swayed up and down with the water. She clung to his arm as they finally stepped onto land.

"Which way, my lord?" asked Jack.

Nicholas squinted up at the sun. "Back to the inn, I think, Jack. 'Tis far too late to travel today. We'll have a good supper and a sleep and then be off at first light. The horses should be well rested. They'll be fresh for the journey tomorrow, and so will we if we rest one more night."

Olivia looked up at him, and their eyes met. The intensity with which he looked at her took her breath away. *How often do I really eat chocolate?* She gathered her skirts, as he offered his arm. They were just about to set off down the busy street, with Jack in the lead, when a small company of soldiers stepped in front of them. Olivia blinked.

"Lord Nicholas Talcott?" the tall, heavily bearded sergeant barked.

"Yes?" Nicholas frowned, eyeing the man up and down.

"We have a warrant for your arrest."

"What?" Nicholas drew himself up and Olivia clutched at his arm. "I'm just returning—I've not been here on English soil for five minutes. On what charge?"

"Treason against the Crown, my lord."

Olivia gasped, and she felt Nicholas stagger slightly. "What?" she whispered, shocked.

"Such a charge is ridiculous—" Nicholas spluttered. "I am Her Majesty's most loyal subject—I've done nothing—"

"You'll have a chance to answer the charge to Lord Walsingham." The sergeant made a gesture and they were surrounded. Olivia shrank against Nicholas, as a burly soldier leered down at her.

"Walsingham!" cried Nicholas. "It was his business I was about!"

The sergeant's disgust was plain on his face. The other soldiers crowded closer, until Olivia could feel their hot breath on her neck. "Apparently he forgot that, my lord. Come now."

"Sergeant, there's been a terrible mistake—I don't understand—"

"It's not for me to understand either, my lord. My orders are to bring you to London. Will you come peacefully?"

"And—and my lady—" Nicholas stopped short and gazed down at Olivia.

"What about the lady?" asked one of the men, leaning on his pike. "Turn her loose? The warrant says nothing about her."

"Bring her. She's part of this. She's with him, right?"

The men surrounded them. Olivia looked through the crowd that had begun to gather and saw Jack standing uncertainly on the periphery. Nicholas caught his eye and gestured with his head. The boy tugged his forelock and took off. *Please,* she prayed, *let him get to Talcott Forest safely. And let Geoffrey come and straighten out this mess as quickly as possible.*

"Nicholas." She spoke as softly as she could. "Where are they taking us?"

"London, missy." The bearded sergeant spoke over his shoulder. His manner was rough, but his voice was not unkind. "To the Tower. The Tower of London."

The road to London was long and rough, and the closer they got to the ancient capital, the more crowded it became. But Olivia, sitting crowded in a wagon with Nicholas bound by her side, was only half aware of all that passed by. They stopped for the night at a tavern that was nowhere near as well appointed as the ones Nicholas had taken her to, and instead of going to a room, they were chained to a pole in the stable. "My God," she murmured, when they'd been left alone in the dark, "they act as if we're guilty."

"They think we are," Nicholas answered grimly. It was impossible to see his face in the gloom, but she pressed against the reassuring warmth of his body. His arm closed around her awkwardly. "Forgive me."

Olivia closed her eyes, burying her face in his chest. She took a deep breath. The odors of the stable, dung and horse, and their own sweat, filled her nostrils. The sweat was acrid and sharp. Fear, she thought. That's what fear smells like.

"Olivia, I'll do all I can, I swear it, to protect you. Even if it means going to the block myself—I'll not tell them anything to implicate you."

In the darkness, she raised her head and stared at the pale smudge that was all she could see of his face. "Nicholas, can't we just tell them the truth?"

He made a little choking noise in his throat.

"Not about me, not that—but, about what happened in Calais? That's what they will question you about—not me."

"Obviously." His dry tone struck her as funny and she giggled. Even to her ears, she sounded hysterical. He leaned forward and awkwardly held her close. "Hush. If we make too much noise, they're likely to separate us and I want to keep you close for as long as I can." He paused. "Are you all right?"

She took a deep breath and forced herself to relax. "Yes."

"Now. Hopefully, Jack got to Geoffrey by now. He wouldn't have stopped, and he may even be home. As soon as Geoffrey hears of this, he'll come right to London. I'm not without friends, you know. And I count Robert Dudley, the earl of Leicester, as one of them. When Geoffrey tells him my story, we'll see how long it takes for the Queen to order us set free."

Olivia closed her eyes, willing herself to believe that what he said was true. "But, Nicholas, we don't even understand the charges. What if it's Geoffrey who's the reason?"

He sat back with a grim laugh. "Then the charge would be witchcraft, not treason." He settled himself against the pole to which they were bound. "Come, lean against me. We better try to get some sleep. I have a feeling tomorrow is going to be a long, bad day."

Tomorrow came all too quickly. They were roused at the very first light of dawn, when the sun was less than a red wedge in the eastern sky over the London road, given a

hard biscuit and a cup of water, and loaded once more
into the rickety wagon. Stiff and sore, Olivia grimaced
every time the wheels jounced over a rut or a pothole.
More than one time, they were pelted with refuse as they
passed through villages, despite the efforts of the soldiers
to stop the abuse. And so slow was the progress, that the
sun had long since passed its zenith by the time they
passed beneath the stone gates that marked the entrance
to the City of London.

Momentarily she forgot their predicament as she gazed
in wide-eyed wonder at the city that rose, massive and
medieval, all around them. Houses were jam-packed along
the narrow streets, some as high as five and six stories,
leaning out so precariously that the streets themselves
were deep wells of shadow. Every house seemed to be a
shop of one sort or another—drapers and clothiers and
glovers of every description all jostling for attention by
means of bright signs and fluttering fabrics. The wagon
lurched around a corner and down another street, and they
passed a church, crooked tombstones in the churchyard
leaning heavily against each other. Here and there, people
paused and stared as they passed: a woman who grabbed
her child away from the wagon wheel; another who
hushed a squalling infant. An apprentice looked up as he
shuddered beneath his master's whip, and schoolboys
tossed an apple over their heads from side to side as they
ran alongside the cart.

And then they turned one more corner, and the road
opened out into a broad avenue, and Olivia's heart rose
in her throat as the rough gray stone walls rose into sight.
This was the Tower of London. This was where Anne
Boleyn and Catherine Howard had met their awful fates—
this was the place where Raleigh and Essex would die.
The so-called Princes in the Tower, murdered most likely
not by their uncle Richard III, but by his usurper, Henry
VII, lay buried somewhere in one of the walls. They
would not be uncovered for more than a hundred years.
Blood stained the walls and tinged the mortar. She swal-

lowed hard as the wagon lurched to a sudden stop.

She looked at Nicholas, and their eyes met. For a split second, time seemed to stand still. In those blue, blue eyes, she read something she had never seen before. "I love you," he mouthed, and then the guards dragged them away and apart.

"Well done, Warren." The thin voice rose above the scratching of the pen, and Warren smiled, even as he inclined his head lower. "I assume you mean to question him at once?"

"Immediately, my lord. I intended to go to the Tower as soon as I placed these plans in your hands."

There was a brief pause as Walsingham scanned the document he had just penned.

"Would you like me to deliver that, my lord?"

"This? Ah, no. I'm not quite ready to turn the plans over to Cecil yet. I think I'll take some time to familiarize myself with them." He looked up at Warren and smiled blandly.

A shiver went down Warren's spine. Copy them, he means, thought Warren. Copy them and commit them to memory, and use them in any way he could to accomplish whatever he thought he could get away with. Walsingham was not so much a master spy as he was a master opportunist. He rose to his feet. "Then if you have no more need of me, my lord, I will go and question the prisoner."

"Yes." Walsingham picked up the pen once more. "Oh, and Warren?"

"Yes, my lord?"

"I'm to understand there's a woman involved?"

Another chill went down Warren's spine despite the stuffy air in the windowless room. Walsingham even spied on his spies, it seemed. "Aye, my lord. Talcott and his leman. I—I thought to release the woman."

"Release the woman? Why?"

"Well, uh—" Warren paused, thinking furiously. The woman was not really part of his plans. He'd only thought to use her to further rouse Sir John, but now that the ruse had worked, he had no more need of her. And the last thing he wanted was for Walsingham, or anyone else, for that matter, to question her. "Why not release her?"

"She may have been a witness."

"Aye, but—she's just whore—"

Walsingham looked up and cocked one eyebrow at him. "I see." There was another silence. "A whore."

"Yes." Warren felt the sweat trickle down his neck. The presence of the cousin complicated the matter in ways he'd not even contemplated when the damnable idea had leapt into his brain. Moon madness! He cursed the moment the sheer stupidity of it had burst into his skull. There was only one solution, which he had grudgingly reached upon long reflection. It had not been his intention to harm a woman.

"Very well," Walsingham said at last. "See that you question her before you release her. The testimony of one whore more or less is scarcely likely to sway the scales against Talcott one way or the other."

Warren drew a deep breath and bowed once more. Walsingham's penetrating black eyes seemed to bore straight into his soul. Warren squirmed. If his master only knew. He pushed the unpleasant thought aside and bowed again. "As my lord wishes, it shall be done."

He shut the door softly as he left the room. Walsingham was biting the end of the quill as he stared into space; he seemed to have forgotten Warren's presence. It was just as well. But the question of Talcott's cousin—well, that was another problem altogether, one he'd been wrestling with ever since he'd seen Talcott and his cousin at the inn in Dover. This was no simple, soft-minded, milk-and-water miss. Despite her youth, she had a strong-minded air about her. She had to be eliminated—wholly and completely. It was perhaps regrettable, but after all, the more members of that damnable tribe who could be eliminated, the better. Releasing her would set her free in the dangerous streets of London, where she'd be vulnerable for at least a little while, without friends or family or even coin. He'd see her released at dusk, when the long shadows would hide the alleys and the crannies where the whores and thieves and cutpurses hid. And murderers.

He glanced up at the sun. Plenty of time to speak to his contacts, and still arrange for the girl's release. He was stopped by Sir John Makepiece as he walked down the stairs that led to the street.

"Master Warren!" The knight turned on his heel and followed him.

"Sir John?" Warren stopped short. "What do you do here, sir?"

"I was looking for you. I was told you were likely to be here—"

"Told by whom?"

"The wench you keep. Said you were likely to be here as anywhere."

"I see." He would have to punish Rose. "What do you want?"

"To talk to you. Where's Talcott?"

"He arrived at the Tower today. I'm on my way there now."

"And how soon—" The knight gripped Warren's arm.

Warren stopped still in the middle of the street. He looked down at his sleeve and the knight dropped his hand. "How soon what?"

The greedy light diminished somewhat in the knight's watery eyes. "My reward. How soon—?"

"These things take time, Sir John. You didn't expect it would happen today, did you?"

The knight drew himself up. "Nay, sir. May I come with you?"

Warren flinched as if struck. "To the Tower, Sir John? 'Tis best you stay as far from Talcott as possible. You'll confront him soon enough."

Sir John straightened up and tugged his doublet into place with an affronted air. "You mistake my meaning, Master Warren. My lodgings lie in that direction."

Mollified, Warren shrugged. "An you will, Sir John. Come, and tell me every detail you remember."

The two men started off, Sir John speaking quietly in his low, dry voice, while Warren pretended to listen. The sooner he got the woman out of the Tower, the sooner she'd no longer be a problem.

"I believe I have the answer." Dr. Dee peered owlishly through his spectacles at Geoffrey and Alison across the table.

"You do?" they chorused in unison.

"Yes, indeed." Dee stroked his long brown and silver beard, looking like a highly self-satisfied squirrel, if a somewhat skinny one. "It *is* here." He tapped the parchment in front of him. "I realized as soon as you mentioned the eclipse that that had to be the answer." He paused.

"Well?" asked Alison impatiently. "Are you going to tell us, or should we guess?"

The older man looked taken aback. "Sometimes I think I spend too much time in the sixteenth century," he said, almost to himself. "I'm sorry. I forget how direct women became in the twentieth century. At any rate, it's going to take two weeks."

"Two weeks?" She leaned forward. "I'm sorry. I don't understand. Why will it take us two weeks to get back when it only took two minutes to get here?"

"It will take two weeks for the angles of sun and the moon, and all the heavenly bodies in fact, to return to the proper positions. It is a gateway, if you will, between now and then. The present and the future, or the past and the present, if you will. But if you do not return in two weeks, you will not have another opportunity for thirty-eight years. Thirty-seven years, eight months, two weeks, five days, eleven hours, sixteen minutes, and twenty-nine seconds, actually, but I don't think you care whether or not it's precise."

"Thirty-seven years?" Alison swallowed hard. "My

God. I'll be an old woman. If I even survive that long. So—why the wait?"

Dee beckoned to her with one long skinny finger. "Look here. It's all in the equations. If t is time, and the value of mass is approximately two hundred and seventy-five pounds—assuming your friend weighs less than you do, being shorter—"

"Doctor Dee," Alison interrupted softly. "I don't care about the math. How come we have to wait two weeks? Do *you* have to wait for this—this gateway to open up? Is that why you're here? You can't get back?"

Dee sighed and scratched his head. "No, no, it's not like that at all. In my time—in twenty-one seventy-six, I mean—the time portal has been perfected to the point where we don't need hedges and mazes and things of that nature. With the discovery of the fifth dimension—not 'discovery' in the sense you understand the word, we'd theorized it existed for years—but with the actual experience of the fifth dimension, using computer-generated space/time realities—" He broke off and sighed again. "The short answer is, I can go back and forth between my time and this one at will. You, however, given the primitive state of just about everything, can't." He picked up an inkwell and candle. "This is then." He held up the inkwell. "This is now." He held up the candle. "You think of these as two different realities, but that's not true. It's really all one. Part of it depends on you, to a great extent. You—the reality of you—extend into every level of existence. The discovery of the integration of the human psyche with the physical world in twenty forty-three was probably the most revolutionary discovery of all time. It goes beyond Galileo. But you, Mistress Alison, like Master Geoffrey to a great extent, aren't quite *there* yet. Do you understand what I'm trying to explain to you?"

Alison nodded slowly. "I think so. It's like my trying to explain genes to someone who doesn't know what the heart does. Am I right?"

"Exactly. Believe it or not, there are things the people

in your time haven't even begun to dream about. And it's all right that things are like that. But what it means for you and for your friend, is that in order to cross the ripple in time, to return to the 'when' you remember as yours, you must wait for the physical world to give you a boost, so to speak."

"Gotcha." She breathed a sigh and looked once more at Geoffrey. He was staring out the window and looked almost dejected. Geez, thought Alison, he looks like he lost his best friend.

Chapter 13

THE CELL DOOR scraped across the uneven floor. From the room's low stone ledge, which served as both bed, table, and chair, Olivia looked up. Even at the height of a summer day, the interior of the Tower chilled her to the bone. It wasn't so much the temperature as the atmosphere, she thought, as the hair rose on the back of her neck. For the first time in her life, she was terrified, truly and absolutely terrified. Nothing she had ever encountered had prepared her for this. Her run-ins with the authorities had been limited to speeding tickets—usually while Alison was driving. Her mouth was dry and her heart was pounding. Despite the chill, her palms were wet with sweat.

She couldn't let them see how frightened she was. Never. She twined her fingers in her skirts to hide how they trembled, and she raised her chin.

The gray-faced, gray-haired jailer peered inside. "Ye can go."

Startled, she blinked. "What?"

"Ye can go. Ye've been released."

"And what about Lord Nicholas? Is all of this—"

"Don't know nothin' about that. My orders was to let ye go. Now, do y' want to leave or not?"

"Of course I want to leave," she said, rising to her feet and smoothing down her skirts. "But what about Lord Talcott? Where's Nicholas? Why are you letting me leave and not him?"

"I don't know nothin' 'bout that either. Get 'er out of here," the jailer said over his shoulder. Two expressionless guards stepped forward and took her by the arms. They half-dragged, half-escorted her down the narrow passageway, to the tiny winding steps. She stumbled on her skirts as they hustled her down and out. Outside, they unlocked the chains that bound her wrist. They took her to the gate and nodded for her to go. Olivia stared back, at the silent, brooding towers, black against the violet summer twilight. She rubbed her wrists and looked back out at the street. Now what? She had no money, no way of getting back to Talcott Forest. What in the world was she to do?

"Please?" she said, as they stood like a pair of robots, staring neither right nor left. "Please won't you tell me how Lord Talcott is?"

For a moment, she thought they intended to ignore her, and then pity flickered across the face of the older one. He glanced down at her but his lips barely moved as he spoke. "He's still inside. They haven't touched him yet, but they will. And may God have mercy on his soul. For surely there's nothing you nor I can do for him."

"You'd best go," the other growled.

She stumbled away, reeling. Go? Go where? She knew nothing of London. She didn't even know how to get to Talcott Forest from here, though by car it was less than two hours away. She walked across the street, dodging pedestrians, and leaned against the nearest wall. *Think,* she commanded herself. *Think.*

She stared up and down the cobbled street, trying desperately to recall the London she knew so well, but nothing was the same. It was all so crowded and dark and dirty. Her stomach rumbled alarmingly and a wave of dizziness nearly overcame her. No, she commanded herself. She couldn't faint now. Perhaps she could find a church—yes, that's what she'd do. Look for a church—any church. Throw herself on the mercy of a priest, whatever his leanings, and beg him to send a message to Geoffrey. Pray God, perhaps they were already on their way. She squared her shoulders and started off across the street, not noticing the dark shape that eased away from the pool of shadows beside the Tower walls.

She hesitated once more, and in that moment, she heard a rough voice say: "M'lady."

She turned and recognized Jack as he approached her out of the twilight. She gasped then, as a heavy hand fell across her shoulders; her legs buckled beneath her at the unexpected blow.

"My lady!" Jack bolted behind her, leaping at the attacker with a raised blade that seemed to materialize out of the air. Olivia scurried forward on her hands and knees, seeking the shelter of the nearest wall, while the two scuffled. Knives flashed in the twilight, and suddenly her assailant ran off, limping and cursing.

At once, Jack bent over her. Blood ran down the side of his face and he clutched his arm. "Are ye all right, m'lady?"

She sagged against the wall, as the blond boy's familiar face loomed out of the growing dark. "Oh, Jack. You don't know how glad I am to see you."

He twisted his hands uncomfortably. "Can you stand? I'm glad to see ye, too, lady. I—I din't quite know what to do. I know Lord Nick wanted for me to go on home and get Master Geoff, but—but I couldn't leave you two. I was afraid they might take you somewhere and I wouldn't know where to tell Master Geoff to go. And there was you—"

She dismissed the thought that Geoffrey wasn't coming yet. "It's all right, Jack. Really it is. I'm so glad to see you—I don't know what I would've done right now—"

"It's good I was here, weren't it, lady?" He grinned down at her.

"Are you all right? Did that—that cutthroat hurt you in any way?"

"Me? Nah, I'm fine. These are just scratches. Come. They grabbed Lord Nick's pack, but they let me have your trunk. I got it down the road a ways, at a tavern called the Red Lion. Will you come? I've got a bit o' money, too—won it dicing this noon, I did. You can get a room—we can have some supper." Talking nervously, as though he feared Nicholas's wrath or another attack, Jack led her through the streets with practiced ease. The hour was growing late, and night had fallen by the time they reached the wooden door. It stood wide open as though in welcome, and through it, she could see a stone-paved room full of long tables and benches, packed with men of all ages and descriptions, who wore the same rough clothing and lifted foaming tankards with uniformly dirty hands.

The thought of Nicholas spending a night in that hellish Tower twisted her heart. She was tired and dirty and hungry. A wave of dizziness came over her, and she stumbled again in the street, nearly falling. Jack turned and caught her arm. "Lady? Are you all right?"

"Yes." She closed her eyes, her head spinning. "Let's go in?"

"At once, m'lady. Forgive me."

Gently, he guided her into the crowded tavern. Raucous laughter greeted them, and the smoke stung her eyes. The odor of roasting meat filled her nostrils, and saliva exploded in her mouth. Her head spun again, as the noise and smoke and smells made her dizzy. She swayed.

"Ho! Easy there, lad—looks as if your lass is done in before the night's a'gun." Good-natured laughter greeted them from the closest table.

"This is not my lass!" said Jack, trying to hold her up. "This lady is cousin to Lord Nicholas Talcott—she's been fallen upon by a robber and needs help!"

"Lord?"

"Aye, Lord Talcott of Talcott Forest—will you help her?"

A burly arm reached out to catch her as she fell, and as the room slowly righted itself, a mug full of foaming ale was pressed into her hands. Nausea rose in her throat, and she shook her head weakly against the shouts of the men to swallow.

"Now, now, let me through, y' oafs! Let me through!" The shrill voice cut through the masculine rumble with shrill efficiency. The crowd parted, although Olivia was aware that Jack hovered, anxious as a mother hen, at her back. A plump woman of middle age, her round rosy face framed by a spotless white coif, her sleeves rolled to her elbows, and her gray, homespun apron spotted with faded grease stains, pushed her way to the fore. She raised Olivia's face to hers with one work-worn hand and shook her head. "Back off, all of ye. Let the lady breathe, for the sake of Christ. Oh, ye poor, poor lamb. What's been done to ye? Such fine clothes, so abused—well, you her squire? Have you been brawling in the streets?" This was said to Jack, who, startled, nodded violently.

"I'm Lord Talcott's squire, aye—" He began, patting his pouch of money at his waist.

"Good, help me bring 'er upstairs, then. And you, Watt, carry that trunk. Meg! A pot of water, now! And a clean towel!" Fussing and bustling like a goose with one gosling, the woman forced a path through the gaping crowd. Somehow, with both her and Jack's help, Olivia got up the steps. She found herself in a small bedroom where a wide bed took up most of the space. A rough table was the room's only other furnishing. The woman pushed her gently down on the bed and set a candle on the small table, where it cast a wan yellow light on the whitewashed walls. The room was stuffy, for the one small window was shut.

"Now, are you faint, lady? No? Good. Meg, put that water down here and open that window so's she can

breathe. You, and you"—she pointed at Jack and Watt—
"back downstairs. Now." She turned back to Olivia, and
put her hands on her hips. "Let's see what we can do wi'
ye."

In a matter of mere minutes, it seemed, Olivia had been
peeled out of her clothes, washed, and put into a clean
smock. A clay bowl, filled with a steaming liquid strongly
scented with spices, was pressed into her hands.

"Have a swallow, m'dear. 'Tis not so fine as what ye're
used to, but 'tis strengthening—will put the flesh back on
yer bones. Don't they feed you?" She looked at Olivia
critically.

Olivia nodded mutely. She sipped at the contents of the
bowl, and found it to be red wine, well spiced with cloves
and ginger. "Your name, good mistress?"

"I'm Deb Althorpe, mistress of the Red Lion tavern.
'Twas my man's till he passed, and there being no one
else, it's mine. Finest run tavern in all of London, you'll
see. And you?"

Olivia hesitated. She'd heard herself introduced as a
cousin of Lord Talcott's—what did it matter who she said
she was? "Olivia."

"Pretty name, but foreign. You stay there. I'll go find
a bit of bread and chicken for you. A nice piece off the
breast'll do you good."

Deb bustled out of the room, leaving Olivia sitting on
the bed, her toes dangling like a child's. She sipped the
red wine slowly. Her stomach rumbled alarmingly, but
now that she was clean and the prospect of food was on
the way, she felt much better. Immediately she thought of
Nicholas, alone in that cold, dank place. Had they fed
him? Given him a candle, or a blanket? What would happen to him?

Thoughts of torture, of the rack and all the other medieval accouterments of justice, brought tears to her eyes.
She remembered the last anguished look they'd exchanged. Had her eyes deceived her? Or had it really been
"I love you" that he'd mouthed?

The door opened, and Deb stepped through carrying a plate. She placed it on the small table next to the bed. "Now, eat." She took the bowl from Olivia and nodded at the plate. "Come now. Slowly."

Her hand shook as she reached for the bread. It was coarser than anything she'd tasted so far. A smear of butter glistened on the surface, and she bit and chewed it slowly. Surprisingly, it had a rich, nutty flavor. "Thank you," she said.

"I'm going back downstairs now. You rest, m'lady. Don't eat that too fast—it'll all come back up."

"I understand. Is Jack downstairs?"

"Yer boy? Aye, in the kitchen with my Meggie getting his arm bandaged. He's quite a talker, that one. You rest now. There's nothing doing tonight. 'Tis nearly nine by the watch."

"I need to talk to Jack."

Deb looked skeptical. "All right, m'lady, an ye will. I'll send him up to ye directly."

"Thank you." Olivia bit off another piece of bread as Deb, with a doubtful shake of her head, left the room.

A hesitant knock came just a few minutes later. "M'lady?"

"Come in, come in, Jack." She smiled up at him and was touched to see the boy blush. "Thank you for everything. I know you took it upon yourself to disobey Nicholas, but—but honestly, I'm glad you did. But listen now. You must go to Talcott Forest tomorrow. You must leave at dawn, for there's no time to waste. God only knows what they'll do to him in that horrible place. Take one of the horses—you brought them, didn't you?"

"Aye, m'lady—one of them. The others I left in Dover. I left the rest of Lord Nick's money wi' the landlord for their care—they'll be well looked after till we fetch them."

"Well, no matter now. You've got to get to Geoffrey and tell him everything. I'll wait here, I suppose. Is there—is there enough money?"

He patted his money pouch with pride. "Aye, m'lady. I was lucky with the dice. But I don't like to leave you, lady. The streets are dangerous, ye saw that for yerself."

Olivia sighed. "There's no help for it, Jack. We've no other way to get a message to Geoffrey, and you can travel so much more quickly alone."

He hesitated, as if he wanted to argue more, but finally shrugged. "An ye will it, m'lady. Here—this'll be enough to cover a day or more." He dug into the pouch with grimy fingers and placed the coins on the table. Olivia smiled up at Jack. "Thank you. I'm sure Lord Nicholas will—"

"Aye, lady. I've no fear on that score." He glanced around the room, clearly uncomfortable. "I'll leave you now, to rest. But I promise, I'll be gone by first light."

She sat back and sighed. "Thank you, Jack. You've been more than kind to me. Lord Nicholas will be pleased."

He tugged his forelock awkwardly. "Aye, m'lady. I think so." With another shy smile, he was gone.

Olivia slipped to the floor and walked around the wide bed to the one small window. It was set into the thatch of the roof, and stood open on its hinges. She leaned out. London sprawled around her, all leaning rooftops and church spires. The Red Lion was the only two-story building on the street. Here and there, a clothesline stretched between houses, and through windows dimly lit by candlelight, she could see dark shapes moving about. The smell of cooking and horses was strong in the heavy evening air. Clouds massed on the horizon, and the air was humid and still. It pressed all around her, stifling as a cloak. She glanced down at the street, where only a few passersby still hurried. The middle of the street was clogged with garbage of every description, from which a rank, fetid smell rose. She wondered if even a strong thunderstorm could clean the streets completely. But at least maybe a storm would clear the air. A dog slunk out of the shadows, sniffing through the refuse. It growled and snapped at something much smaller, which scampered out from under its paws. A rat, most likely, she thought as she averted her eyes with a shudder.

She craned her head, trying to see the Tower, but her window faced the wrong direction. *Don't let them hurt him,* she prayed. *Let them listen to the truth.* A cold, uneasy feeling settled in the pit of her stomach despite the heat. She had been instrumental in getting those plans for him. If she'd not spoken up, maybe there would have been trouble with the Spaniard, but surely Nicholas, being younger and perhaps just as well schooled in fighting, could have bested him. They would've gone home empty-handed, and then there would be no damnable evidence to point to.

But who accused Nicholas, she wondered. Sir John? Was that why he'd been lurking around the church? But how had he known to watch for them there? She pressed her hands to her temples. Oh, for an aspirin, she thought. If ever there was an Excedrin moment, this had to be it. She padded to the table and drained the contents of the bowl. There was nothing she could do. She climbed into bed and blew out the candle. *Please God,* she prayed. *Let him be safe. Let him be whole. Let him be free.*

"You concocted this scheme. And used it against me." Bruised and battered by the treatment of the guards, Nicholas held himself rigid. He would never let this bastard see any weakness.

Christopher Warren shrugged. "You can't prove that."

"When my brother goes to Leicester—"

"Leicester's with the Queen on summer progress. Remember? And by the time your brother finds Leicester, you'll be dead, my lord. The only question here is how."

"I've not been convicted."

"You were arrested with the plans for the invasion of England on your person. You've already been convicted. The sentence has but to be carried out."

"So you mean to put me to death? Without so much as a trial? You can't do that."

Warren shrugged again. "That is the penalty for treason against the Crown, my lord. Surely you are aware of that."

Nicholas did not respond.

"But I'm here to make you an offer. The usual sentence, as you know, is death by hanging, drawing, and quartering—a most painful method, as you can imagine, and one possibly only surpassed by burning to death. If you sign this confession, admitting your treachery, then you'll be beheaded—which is, after all, quite possibly the swiftest and cleanest of deaths. But if you don't, I'm afraid the execution will be by the former method. And it will be quite prolonged and painful. I can assure you. I've watched."

The expressionless tone, and the flat, hard look in the man's eyes, chilled Nicholas. He had no doubt at all that Warren intended to see him die in the most painfully protracted way possible. "Why?"

Warren seemed to falter for a moment. "Why what?"

"Why do you want me dead?"

"What makes you think *I* want you dead?"

"This whole, elaborate scheme—clearly it was concocted by you. Why? I don't even know you. What reason do you have?"

"No, you wouldn't know me, would you, Lord Nicholas? The son of the lord of the manor would have no reason to consort with the snot-nosed son of the local schoolmaster, would he? Of course you wouldn't know me. But I know you."

"What of it?"

"My father was the schoolmaster in Sevenoaks. You don't recall it—you had a tutor. Not for you the creeping from the house at dawn in the gray winter light. He kept eight of us on his schoolmaster's pittance. But no mind— we were happy. Until the day Lord William Talcott of Talcott Forest caused him to be arrested for heresy. And treason. And saw him sent to Canterbury and burned at the stake for the sin of reading an English Bible."

"Sweet Jesu," Nicholas murmured. "This is about your
father? You seek to avenge his death?"

"Aye. The sins of the fathers shall be visited upon the
sons even unto the seventh generation. That's in the English Bible—have you read it?"

"Of course I've read it. The Bible also talks about forgiveness."

"Forgiveness? Should I forgive the son of the man who
saw my father die in agony? Who saw my mother turned
out of our home and forced from the parish? She died in
a ditch in London with no more than a bundle of sticks
for a roof above her head. 'Twas the best I could build
for her. I was ten at the time."

"Warren, I'm sorry for your losses but these things
were not my fault—"

"Your fault? Your fault is not the issue. What I want
from you is payment, and you shall pay. I swore that day
I would see the Talcotts brought down."

"Let me make amends to you—"

"Amends? Can you raise the dead? Can you bring life
into my father's ashes? Or flesh to my mother's bones?"
Warren got to his feet, a light burning in his black eyes.
His face was pale, and in the flicker of the candlelight,
his eyes glowed like twin lamps. He twisted his hand in
Nicholas's hair and pulled it, so that Nicholas was forced
to face him. He put his face so close to Nicholas's, he
could smell the wine on Warren's breath and the sour
smell of decaying teeth. "You'll make your amends. I will
forgive when the house of Talcott falls—when I see your
bones crushed and ground into powder and scattered to
the four winds—then the debt between us shall be repaid.
But I shall never forget." His voice shook with suppressed
emotion, and his eyes burned with a mad light. He released Nicholas's hair with a savage twist and backed
away. His boots echoed on the stone floor.

"You have a choice, my lord." When he spoke once
more, his voice was much more composed. He tapped the

parchment. "I give you twenty-four hours to sign this confession. If you do, you will die far more swiftly and cleanly than either my father or my mother. But if you do not, I shall watch with the greatest pleasure as you are sliced and burned and battered into shreds."

He spun on his heel abruptly and slammed the door shut, leaving Nicholas alone with the sputtering candle and a sickening sense of doom.

Warren pounded down the winding steps, his heart thudding in his chest, his veins throbbing in his head. He had to force Talcott to sign the confession—he had to. It was the only way to ensure a speedy execution. And after the botched attempt on the wench—He closed his eyes and paused near the bottom. He would have to see to her himself. He recoiled from the thought of actually having to kill her himself, but he had no time to find another assassin. And as for Talcott . . . He glanced back up the stairs. If Talcott refused to sign the confession there would be an inquiry at least, and a trial. A dagger between the ribs at night would give nearly as much satisfaction, but who could he trust to do the deed? He'd never intended to bloody his own hands. His mother's anguished face rose before him, and the remembered sound of her hacking cough as she struggled to breathe filled his ears. And the eyes—those tormented eyes—they tortured him more than the memory of his father's screams. Whatever was required he would do, he decided suddenly. No matter how distasteful.

Chapter 14

"SHE'S BEEN TAKEN where?" Alison rose to her feet, her face flushed, eyes flashing. "What in the name of God is going on? Damn it, I knew there was a good reason she shouldn't go. I knew she might be risking her life—"

"Alison." Geoffrey touched her hand. "Come, sit. This is distressing, but nothing's to be gained by shouting. We must think."

Their eyes met in a long look, and, abashed, Alison sat. "Go on, boy. Tell us what happened next."

Jack glanced nervously at Geoffrey, who nodded. "Well, after they got arrested, m'lord told me to go to the inn and get the horses and bring 'em home. But I thought better to follow 'em to Londontown, and that's what I did. They let Lady Olivia go—"

"Oh, now she's Lady Olivia," interjected Alison.

"Sh," said Geoffrey. "Go on, Jack."

"So they let 'er go and I found a place for 'er, but she told me to come straight to you and here I am."

"So Olivia's alone in London? Without money? Or anyone to help her?"

Geoffrey patted her arm. "You did well, Jack. Go to

the stables. Tell Adam to saddle my horse—"

"I'm coming with you," Alison interrupted.

Geoffrey raised one eyebrow, but didn't argue. "All right, two horses—"

"What's all this shouting for, Geoffrey?" Dr. Dee was slowly walking down the staircase, his academic robes whispering around him.

"My brother, Dr. Dee. Nicholas is in the Tower, accused of treason."

"Treason?" Dee looked shocked. "What's this all about?"

Geoffrey exchanged a look with Alison. "To tell you the truth, we're not quite sure. But that's all, Jack. Oh, and see if Miles is about. I'll need some money from the strongbox."

"Aye, sir." Jack tugged his forelock and practically scampered from the room.

Alison paced between the fireplaces. "I knew it, I just knew it. . . ."

"Come, come, Mistress Alison, we're not without friends at court," Dee said kindly. "We'll get this mess straightened out. I promise. Tell me more, Geoffrey. What has your brother involved himself in?"

" 'Tis all because he seeks favor at court." Geoffrey ran his fingers through his hair.

"He's not alone in his ambitions, my boy."

"No, maybe not, but Nicholas pursues his with a single-mindedness that blinds him to other possibilities, I'm afraid. At the Queen's visit, just a fortnight ago, Nicholas was approached by one of Walsingham's agents, a Master Christopher Warren."

"Hm, the name is unfamiliar, but no matter. I avoid Lord Walsingham's men at all costs." He winked at Alison. Only in private did Dee drop the mask he wore so expertly. In public, Alison had a hard time remembering he was from her own future.

"So should we all," Geoffrey put in. He quickly outlined the plan that Nicholas had so enthusiastically embraced. "And then there was a bit of trouble, which I thought very odd—Warren returned the next day and said Nicholas would not suit, since he was not possessed of a wife. And thus, Mistress Olivia offered to play the role, and the two of them left nearly a sennight ago. And now, this."

"So Nicholas obtained the plans as he was bidden, and then the moment he stepped foot on English soil, he was arrested? And taken to the Tower?"

"Aye. That's the story Jack told."

"And Mistress Olivia—she was released?"

"Aye. Without questioning."

Dee stroked his beard. " 'Tis most odd—the whole business. One would almost think they discounted what she had to say, or did not want to hear it at all."

Alison glanced over her shoulder and bit back the retort that rose so readily. *Odd* wasn't the word that came to her mind. But nothing would be accomplished by antagonizing either Geoffrey or Dee, so she stayed silent.

"The Queen is still on progress," Dee was saying. "I don't believe she'll be back at court for another fortnight or more. If there were some way to send a message to her—"

"Excuse me, Master Geoffrey?" Miles Coddington stood in the door, his shirtsleeves rolled to his elbows, his breeches dusty. Obviously, he'd been in the middle of working. "Jack has brought me extraordinary news—is it true, sir?"

"Aye, Miles, I'm afraid so. Come in, come in."

"How has this happened?"

"I believe my brother has an enemy he knows not of, Miles. 'Tis the only explanation possible."

"So it would seem," said Dee. "But if we can get a message to Her Majesty—"

"I'll take it," said Miles at once. "Allow me, Master Geoffrey."

"I am not quite certain where Her Majesty is," Dee said. "I shall go to Leicester House in London. The earl's men will know where she is," offered Miles.

"Excellent," said Dee. "I shall pen the letter myself immediately." He gathered his robes and ascended the steps, his face creased in a frown.

"And I'll make ready to leave, with your permission, Master Geoffrey?"

"As will I and Mistress Alison. We'll ride to London together—tell that young rogue Jack that we'll need him as well."

"Very good, Master Geoffrey. I shall see to the preparations at once." With a brief bow, Miles was gone.

When they were alone, Geoffrey walked over to Alison and put a gentle hand on her shoulder. "Allie."

At the sound of her nickname, Alison looked at him over her shoulder. She blinked back sudden tears. "I'm really scared."

"I know." He pulled her close and, for a moment, she allowed herself to relax against his chest.

"I mean, Olivia's all by herself. . . ."

"Allie, we'll be there as soon as possible. I promise. Jack will take you right to her, while Miles goes to Leicester House and I see if I can get to Nicholas."

"Will they let you in to see him?"

"I can but try." He gave her a crooked little grin and chucked her under the chin. "Chin up, now. Go see to your packing. I'm sure old Janet doesn't move as fast as she once did."

They broke apart, and Alison started up the stairs. Halfway up, she paused and turned back. Geoffrey was standing by the hearth, stroking his chin. He looked troubled, and a pang went through her. "Geoffrey?" At once he looked up. Before he could speak, she went on, "I'm sorry about Nicholas. I don't mean to act as though your brother's life isn't important. I'm sorry."

He gave her another crooked smile that didn't reach his eyes. "I understand, Allie. Believe me, I do."

• • •

A shaft of afternoon light fell across the rough plank table. Olivia sat against the wall, stabbing fruitlessly at a piece of embroidery. Every now and then she stabbed herself with the needle. She held the linen square out and surveyed it. Between worry about Nicholas and her own inept attempts at sewing, she knew Deb was going to be sorely disappointed with her handiwork. The kindhearted soul had obviously wracked her brain to find an occupation she considered suitable for a lady of Olivia's supposed stature. She threw it down with a frustrated sigh and rubbed her temples.

"Lady?" Meg's soft voice broke her reverie.

She looked up. "Yes?"

The girl's pink cheeks glowed from the heat of the kitchen, and she smiled shyly. "Message come for ye. Mistress said I was to give it to ye. If ye cannot read it, we can send down to the church for the clerk."

Olivia started at this fresh evidence of how different this time was from her own, then held out her hand. "No, no child. I can read it. Please, give it to me."

The girl put the folded parchment in her hand and bobbed a rough curtsy. Olivia smiled and carefully opened the folded sheet.

In a labored secretary script, the message read, "Greetings, Olivia. Meet me at the Rose and Quill tavern at the Bishopsgate. Your loving cousin, Geoffrey."

She rose to her feet. Surely Bishopsgate wasn't far— nothing in London could be that far. She stared at the script. But why hadn't Geoffrey come here? Hadn't Jack said he'd bring Geoffrey here? She looked out the window, frowning. Maybe she'd better ask Deb who'd brought this. If Jack had been going to bring them here, and for some reason they went someplace else, why hadn't Jack, at least, come for her? Surely Jack would not have stayed behind. The sun was shining brightly and the street bustled with people about their daily routines. Perhaps Deb could find one of the stable boys to escort her. Or maybe it was close enough that she could walk by herself. At least Mistress Deb could answer those questions.

Lounging in the afternoon sun, Warren watched Olivia leave the tavern, a simple shawl clutched close around her shoulders. She looked both right and left, then stepped into the human current that jostled through the street. He followed her as she headed with purposeful steps toward the Rose and Quill tavern.

Darting through an alley shortcut, Warren emerged in time to see Olivia cross the street. He pulled back just as she walked past his hiding place. Swiftly, his arm snaked out and drew her into the alley. A swift chop to her throat rendered her momentarily speechless, and another punch to the stomach doubled her over in pain. He spun her around and raised his knife for a quick underthrust through the ribs. But his arm was caught by a strong hand, and he looked up—into a surprisingly familiar male face. "You again!" Warren cried, jerking away. It was the same one who'd stopped him from harming the pickpocket a few nights previous.

The young man reached for him, but Warren fleet-footed, sped off, down the narrow alley. He glanced back over his shoulder, but the man was not in pursuit. He bent instead over the woman, where she knelt, groaning. Warren stopped behind a stack of crates, took a deep breath, and adjusted his doublet. He ran his fingers through his hair and smoothed his beard while his pounding heart slowed to nearly normal. When he could no longer feel it thumping against his chest, he peeked out from his hiding place and started off. Talcott's pretty cousin persisted in being a complication. He could feel the pressure begin to rise in his veins. Something had to be done—something soon.

"M'lady? M'lady?" Deb's rough voice was soft with kindness. "Ah, here you are now."

Olivia's eyes fluttered open. Her throat hurt and she

ached all over. Deb's face slowly came into focus. "What—what happened?" she managed to croak. Her throat felt as though she'd tried to swallow a brick.

"Ye were attacked on yer way to the Rose an' Quill, m'lady. And Master Will saved ye."

"Master Will?" Olivia repeated painfully.

"Aye, he's downstairs. He comes here between plays sometimes. I sent to the Rose an' Quill, lady, but there's none there who know ye."

Olivia shut her eyes. "I don't understand."

"We'll look into it, lady. Don't worry yerself on that 'count." Deb paused a moment. "But ye were lucky that Master Will happened along when he did."

Olivia tried to move. Her midsection was sore, and pain radiated across her abdomen. "Very lucky, I'd say."

"Do ye want to try and get up? Or would ye rather rest here?"

Olivia sat up slowly. "This Master Will, the person who saved me. You said he was here?"

"Aye, he brought ye back here, since he'd seen ye here last night. He's downstairs scribbling one of his everlasting poems. Forgive me, lady, for not sending one of the lads along wi' ye. I never thought in broad daylight—" She broke off, her anxious face creased with concern. "You stay here with us, lady, 'til your lad comes back fer ye. Are ye feeling up to going downstairs?"

She nodded. "I must—there must be some way to send word to the Rose and Quill. . . ."

Deb nodded. "I'll help ye dress, m'lady. And then I'll roust Dickon's lazy bones—he's not much good at doing much besides wasting the day away, but a shilling or two might get 'im going. If ye tell him exactly who to ask fer—are ye sure ye're up to being about?"

"I'll be fine, really." Wincing, Olivia sat up and swung her legs over the side of the bed. She felt battered all over. She felt cautiously at her throat. The skin was swollen and tender, and she knew without looking that she had a bad bruise. Deb helped her down the stairs, guided her to a seat near the hearth, and, with an admonition not to go anywhere, bustled away to the kitchen.

Olivia looked around and met the gaze of a mild-eyed young man, who gnawed a quill, on the other side of the tavern.

At once, the young man smiled, leapt to his feet, and bowed with as much accomplished grace as Nicholas, a bow far more polished than his clothing and ink-stained fingers augured. "I'm pleased to see you looking better, my lady."

"You are—you're the one who saved me?" she managed. "Sir, I am most grateful to you."

"I'm only happy I was able to render you the service, lady. To think in broad daylight . . ."

Olivia glanced up and out the window, where the street was still sunny, but less crowded in the afternoon heat. "Did you see who it was, sir?"

The young man shrugged and spread his hands. "I could try to recollect a description, but in truth . . ."

Olivia sighed. In this rough section of London's streets, a well-dressed woman alone was an attractive target. She'd been foolish to rush out by herself. Jack had been right. "I understand. May I have the honor of your name?"

He bowed again in the same graceful, easy movement as before, and she knew, somehow at once, that he was an excellent mimic. "Will Shakespeare at your service, my lady. Player, poet, aspiring mountebank, and sometime rogue."

She knew the color drained from her face. The room spun and righted itself as a wave of dizziness swept over her. She stared, helplessly, at the man before her. He could not be more than her own age, she thought, calculating furiously. Born in 1564, dead in 1616, he was now about twenty-three.

"Are you all right, lady? Do I distress you in some way? Should I call for Mistress Deb?" The heavy country burr was mitigated by the gentle manner of his speech.

She swallowed hard. "No—no, not—not at all." *Stop*

stammering, you ninny, she hissed to herself. *You're behaving like a groupie. And he has no idea why.* "I'm quite
all right, really. You, uh, you write poetry, you say?"

"I wrestle with it." He smiled.

At that she laughed. "How—how did you come to be
a player?"

He scratched his head and looked at his nail. " 'Tis a
simple story, lady, and one without much amusement. Tell
me, do you enjoy the theater?"

"Very, very much," she answered, feeling as though she
ought to pinch herself. Her throat gave a throb as she
swallowed hard in an attempt to control herself. "Uh, what
did you mean, sometime mountebank and aspiring
rogue?"

"Aspiring mountebank and sometime rogue, lady," he
corrected with a merry twinkle in his eye. "The words
mean all, you know."

Blessed God, he would say that, wouldn't he? She
forced herself to smile as casually as she could. "Yes,"
she answered softly. "I know."

He cocked his head, pinning her with a gaze that was
as penetrating as it was benign. "May I inquire what you
do here, lady? I've seen you in the past two days, haunting
the inn like an unlikely ghost. You're waiting for someone?"

She looked up at him. *You wouldn't believe me if I told
you,* she thought. She drew a deep breath. "I'm waiting
for my—my cousin. Lord Nicholas Talcott. Do you know
the name?"

"Alas, lady, I am ignorant. And where is your cousin
that he would leave a lady in—" Shakespeare paused and
looked around. "Well, forgive me, but this is not a place
much frequented by the gentry."

"He didn't leave me here," Olivia replied. "He's been—
detained, I suppose you could say."

"By whom or by what?"

"He was arrested for treason and brought to the Tower.
Yesterday."

At that Shakespeare looked around. He crossed the floor between them in a few long strides, took a chair, and straddled it backward beside her table. "In truth, lady?"

"Aye," she murmured, thinking of Nicholas. "Unfortunately."

Shakespeare glanced over his shoulder. "Lady, you are gently born, and should not be here. Good Deb, the landlady, is a decent sort who'll not take advantage of your bad fortune, but there are plenty around here who would. Do not bandy such a thing about, it you can help it. But a lady like you shouldn't be alone in London. Have you no friends? No one among the nobles to come to help?"

"His brother—Geoffrey. But he's in Kent—or he was. I think he's at the Rose and Quill tavern—my servant went to fetch him. I was there in the Tower, too, till yesterday."

"Sweet Jesu," Shakespeare breathed. "What did they think you'd done?"

She shrugged. "They let me go. It's Nicholas who's in danger."

"And you love this Nicholas?" He leaned forward, speaking softly, but his words caught her by surprise.

"Why—" She gave a little laugh. "What makes you say so?"

It was his turn to shrug. "The look in your eyes when you speak of him, perhaps. Forgive me. I have been told much that I should not speak of things which are only shadows in the eyes of others."

"You see too well, perhaps."

It was his turn to flush and drop his eyes. "You flatter me, lady."

Oh, no, I don't, she thought. *If only you knew.* "I don't mean to. It was only an observation."

"You're very kind." He leaned forward again and whispered conspiratorially, "But of what is he accused? What do they say he did?"

"He was arrested for bringing in plans for the invasion

of England by Spain. But—he had no part in the plot— he thought he was working for the government. . . . He believed he was helping—oh," she said in frustration. "No one will believe this."

Shakespeare frowned. "I will believe it, if you tell me, lady. What exactly has happened?"

Touched by his air of genuine sympathy, Olivia haltingly recounted the story of their trip to Calais, their encounter with the Spaniard, and their subsequent arrest in Dover. "They took me to the Tower, too, but they released me almost at once. And I am very grateful to you, sir, for this was the second time I've been attacked."

"Twice? Since yesterday?" Shakespeare leaned forward with a frown. "In truth, lady, the streets are rough, but— twice?" He shook his head and sighed. "Lady, has it occurred to you that someone wants you dead?"

"Me?" Olivia sat back with a troubled stare.

Shakespeare shrugged. "I was here last night when your boy brought you here. And believe me, you didn't look as though you'd anything worth stealing, save perhaps your clothes. Could it be that someone seeks to take advantage of your state, and is trying to lure you away from this inn?"

Startled at the suggestion, Olivia gazed once more out the window. She knew there was a lively trade in used clothing in sixteenth-century London, but the thought that she could be attacked for the very clothes on her back had never occurred to her. Suddenly the streets outside the window appeared far more menacing than she had ever considered they might be. She remembered Nicholas's words at the inn that first night in Dover, when he'd essentially stood guard while her bath had been prepared. That night seemed so long ago now, even as she realized there were very good reasons men went about armed in broad daylight. Still, her mind veered away from the possibility that someone could be deliberately trying to kill her. "I see that I was foolish to venture out by myself, Master Will. But why would I have been set free?"

Shakespeare spread his hands in an expansive gesture and shrugged. "Methinks this mire goes deeper than you have yet to fathom, lady. 'Twould seem to me that if this is truly a plot against your Nicholas, the one who plots against him has realized the danger that you are. You cannot be allowed to testify to the truth of the matter, and thus you were released, and yet, you cannot be allowed to live. Lady, forgive me if I alarm you, but I think you are in the most desperate danger until your cousin arrives."

Olivia sat back, as the truth of Shakespeare's words struck home.

"And let's hope he arrives post-posthaste, lady. Such a place as this is no place for a lady. As well you've come to learn." Their eyes met in a long, significant look.

With a troubled sigh, Olivia looked away. The afternoon light was nearly gone. They were no longer alone— two roughly dressed men had come in and appropriated a seat on the other side of the fireplace. They eyed her with speculative interest, and Olivia was glad that she was no longer alone, if only temporarily. Olivia hesitated as Meggie, the girl who had served her last night, entered the common room to light the tapers on the walls and the candles in the center of each table. "You're right, Master Shakespeare. But Geoffrey and Nicholas are very close. I know he'll come as quickly as he can."

"And he's in Kent?"

"Yes. Hopefully, he's at the Rose, and if not, he will come no later than tomorrow."

"Will ye have a cup of cider, lady?" Meggie's broad face was flushed from the heat of the cook fire in the kitchen.

"I will, thank you. Will you join me, Master Shakespeare?" she asked, wondering a little at her own boldness.

"If I might have the honor of your name, lady." He grinned back, his deep-set eyes alight with humor and something else—something as flattering as it was unexpected. He was attracted to her.

She felt herself blush. "My name is Olivia."

"Lady Talcott?"

She hesitated and glanced up at Meg. Her stolid face bore no hint of impatience, but Olivia paused before answering. She knew instinctively that the reason the landlady treated her so well was because she believed Olivia to be part of a noble family. She glanced involuntarily at the kitchen door. If the goodwill of the lady of the establishment depended upon the belief that she was a "Lady," she didn't want to destroy the illusion. Still, she couldn't lie. "Two ciders, Meg, please."

When the girl had gone, she looked at Shakespeare. "I'm not Lady Talcott, Master Shakespeare. My name is Lindsley—Olivia Lindsley. But—"

"Your secret is safe from good Deb with me." He patted her hand. "I'll take it to the grave if necessary."

"Oh," she breathed, as Meg returned, carrying two tankards. "Let's not speak of graves, Master Shakespeare. I have the uncomfortable feeling I'm standing far too close to my own."

Chapter 15

A CURVED SICKLE of a moon hung high above the dark walls of the Tower of London, a sight that reminded Nicholas all too well of Death's scythe. He flexed his shoulders and paced in frustration. He might as well have been entombed alive, for all the attention the guards paid him. They'd opened his door once all day—to bring him the day's rations of stale bread, moldy cheese, and water, silently setting the items on the table beside that damnable confession. Otherwise they ignored him, refusing to acknowledge his demands for a messenger to send to Lord Leicester or an opportunity to talk to Walsingham himself.

On the rude table in the center of the room lay the parchment confession. He'd read it—and had to restrain himself from tearing it to pieces. He understood perfectly why they wanted him to sign it. His estates would automatically revert directly to the Crown, and Geoffrey would never inherit either title or lands. The Talcott line would effectively end. If he refused, and was posthumously found not guilty, the title would pass to Geoffrey and the line would continue. So much for all his hopes of restoration, he thought bitterly.

He rubbed his hands together. The stones were cold,

and his shirt was thin. The parchment lay on the table, silent, mocking. A swift, sure death, or one in agony? it seemed to taunt. And what about Olivia? Where was she and what had they done with her? Was she condemned to die as well?

The door shrieked open on rusting hinges, and he spun around. Christopher Warren stood in the door. "Thank you, jailer. I'll take the lantern." He walked into the room and set the lantern on the table. The sputtering light threw up huge shadows and cast a weird orange glow on Warren's face. "Well, Talcott?"

"Go to the devil."

"You refuse to sign?" Warren shrugged. "I thought as much. It matters not to me." He picked up the lantern and the parchment.

"I'll see you in hell, Warren."

"You'll see me on the scaffold first." He turned as if to leave, and Nicholas forced himself to stand rigid.

"Where's Olivia?"

"Ol—? Ah, your leman? A tasty tempting morsel, if ever there was one, Talcott. We all enjoyed her. And then put her out on the streets where she belongs." He dodged out of the room just as Nicholas rushed for his throat.

Nicholas hit the door as it slammed shut in his face. Damn the bastard to the hottest pit of hell. He pounded on the door with both fists, until his rage was spent and he slumped, exhausted, against the heavy door. Olivia, where was she? What had they done to her? He imagined her hurt, bleeding and abused, lost and alone on the savage streets of London. Pray God Jack had reached Geoffrey. He trusted his brother would do all he could to set him free, but what about Olivia? Friendless, she was at the mercy of every cutthroat, rapist, and thief. They'd steal her clothes off her back, if given half the chance. He slid to the floor and buried his face in his hands, shutting his eyes against the awful picture. This was all his fault. He should never have agreed to take Warren's bait. He saw now, so clearly, how he'd walked so willingly into the trap. And he'd taken Olivia with him—intelligent, gentle, beautiful Olivia, whom he'd come to love as much as he desired her. If only he could see her one more time, he'd throw himself at her feet and beg her forgiveness with his last breath, if necessary.

He dragged himself up, flexing his aching hands. The knuckles were raw and bleeding from his assault on the door, but he paid them no heed. He wrapped his hands around the bars of his window and stared out at the silent moon. *As God is my witness,* he prayed, *as God is my witness, I'll get out of here and I'll see Warren flayed alive, with my own hands if necessary, if he's harmed one hair of Olivia's head. Just one.*

The insistent knocking roused Olivia from her uneasy sleep. Her dreams were darkened by images of Nicholas in chains, faces leering out of the shadows, and rats that swarmed up and down the walls. She sat up, rubbing her temples. "Who is it?"

"It's me, Livvie!" Alison burst into the room in a swirl of russet cloth. She was across the narrow room in two strides and hugged Olivia fiercely. "Are you okay? Please tell me you're all right. They didn't hurt you in any way, did they? Did they?"

Olivia stifled a squeak of pain as Alison crushed her bruised body. She sagged with relief against her friend. "Oh, God, Allie, I can't tell you how glad I am to see you. I'm fine—really, I'm okay," she said again, as Alison drew back with a dubious expression. "I could use a bath. . . ."

"Yeah, who couldn't?" Alison wrinkled her nose. "But what's this about you being attacked? The lady downstairs said you'd been attacked by some ruffian. What happened?"

"Well, I—I guess you could say I was set upon by— I'm really not sure. He ran off like a common cutthroat, but I'm beginning to think it has something to do with this mess, too. But really, physically, I'm fine. Just a bit bruised. Is Geoffrey downstairs?"

"He's gone to the Tower, to see if they'll let him see Nicholas. And Miles Coddington's gone to Leicester House with a letter from Dr. Dee—you know, the u-Queen's—"

"Yes, her astrologer."

"And personal physician. He wrote a letter on Nicholas's behalf as soon as he heard about what happened, but no one is sure where the Queen is, you see."

"She's on her summer progress."

"Yes," Alison said. "You knew that?"

Olivia shrugged. "I know too damn much. Allie, this whole thing is my fault."

"Your fault?" Alison wrapped one arm around her and would have squeezed again except for Olivia's wince. "What in the name of God are you talking about? How could any of this be your fault? And how did you get hurt? What happened to you?"

Olivia ran her fingers through her hair. "It's a long story."

"I've got all night. Tell me everything that happened."

Olivia took a deep breath, then plunged into the story. "Everything went as we expected until we met the Spaniard. And then it turned out that whoever this Warren had gotten his information from had either not known or neglected to tell him that the woman who was supposed to show up was one of the ladies-in-waiting to Mary, Queen of Scots, and had been with her when she was executed. And the Spaniard was supposed to get details of her death from this woman—sort of as a trade, I guess. Well, if I hadn't been there, Nicholas wouldn't have gotten the plans, because—"

"Oh, no, Olivia, you knew all about it, didn't you?"

"Well, enough to convince him to hand over the plans." She buried her face in her hands and her hair spilled over her shoulders. "It's my fault, Allie. He's going to die as traitor, and it's all my fault."

"But—but won't there be a trial? Won't they at least listen to him? Get his side of the story? We can all be witnesses."

Olivia shook her head. "Elizabethan justice is fairly medieval. Nicholas was caught red-handed with the plans. I don't know if they'll bother with a trial. I guess in theory there ought to be one, but it isn't like in America. Under English common law, they assume you're guilty until you're proved innocent—not the other way around. And if you look at it from that point of view—"

"Well, what about this Warren? Where's that little weasel? He's the one who set Nicholas up."

"I don't know, but I wouldn't be surprised if he's behind the attacks on me. The last thing he'd want is for me to corroborate Nicholas's story." She described the events of the day. "I was lucky Master Will happened along."

"Good God. What a mess. Geoffrey was right." She shook her head and plopped beside Olivia on the bed. "Well, the good news is Dee thinks he found a way for us to get home."

Olivia raised her head and stared at her friend. "And you think it will work?"

"It damn well better." Alison paused. "You might not believe this, Liv, but he's from the future, too."

"What?" Olivia stared at Alison in disbelief. "From our time?"

"No. From *our* future. Over a hundred years ahead of us. And in his time, they've perfected the technique, apparently—"

"Do you think there're more people from the future, then?"

"You mean here?" Alison waved a dismissive hand. "You know, Liv, I guess that could be. But you know what? I really don't care. I just want to go home."

Home. The word echoed in her mind. Olivia wrapped her arms around herself and stared out the tiny window. A tiny smidgen of sky was all that was visible between the buildings. "Aye," she murmured. "Home."

Alison gave a short laugh. "Geez, you even sound like them now. How long have you been here?"

"Since last night. Jack found this place—it's not the best inn, but the landlady's sweet." She looked at Alison. "You'll never guess who saved me this afternoon."

"Who?"

"Shakespeare."

"Huh?"

"William Shakespeare. He's really very nice."

Alison's eyes were two round blue saucers. "I can't believe what I'm hearing. No one is ever going to believe us, you know that? We might as well say we were kidnapped by drug lords or something."

"We don't have to worry about that yet, do we?"

"No. Not for another two weeks."

Olivia drew a deep breath. "Allie, I don't want to go back if Nicholas is still imprisoned."

"What? You have to go back. The next time you can go back won't be for another forty years almost. Don't be ridiculous, Liv. Of course you have to go back."

Olivia turned away. "You have to go back, Allie. I don't know that I do."

"Livvie, you're upset."

"I love him. I don't want to leave him in prison."

There was a long silence as Alison stared at her in shock. "You're serious, aren't you?"

Olivia nodded.

Alison slowly shook her head. "I—I just don't believe you'd want to stay—"

Olivia spread her hands. "Well, not permanently. I just don't want to leave without knowing what happens—"

"You can look up what happens. Didn't you see what happens when you looked at the records? You were reading them right before we came back. Don't you remember?"

"Don't you think it's all changed now?"

"Liv, if we don't go back in two weeks, we won't be

able to go back for almost thirty-eight years. We could die in that time!"

"I didn't say you couldn't go back, Allie. I just don't want to go back yet."

"Me go back without you? How could I—" Alison broke off. "Liv, you're just upset. You've been through a terrible experience. This whole thing has just been an awful experience for both of us. We'll all put our heads together and do the best we can to get Nicholas released and this whole awful mess resolved, and then—" She broke off. "And then I guess we'll see." She patted Olivia's hand, and in her blue eyes Olivia read a troubled sort of acceptance. "I—I guess I sort of understand how you feel."

"You do?"

"Well, not about staying here." Alison waved a dismissive hand. "I think the first thing I'm going to do when I get home is take a three day shower. But I guess I understand about Nicholas."

"Why? What do you mean?"

Alison shrugged and looked sheepish. "Geoffrey's really sweet."

At that, despite everything, Olivia burst out laughing. "He's sweet? That's a real change of heart!"

"Well, um. Yeah. It is. I guess he's the sort of person who grows on you, you know?"

"He is?" Olivia giggled at her friend in spite of herself. "Are you telling me that Alison O'Neill has been swept off her feet by a sixteenth-century geek? Alison O'Neill, who's broken hearts more times than the Yankees beat the Red Sox? This is one for the history books!"

"Oh, cut it out." Alison cuffed Olivia on her uninjured arm. "How about you, Miss I-don't-want-to-leave-my-love-in-jail?"

"Sounds like a country-western song." The two women exchanged grins, and then reality crashed down on Olivia once more. Tears filled her eyes and she brushed them away. "I just don't want to see anything bad happen to him, Allie, and I don't think I could stand not to know."

Alison gathered Olivia in a motherly hug. "I know, honey. I understand. Try not to worry, though. Mother O'Neill's here now, and we'll make it all right. I promise."

And clinging to Alison like a child, Olivia desperately tried to believe that was true.

"What word, Miles?" Geoffrey ran his fingers through his hair. It stuck up in all directions, but for once, Alison didn't think it the least bit funny. Olivia had finally fallen back to sleep, and the night watchman had announced midnight on his rounds through the nearly empty streets. Empty of humans, that is. Dogs skulked in the shadows, snarling over bones, and alley cats slunk up and down the ledges of the buildings, eyes glowing green on the hunt. Even the raucous noise in the tavern below had faded, as the patrons had stumbled in twos and threes out the door and down the street, most by ten or eleven.

Miles Coddington shifted on his feet. His face was gaunt with fatigue, and his limp was even more noticeable. Dark bags hung below his eyes. "Lord Leicester's in Sussex with Her Majesty, Master Geoffrey. They are not expected to return to London for another week or more."

"A week. And the women must be back at Talcott Forest in less than a fortnight," Geoffrey breathed.

"Did they let you see him?" Miles asked.

"They told me to come again tomorrow at noon."

"Now what do we do?" asked Alison. "We're not going to just sit and wait for a week to pass, are we?"

"No," sighed Geoffrey. "But I wish I could think of some way to ensure that Dee's letter would be delivered to the Queen. There's always the possibility she might not read it—or be given it—until it's too late."

"If Lord Leicester gave it to her—" Miles began.

"Aye, but how to ensure he gets it? How to make certain he understands how important it is?" Geoffrey stroked his chin and rubbed his temples.

"Can't you just show up and ask for an audience?" Alison put in.

"Oh, certainly. But will we get one? That's the question. While she's on summer progress, the Queen refuses to be troubled by requests from petitioners. Nothing must interfere with her sport and her delight. And she's sure to be besieged by such requests by those who seldom, if ever, have an opportunity to come to court. So though we might get the letter to her, how to make sure she doesn't let it languish . . ." Geoffrey rose to his feet and paced to the window, his long strides as restless as a caged tiger's in a crowded cage. "There's the rub."

"Well, we should at least show up, don't you think? The squeaky door gets the grease, as my mother always said."

"Ah, but it will be all for naught if the Queen's humor—" Geoffrey slammed a fist against the wall. "I'd like to wring his neck."

"This is a matter of life and death," Alison said. "She wouldn't interrupt her sport for that?"

"The Queen answers to no one, Mistress Alison." Miles looked grave. "According to Lord Leicester's agent, the Queen may be at Greenwich one week hence, but that is the soonest anyone expects her."

"Greenwich, hm?" Geoffrey stroked his chin. "Perhaps there. . . ."

"Why? What's so great about Greenwich?" Alison asked.

" 'Tis one of her own residences, mistress," Miles answered. "Once she's there, the pressures of her councillors will begin to bear on her. She may be more open and receptive to requests, although she's sure to be besieged by court business—"

"Well, this is court business, too," Alison snapped.

"We've a better chance of an audience, Alison, that's true. But she may keep us cooling our heels for who knows how long." His voice trailed off and he stared into the fireplace. Finally he shook his head, as if to shake off the worry, and turned back to face them both. "All right, Miles. Let's to bed. We've done as much as we can do this night."

"I'll come with you to the Tower, tomorrow, if you will, Master Geoffrey."

"Of course." Geoffrey nodded a dismissal. "Good night, Miles." He looked at Alison when the older man had gone. "The hour's late, Allie. We'd best go to bed." Their eyes met and held, and Alison felt the color rise in her cheeks.

She picked up the candle. "I'll be right next door, then. With Olivia."

"Allie—" He held out his hand. "You can stay here, an you like."

She shook her head slowly. "Geoffrey, that's not a good idea. We both know that." *Look at what's happened to Olivia,* she wanted to say. *She wants to stay in this benighted time, all because of your brother.* But she held her tongue, and smiled sadly instead. "Good night, Geoffrey."

"Good night, Allie. Sleep well."

She nearly responded, "Sweet dreams," before she stopped herself. Surely if any of them dreamt tonight, there'd be no good dreams at all.

Chapter 16

"THEY WOULDN'T LET me in to see him." Geoffrey strode over to the table where Alison and Olivia waited. He slapped his gloves down and stared, grim-faced, into the empty hearth.

"So now what?" asked Alison with her characteristic practicality.

"I was told to return at two o'clock."

"Will they let you see him then?" Olivia asked.

"I don't know." Geoffrey shook his head. He wore an expression that could only be described as disgust.

"May I come with you?" Olivia refused even to consider the possibility that the trip would be for nothing.

Geoffrey glanced down at her, surprise clear on his face. "Mistress, that place—the Tower—'tis no place for a lady, and especially not one—"

"I was there, too Geoffrey." She reminded him gently.

He heaved a sigh. "An you will, then, mistress. 'Tis not—"

"That's all well and fine," interrupted Alison, "but don't you think we ought to give some thought to exactly what might be going on? And try to figure out how this happened, and what's the best way to get him out of there?

All this wringing our hands and moaning and groaning isn't going to help much."

Geoffrey sat down heavily on the bench next to Alison. "Well, Mistress Allie, what're your thoughts?"

Even Miles, silent up to now, leaned forward.

"Ok—" Alison began, then stopped, remembering to watch her speech in such a public place. "All right. This much we know for sure. Nicholas—and Olivia, too—was set up by someone, most likely this Christopher Warren, right?"

"Aye." Geoffrey nodded, stroking his chin.

"All right. We know that Warren knew *something*, because the information he gave Nicholas was accurate to a degree, but that there were things he didn't know, like the fact that a woman who served Mary, Queen of Scots, was supposed to show up, too, right?"

Again the men nodded, and Olivia plucked listlessly at the embroidery on her sleeve.

"How'd Warren get his information? I mean, who does Warren work for? Is that person Nicholas's enemy too? It seems unlikely, as far as I can tell. Warren's the one with the ax to grind. So what if we go to Warren's boss and tell him what happened? Think that might work?"

The men exchanged glances. "It might," Geoffrey said, with a puckered brow.

"It's worth a shot, isn't it?" Alison looked from one to the other. "I mean, what do you think, Liv?"

Olivia spread her hands. "I suppose that's a good idea. I guess I'm not sure that it's going to be as simple as knocking on Sir Francis's front door and saying, 'Hi, we're here to talk about Nicholas Talcott.' I mean, I just don't know. What do you think, Geoffrey? Master Coddington?"

"I'll be happy to take a letter to Sir Francis, mistress, wherever he might be," said Miles.

"I guess it can't hurt," said Geoffrey. "I wish I could get my hands on that Christopher Warren myself."

"Maybe we should look for him," Alison suggested.

"And do what? Beat him to a pulp? Force him to tell the truth?" Geoffrey shook his head. "If this whole scheme was his idea, to bring down Nicholas, the last thing he'll ever want revealed is the truth. Especially to Sir Francis Walsingham. He'd go to his grave denying it, and if that happened, then who's to say Nicholas is innocent?"

"Who's to say he's not?" Olivia asked softly.

Alison stared at her. "Are you saying let's commit murder, Livvie?"

Olivia shook her head. "Of course not, Allie. This whole situation is just a mess. And we've got this time constraint thing—"

"Miles will take you back to Talcott Forest when the time comes, mistress," Geoffrey said. "Have no fear on that score."

"That's not what I'm afraid of, Geoffrey." Olivia took a deep breath. "Don't you see? The only reason Nicholas was able to get the plans from the Spanish agent was because I was there to tell the Spaniard what he needed to know. That's the reason Nicholas was found with the plans, and that's the ultimate reason he's in the Tower now. We have to find a way to get him out of the Tower, or, when we go back, we might not go back to the same place we left."

Alison stared at her in dismay. "What are you talking about, Liv?"

"Don't you remember practically the last thing I did before we went through the maze, Allie? I was checking the Talcott family records. There's no mention that Nicholas Talcott died a traitor's death. If this happens, the past we knew will be irrevocably changed. If Nicholas dies, God only knows what the repercussions will be. How can we return?"

With a shocked and troubled stare, as the implications of all Olivia said slowly penetrated, Alison shrank on the bench, her face pale, her eyes wide. "Good grief, Liv," she breathed. "I think you're right. What in the name of God are we going to do?"

"Let's think," said Olivia. "No matter how silly or ridiculous the idea, we have to think." She looked up at Geoffrey, who wore a look very similar to Alison's.

"Nicholas said no good would come of the maze," he said, so softly it was hard to hear him.

"There's no time for feeling bad about that now," Alison snapped. "Two things are going to happen in the next two weeks. Nicholas is getting out of that Tower, and Olivia and I are going home."

"Has the prisoner signed the confession?" Walsingham paused long enough from his writing to stare up at Warren with his black, deep-set eyes.

There was something of a Spaniard about his master, thought Warren suddenly—the black, piercing eyes that seemed to bore right through to a man's soul, the thick dark hair, and the sallow, pockmarked skin. "No, my lord, not yet."

"He refuses?"

"Yes, my lord. But with your permission, I've prepared this warrant. . . ." Warren placed the rolled parchment gingerly on Walsingham's desk.

"And this is?" The dark eyes seemed to stab all the way into Warren's most private thoughts.

"A warrant, my lord. For the execution of Lord Nicholas Talcott—"

"You want this man dead, don't you, Warren?" Walsingham toyed with the parchment scroll. He sat back in his chair with a long sigh. " 'Tis not so easy as Master Steele, Warren. Lord Talcott is just that—Lord Talcott. Only a court of the high steward, or the Queen herself, can command that a peer of this realm may lose his life for treason. And while Her Majesty makes merry on her summer progress, there is no hope at all of this matter coming to her attention. Even when she returns to Greenwich, a return most devoutly to be wished, she won't want

to give this sordid little matter her attention unless cajoled.
She likes Lord Talcott, remember?" Walsingham drew a
deep breath, stared into space for a long moment, and then
shrugged. "Let him cool his heels in the Tower a few
weeks. The case against him is strong—he was, after all,
caught with the plans—"

"And there's a witness, my lord."

"Ah, yes, so you did say. Sir John? Sir John Makepiece?"

"Yes, my lord."

"He's known to me." Walsingham steepled his fingers
together and pressed his lips to the tips of his forefingers.
"That's all, Warren."

"But—but—but, my lord—"

"Yes, Warren?"

"What about the confession? Should he not be—"

"Racked? You forget, Warren. This is a peer of the
realm. Lord Talcott may go to the block. But for the in-
terim, you cannot touch him. Do you understand?"

"Yes, my lord." Warren bowed, forcing his face to re-
veal nothing of the frustration he felt. As he reached the
door, Walsingham's cold, dry voice stopped him in midstride.

"Warren? Tell me again. Who gave you Talcott's
name?"

"Stephen Steele, my lord."

"Under torture?"

"Yes, my lord."

There was a long silence. Walsingham seemed to mull
over this information in his mind. Finally he nodded.
"That's all, Warren. You may go."

Suppressing a sigh of relief, Warren made his escape,
ignoring the servant who politely held the door open.
He'd have to tread carefully lest Walsingham discover
what he'd done. He had the terrible suspicion that Walsingham suspected something. He'd have to go once more
to his contacts, and see if there were some way to reach
the Talcott cousin while she stayed within the inn itself.

Now that the brother was here in London, she'd be better protected. Perhaps one of the servants could be bribed—or even the landlord himself. Surely there'd be a way to silence her, he thought with a growing sense of desperation that required a greater effort than before to suppress. But why should Walsingham care, he rationalized. Intercepting the plans for the invasion of England was as great a coup as he was ever likely to score. Surely that alone would warrant gratitude from the Queen herself. He went out the door with almost a light heart as he envisioned bowing low to receive Elizabeth's grateful thanks.

As he was walking down the steps to the street, he was surprised to meet Sir John Makepiece walking up them. "Sir John! What do you here?"

"I was told I could find you here, Master Warren." The tall knight reversed direction and followed Warren down the steps. When they reached the street, he paused and put his hand on Warren's arm. "Well? What news?"

Warren stiffened. "News?"

"Of the traitor? Has he confessed? Has his property been attainted?"

Warren shook his head and started off, Sir John following as eagerly as a puppy at his heels. "Not yet."

"Not yet? You have him with the plans in hand—I'm the witness—what do you mean, not yet?"

"He refuses to sign a confession."

Sir John narrowed his eyes and drew himself up, his thin lips pursed in disdain. "I see."

"These things take time, Sir John. Surely you didn't believe Talcott would be executed immediately? He's a peer of the realm—only Her Majesty can sign his death warrant." Surreptitiously yet savagely, Warren crumpled that document, which he still held in his fist.

"I see."

"I promised you nothing, Sir John."

At that, Sir John dropped his eyes. "You're right, Master Warren. I am, perhaps, overzealous in my desire to see the traitor punished."

Aren't we all, Warren wanted to say, but all he allowed himself was a mild, "It is quite understandable, Sir John. I bid you a good day."

"And a good day to you, sir." Sir John bowed his head politely and stood aside as Warren nodded in return and took off down the street. He had the unpleasant feeling that the knight watched him every step of the way, until he was swallowed by the crowd.

"A quarter hour, that's all." The jailer swung the door closed with a satisfying bang. Olivia raised her eyes to Nicholas. His chin was rough with his unshaved beard, dark circles ringed his eyes, and he looked pale and drawn. His shirt was wrinkled and filthy, but at least he clearly had not been harmed. The two of them hesitated, and then she rushed across the room and clutched him in her arms, as his closed around her.

"Are you all right?" they asked in unison.

They drew apart and looked at each other, smiled, and both laughed.

"I'm fine—" she began, trying not to wince.

"Well enough—" he said.

They stopped once more, and their eyes met again. "You first," she said.

"Let me look at you." He traced the outline of her face with the tip of one finger. "Sweet Jesu, I've been so worried about you."

"Me? I've been frantic for you. What's happened? Are you all right?"

Nicholas nodded and turned away. "Aye, as well as I can be. Warren tried to threaten me if I didn't sign his confession. I refused, of course."

"Can they force you?" She picked up his hand and held it between both of hers.

"Rack me, you mean?" He shrugged. "Not without some sort of royal approval from some level. But given the seriousness of what they say I've done, who knows?"

"Oh, Nicholas." She dropped her head and closed her

eyes against the tears that threatened to spill down her cheeks. "This is all my fault."

"Stop that nonsense, lady. You and I both know that's not true. 'Tis my own folly that got us both tangled in this web, nothing more. My own folly and ambition. I should've listened to my brother."

"He's here."

"I know. They told me." He hesitated. "But I'm glad they let you in first."

"He's found a way to send us back."

For a moment there was a long silence. Finally Nicholas nodded. "I see."

"He says we must leave in less than two weeks, and if we don't go back then, there will be no going back for another forty years."

"I see." He turned away, flexing his shoulders. "So you've come to say good-bye."

"No!" she cried. "I came to see how you are. I've been so worried about you, shut up here in this terrible place. You don't belong here."

He looked at her with a sad smile. "Neither do you."

"Oh, Nicholas, let's not talk about that now."

"If you wish, lady." He slumped down in one of the wooden chairs. "Will you sit?"

She sank down in the other. It creaked dangerously beneath her weight. "We're trying to set you free."

"Thank you." His face was shuttered, closed, and his eyes avoided hers.

"What is it, Nicholas?"

"No matter, lady."

"It matters very much to me. Nicholas, what's wrong? Is it—" She leaned forward, and understanding dawned. "Is it—"

He shrugged and shook his head. "You'll think me even more of a fool than you must already, lady."

"I don't think you're a fool at all, Nicholas. I think you're brave and—" She broke off. "Not a fool at all."

"I meant what I said the last time I saw you, lady." His

eyes met hers, and the intensity with which he looked at her took her breath away. "I love you. I don't want you to leave."

She caught her breath and swallowed hard. "I don't think I want to leave, either, Nicholas."

He reached out for her hand. "And what about me?"

Her fingers twined with his. "I—I've been afraid to let myself love you, Nicholas, because I've believed that I had to go back."

"Why?" The word seemed to burst from the depths of his being. "Why must you?"

She looked around, as if searching the barren stone walls for a way to explain something that seemed to have no explanation. "Well, don't you think I belong there?"

"Do you?" he asked, his eyes penetrating, his voice low. "Do you really?"

"I—I—" She stopped, then got to her feet. She paced to the window, where she could see the multileveled roofs of the towers that comprised the Tower of London. Flocks of ravens swooped and circled, screeching in the afternoon sun. She heard him rise and come to stand behind her. He put his hands on her shoulders.

"Do you really, Olivia?"

She turned her head to answer, but as she opened her mouth, his lips came down on hers, gentle at first, tender and searching, and then, gradually, the kiss deepened, until they stood locked in each other's arms.

"Oh, Nicholas," she murmured, burying her face in his shirt when he finally drew back.

"You need not answer now, Olivia. God knows I have little to offer you, and now, next to nothing. But I think 'twas more than a mere trick of my brother's that brought you here to me, in this time and place. I think 'twas Fate herself intervened across an ocean of time. I think you were meant to come here. I think I was meant to love you." He bent his head once more, and she gave herself up to the sweetness of his kiss.

Finally she broke away. "Nicholas, we must find a way to save you."

He raised her chin. "My only regret would be to lose you and the possibility of a life with you."

Olivia walked away, twisting her hands together. "You—you don't understand."

"Then, tell me, sweet, but tell me quickly, for the guards will come back."

"You never asked me why I was at Talcott Forest that day. I was there doing research into your family."

"Mine?"

She nodded miserably. "You didn't die a traitor's death."

"Ah, well, that's good then." He grinned.

"No, don't you understand? The only reason you got those plans was because I was there—otherwise you'd never have had the information the Spanish agent wanted. You would never have been given the plans—the whole awful mess would have gone awry. There's no mention of it anywhere that I saw. Whatever was supposed to have happened, didn't happen because of me. And somehow, we need to find a way to save you. Because—"

"Because the line will end, otherwise? And all of history will be changed?"

"And I'm afraid the whole world might be changed with it." *And because your wife is named Olivia. And I think she might be me,* Olivia finished silently. She raised her chin and met his eyes squarely.

"Would you marry me, my lady? If all of this"—he waved his hand—"if all of this were different?"

Had he read her mind? She was stunned. The sudden question caught her by surprise, and all she could manage was, "Oh, Nicholas." Her eyes filled with tears, but before she could answer the guard banged on the door. The rusting hinges shrieked as the door slammed open.

"Time's up."

"Oh, Nicholas." She reached out to take his hand, but the guard pulled her arm.

"Let her go," Nicholas barked.

"Time's up, me lord."

She only had time for one more anguished look at Nicholas as he stood with rigid shoulders against the backdrop of the cold gray stones.

"I think the answer's obvious," Alison said with her characteristic decisiveness. "We have to find a way to make the Queen pay attention."

Geoffrey let out a long sigh, and Miles nodded slowly. Olivia said nothing. Her conversation with Nicholas had unnerved her beyond all expectation. The imminent threat that he could die, coupled with her own heretofore unrecognized realization that she could be the Olivia he had married, or would have married, jumbled her thoughts into a confusing swirl that somehow defied every attempt to set them aside. Did she want to stay here, with Nicholas? As his wife? Was this the final outcome all along? Olivia, Lady Talcott—the words seemed to reverberate over and over in her mind. The portrait in the pub—had Alison been right all along? Had it resembled her so closely because it *was* her?

She sat back, scarcely paying attention as the others talked.

"Well, what do you think, Liv?" Alison asked. "You're one of the resident experts. How do you think we can get the Queen's attention?"

At that moment, a laughing group of men invaded the tavern.

"Damn," Geoffrey muttered. "I knew we should've gone to another place. This one's frequented by too many . . ."

Olivia raised her head, her eye caught by a familiar face. At once, Shakespeare was by her side, bowing over her hand, his large eyes roving over each face in turn. "Mistress Lindsley, how do you do?"

"As well as can be expected, Master Will." She felt an unexpected pang of fondness for him. He was so—so human and so kind in every aspect. "These are my—my kinsmen—Master Geoffrey Talcott of Talcott Forest in Kent, and Mistress Alison O'Neill, and Lord Nicholas's agent, Miles Coddington."

Shakespeare bowed and nodded to each in turn. "My deep sympathies for your troubles, good gentles. Mistress Olivia was kind to share something of them with me. I stand at your disposal if there's aught that I could do."

Raucous laughter broke out from the other side of the room. "What ho, Will, don't you ever need respite from the ladies?"

"Come, your ale is going flat, even as you dally."

"Flat ale is a small price to pay for dalliance," Shakespeare replied good-naturedly over his shoulder. "I'd rather dally than dither like the rest of you lot." He turned back to her and bowed. "Duty calls, good gentles."

"Wait," Olivia said, half-rising. "Who are your companions?"

Shakespeare grinned. "These rogues are but members of Lord Leicester's Men, mistress."

"Come here and meet us, sweeting, you'll see we're much nicer than half-wit Will."

"Half-witted, but full talented," Shakespeare shot back. "Why do you ask?"

"Master Will," Olivia began, thinking furiously, "you write, do you not?"

"If you can call his poetry writing, sweetheart," shouted another wit.

Shakespeare shrugged. "As they say, mistress. Doggerel at best, perhaps."

"That's not true," she said with such conviction he turned back to her. "You know it."

He shifted on his feet. "Methinks you hold me in higher esteem than ever I could warrant, mistress."

"Have you ever written a masque? Or a play?"

"Oh, aye, our Will's taken his hand to a few scenes already, haven't you, Will? Tell her, lad."

Shakespeare sank down beside her on the bench, his

eyes searching hers, ignoring all the teasing shouts. "I—
I have begun to dabble in such things."

"Would you write one for us?"

He glanced around the table. Geoffrey was listening, a
guarded look on his face as if he realized what Olivia was
leading to, while Alison and Miles watched. "Good mistress, methinks there's more to your request than I yet
know."

Geoffrey leaned forward. "We need a way to get the
Queen's attention. She returns to Greenwich less than a
fortnight hence."

"It wouldn't even require lines, Master Will." In her
enthusiasm, Olivia gripped his arm. "A dumbshow—we'd
tell you what to do—tell you what must happen. You
know, the play—the play's the thing—" She broke off,
flustered.

Shakespeare stared at her. "The play's the thing?" he
repeated slowly. "What play can you mean? You speak
in such riddles, mistress, and yet—" He broke off and
stared at her. "Are you to be my muse, mistress?"

She dropped her eyes. Oh, great, she thought. Now
what do you say—never mind, you haven't thought of
that yet? "I—I was only thinking that a play within a play
might be a way to get the Queen's attention. And if we
could have Leicester give her the letter from Dr. Dee—
while she's watching it—"

"By God, that might work," Geoffrey said. "There's
nothing Her Majesty loves more. Can you do it, Master
Shakespeare? I'll pay—you and your fellows. 'Tis as
good a way as any I've heard—what do you think, Alison?"

But Alison was staring at Olivia.

"Allie?" Olivia asked.

Alison's eyes moved slowly from Shakespeare to Olivia and back again. Finally, she looked at Olivia. "I told
you, didn't I?" There was a quiet finality in her voice,
which made all three men cock their heads, confused.
"That portrait—that picture in the pub. That was *you.*"

Chapter 17

THE GREAT HALL of Greenwich Palace was alight with thousands of candles, and the costumes of the courtiers twinkled with hundreds of jewels of every color and description. Olivia looked around, wide-eyed, as she, Alison, and Geoffrey slipped in with the actors and mingled among the throng that clustered like moths about the flame that was Queen Elizabeth of England.

All the accounts of all the history books she had ever read could not prepare her for the reality of the English court, the abundance and the opulence of the feast that was spread out on tables before their eyes. Musicians played sweetly in the gallery overhead, and courtiers mingled, dancing, laughing, drinking, presided over by the Queen herself, who sat flanked by Lord Leicester on the one hand and the Spanish ambassador on the other. Geoffrey had delivered the letter from Dr. Dee to Leicester himself that very afternoon, and Leicester had promised not only to deliver the message to the Queen as she watched the masque, but to inquire himself into the charges against Nicholas.

Elizabeth wore a fantastic gown of silver brocade, heavily embroidered with diamonds and pearls. On her dark red wig, she wore a glittering tiara, from which diamonds winked and sparkled. Against the backdrop of the court, she shone like a pale moon. Olivia's heart beat faster as the musicians finished their song with a flourish. The dancers bowed and drifted off the floor. A drum roll from the musicians's gallery and a flourish of trumpets brought conversation to a muted standstill. Even the Queen looked up expectantly. She leaned toward Leicester and whispered behind her fan.

Shakespeare strode out into the center of the hall and bowed low to the Queen. He bowed to each side of the room. "Most Gracious Majesty, noble lords and ladies, sweet people all, turn your eyes to this small space, and let it, for one brief moment, an you will, encompass England's sunny fields of amber corn."

Olivia clutched Alison's arm, and her friend gave her a reassuring squeeze. "It'll be okay, Liv," she whispered.

"That's not what I meant, Allie. Look, over there, I think that's Christopher Warren—the one who set this whole thing up!"

"Really, where?" Alison craned her head.

"Over there by the door—see? Next to the guard? He's in dark brown—damn. I don't see him. But the play doesn't sound bad, does it?" Olivia whispered back.

"Not bad for his first attempt." Alison winked, as a serving girl shushed them both.

Shakespeare ended his prologue with a flourish, and the other actors leapt to their parts. Olivia scarcely watched the performance at all. She was much too engrossed with watching the reaction on Elizabeth's face. The Queen chuckled heartily a few times and even slapped her thigh once or twice. The Court erupted in spontaneous applause several times. The musicians played softly in the background. Then the music fell silent.

Elizabeth leaned forward with interest as white-faced players dressed in motley scampered into the center. With deliberate, exaggerated steps, they enacted silently Warren's offer to Nicholas, Nicholas's acceptance of it, and the meeting with the Spaniard.

On the other side of the room, Christopher Warren began to sweat. His face paled as the actors continued. The Queen was frowning as the dumbshow went on, and Olivia, peering through the crowd, saw Leicester hand her the rough parchment that contained Dr. Dee's letter. With a puzzled expression, the Queen broke the seal, scanned the letter, and looked at Leicester, a frown deepening the lines on her face. Leicester whispered something to the Queen. Elizabeth looked at the Spanish ambassador and down at the letter. Through the layers of white makeup the Queen wore, Olivia saw the color unmistakably rise. She glanced up at the players, who had reached the part in the drama where Nicholas was dragged off to the Tower.

The courtiers closest to the Queen, noticing her reaction, began to whisper among themselves, and the low rustle of voices swept like wildfire through the hall, as the silent actors reached the end of their performance. The actors scurried away, and the musicians struck another note, when the Queen rose to her feet, holding up her hand for silence. The entire room fell silent. Tension quivered through every line of Elizabeth's body, and when she spoke, her voice echoed to the roof. "Is Master Geoffrey Talcott present?"

There was a moment of profound and utter silence. Then Alison gave Geoffrey a little nudge. He pushed through the crowd of lesser nobles standing at the back of the room, and strode into the center, his boots clicking loudly on the polished parquet floor. "At Your Majesty's service." He sank down on one knee, head bowed low.

Elizabeth took a deep breath and glanced at Leicester. "Where is your brother, Master Talcott?"

"He has been detained in the Tower of London, Your Majesty."

"On what charge?"

"Treason, Your Majesty."

Whispers swept like wildfire through the room, and on the other side, Olivia caught Shakespeare's eye. He winked.

"Come with me, Master Talcott, and you, too, my Lord Leicester. We like it not that a peer of my realm should be so imprisoned upon such a grievous charge and we know nothing of it."

"If Your Majesty will allow—" Olivia looked toward this new voice and saw a dark-haired man push his way into the open space before the Queen. His costume was black like a Puritan's, but far too lavishly embroidered. His lacy ruff was small, but starkly white against the otherwise unrelieved black, and Olivia recognized him at once from his portraits. Sir Francis Walsingham spoke with a dry and humorless air. "There is evidence. And a witness."

"The evidence is contrived!" cried Geoffrey.

"Contain yourself, Master Talcott." Elizabeth frowned at his outburst. "Sir Francis, you, too, then, will come with us."

Walsingham looked startled, but bowed immediately. "As Your Majesty requires."

"I have a witness, too, Your Majesty," said Geoffrey.

"Oh?" Elizabeth paused in midstep. "Who?"

"Mistress Olivia Lindsley." He turned and beckoned to Olivia.

Heart pounding, throat dry, Olivia glided forward and sank into a deep curtsy before the Queen.

"We know you, chit," Elizabeth said. "You sang a song for us, and bid us avoid the company of men. 'Twould have been wise if you'd heeded your own advice, no?"

"Yes, Your Majesty," Olivia breathed, scarcely daring to look at the Queen.

"Come along, then, all of you. 'Tis a tangled coil indeed when dinner must be interrupted to deal with it."

They followed the Queen from the hall, Olivia clinging to Geoffrey's arm. The musicians struck up a merry tune, but even they could not disguise the babble of speculation that rose in the Queen's wake.

Elizabeth led them to a room furnished with one chair on a raised dais and a long table surrounded by chairs. "Now, Master Talcott. My own physician vouches for your verity. What's this all about?"

As quickly as he could, Geoffrey told the whole story, explaining how Nicholas had believed himself to be the agent of the government, risking himself and Olivia to retrieve the plans for the invasion of England.

Walsingham said nothing. Finally Geoffrey fell silent. Elizabeth looked at Olivia. "Well, mistress? Is all as Master Talcott tells it?"

"Yes, Your Majesty."

"You aren't so saucy today as you were before. What ails you, mistress?"

"Lord Nicholas is unfairly accused, Your Majesty. 'Tis hard to make merry when he lies in prison under threat of losing his life."

Elizabeth did not reply, but her bright black eyes slid over to Sir Francis. "And what say you, Sir Francis?"

"There is a witness, Your Majesty."

"Who?"

"Sir John Makepiece, Your Majesty. A knight of unassailable reputation, and a Protestant of unparalleled virtue."

"That well may be," Olivia burst out, "but why was he there in the first place? We saw him in the church—a Catholic church, Your Majesty." Elizabeth narrowed her eyes, and even Sir Francis started. "Who told him to look for us there? Sir John would no more darken the door of a Papist Church than he would a house of prostitution."

"Hold your tongue before the Queen, hussy!" Sir Francis burst out.

But Elizabeth burst out laughing. "You have a rare spirit, wench." She glanced at Sir Francis. "Sir Francis. You agree this is most irregular?"

Sir Francis shrugged. "I would have to speak to Sir John, Your Majesty."

"Then do so. And as for you, Leicester, Talcott is a friend of yours, is he not?"

Leicester, who up to now had stayed silent, started. "Well, Your Majesty . . ."

"Do not equivocate, Robin, 'tis not your head upon the block."

"He is my friend, Your Majesty."

That seemed to satisfy Elizabeth momentarily, but soon she looked up with a puckered frown. "This Christopher Warren. Where's he?"

Walsingham looked up. "He's here, Your Majesty."

"Summon him. Now."

At once Walsingham bowed and went to the door. He whispered something to the guard outside and turned back. "He'll be here momentarily, Your Majesty."

"Good." Elizabeth nodded with a self-satisfied air. "We'll get to the bottom of this."

The minutes dragged. Olivia shifted on her feet and stole a peek at Geoffrey. He glanced at her and winked. Finally there was a tap on the door.

"Enter," cried the Queen.

A puzzled-looking guard stood in the doorway as the heavy door slowly swung open.

"Where's this Master Warren?" asked Elizabeth.

The guard bowed. "In truth, Your Majesty, he's not to be found. He was seen to leave shortly after the play began. He did not look well, according to those who saw him go."

"Ahh!" Elizabeth turned to Walsingham. " 'Twould seem there's more afoot here than even you know, my lord. Robin, I charge you to look into this matter, in my name." Elizabeth gazed around the room and her black eyes settled on Geoffrey. "Well, Master Talcott? Does that satisfy? My Lord Leicester shall inquire early tomorrow into this matter."

Geoffrey bowed. "Completely, Most Gracious Majesty."

Elizabeth fixed Walsingham with a hard stare. "And I shall expect, Sir Francis, that both your agent, Master Warren, and Sir John shall be present to accuse Lord Nicholas face-to-face."

"It shall be done, Your Majesty." Walsingham bowed low.

With another satisfied nod, Elizabeth swept from the room, Leicester and Walsingham trailing in her wake.

Olivia looked up at Geoffrey. "At least we got her attention."

He nodded, his expression not quite so grim as before. "Indeed, mistress. Now, let's hope that there's no more to this coil than we already know."

A shower of stones hit the window of Olivia's bedroom, striking the thick panes of glass with a sound like falling hail. Startled out of her sleep, she lay awake a moment, trying to place the sound, and then realized what it was when the sound came again. She scrambled out of bed, Alison sleeping as soundly as usual by her side.

She unlatched the window and peered out into the dark night, looking down into the deserted street. London lay sleeping, but a figure, as familiar as it was unexpected, stood looking back up at her, a sheaf of parchment clutched in one hand. "Master Will!"

"Mistress Lindsley." He swept the flat cap off his head and bowed low, in an actor's version of a polished Court bow.

Olivia looked back over her shoulder. Alison rolled over on her back, muttering softly. "What do you want?" she asked in a loud stage whisper.

"Forgive me for disturbing you so, but I didn't see you after the performance—you left with your cousins and—" For a moment he looked sheepish, and Olivia remembered that the Bard of Stratford was no more than barely beyond boyhood, the full force of his talent years from flowering.

"I'll be right down." She pulled the latched window shut, thrust her feet into her slippers, and threw on the loose robe over her shift, which served as her nightdress. She scampered down the silent hall, down the stairs, and into the common room, where the low glow of the banked fire gleamed a soft red in the shadows. She struggled with the great beam that barred the door. It fell aside with a thud, and she opened the door, wondering if Mistress Deb would forgive her for opening the door so late. Shakespeare slipped inside.

"I'm sorry to disturb you so, mistress."

"No trouble, not really. But why did you come here? What's wrong?"

"I must return to Stratford, mistress, on the morrow. My—my wife has been taken ill, and—well, the message reached me at my lodging—and I had no other way to contact you so I—"

"I understand, but—"

"I wanted to give you this." He pressed the sheaf of parchment into her hands. " 'Tis my first play, mistress. You—you were right. In some way I cannot name, this play, tonight—poetry is still my first love, but, oh, Mistress Olivia—I think I can be as capable as Marlowe himself in the penning of these plays. And if you'd not suggested it . . ."

Olivia stared at the parchments in her hands. Stained with ink spots, lines crossed out and others substituted in a wayward scrawl, creased and dog-eared, they were still a priceless possession.

"I owe you a great debt, mistress. I—I hope all works out for you as you hope, and that if you come again to London you will seek my company out. 'Twould be a great honor to know that you were in the audience. With your cousins, of course."

"Of course." She stared up at him, scarcely able to speak. "Master Will, I—"

" 'Tis you should be thanked, mistress." He caught up both her hands and pressed a kiss on both of them. "I must away to Warwickshire at first light, but I could not leave without telling you."

"You are more than welcome, Master Will. I shall treasure this play all the days of my life." *And all the days after that,* she added silently. "Did you sign it? Date it?"

"Ah!" He strode to the fire, reached for a piece of charred wood, and scrawled his name across the last page. "There. 'Twill suffice, I think? You and I both know it is from me, to you." He grinned. "My muse."

She felt herself blush. "You're too kind, Master Will."

"I must go." He clutched his cap and bowed. "You will let me know if you ever come up to London?"

"Of course," she promised, still stunned by his gift and scarcely capable of speech.

He was gone with another bow. She placed the parchment sheets reverently on one table while she struggled to bar the door once more, then picked them up and carried them upstairs to the bedroom as gently as she might an infant. She was still nearly speechless when she climbed into bed.

"Livvie?" muttered Alison. "Where'd you go?"

"Allie, you'll never guess who was here."

"Nicholas?"

"No! No, Shakespeare. Shakespeare was here—you know we left Greenwich before we could see him. He brought me his play."

"He did what?" Alison struggled to sit up.

"Look." Olivia reached over and spread out the parchments. "It's his play. His very first play."

"Cool." Alison yawned.

"Allie, don't you understand? This is priceless! A play by Shakespeare—his first play. Look, he dated it—and signed it—Allie, can you believe what he gave me?"

"What are you going to do with it?"

Olivia sat back. "I don't know. Try to take it into the future somehow, I guess. If I just show up with it, it's going to raise all sorts of questions—" She broke off and sighed. "Well. We have enough to worry about right now."

"I'll say." Alison patted her hand. "Let's get through the next day or so, okay? We can talk about how to get your gift home later." She turned on her side and pulled the sheet up to her ear, yawning. "God knows I can't wait to get back."

Olivia placed the parchments reverently on the tiny table and lay down beside Alison. In the shadowy room, the sheaf was a pale smudge. Who would ever have imagined anything like this?

Chapter 18

NICHOLAS KNEW THAT something was afoot when the jailer threw a clean shirt and hose on the table, along with a bucket of water, soap, a towel, a razor, and a sliver of a mirror. He leapt to his feet from the narrow cot.

"Make ye'self ready, m'lord," the jailer growled.

"For what?" Nicholas demanded.

"Lord Leicester's come to see ye." Before Nicholas could ask anything else, the jailer slammed the door shut.

With hands that shook from anticipation he soaped and shaved and rinsed and toweled himself as best he could. He laced on the clean shirt and hose as quickly as possible. When he was ready, he went to the door and banged on it. There was no response. Then heavy footsteps sounded in the corridor and the door opened once more, this time to admit the jailer accompanied by Robert Dudley himself.

"Leicester!"

"Nicholas." The older man stepped inside the room and peered around. "Mine was worse." He glanced at the jailer. "That'll be all, my good fellow."

"Ye want me t' see t' the rest of 'em, m'lord?"

"Aye," answered the earl. "Do that." When the jailer had gone, he grinned at Nicholas. "Now, perhaps you could explain to me why Walsingham's crowing like a cock at daybreak over the fact that you're here. Have you taken leave of your senses, man? I never thought to see the day that you'd be accused of consorting with the Spanish."

Nicholas groaned and ran his fingers through his hair. "Blessed Jesu, Leicester, 'tis the last thing I ever thought to be accused of, believe me. I thought I was performing a service for my country—not consorting with anyone."

"Hm. Except perhaps for that tempting little Olivia. I hear you're also accused of masquerading as man and wife."

"And that's a crime now?"

Leicester cocked his head and wagged his finger. "Nicholas. In the church courts, you know it is." He shook his head. "All right. Tell me how this all happened."

" 'Twas the day the Queen came to Talcott Forest. Master Christopher Warren approached me and asked if I'd do Her Majesty a service. I said of course. So he told me that a traitor had been apprehended and that someone was needed to go to Calais." Haltingly, careful of any mention of Olivia, Nicholas explained the story.

At last, when he was silent, Leicester nodded, stroking his chin. "And there's no witnesses to any of this? Save your brother and Mistress Lindsley?"

Nicholas shook his head slowly. "But—surely you see—"

"Aye," Leicester said, "I do. 'Tis a question of whether we can make Sir Francis and his agent—"

"Give me five minutes alone with Master Warren," Nicholas said, clenching his fists.

"Now, now." Leicester wagged another finger, about to say something else when a knock on the door interrupted him. "Enter."

"Ye said to tell ye, m'lord, when Sir Francis and 'is

man arrived." The jailer peered around the corner of the door.

"Ah, good. Well, come, Nicholas. Her Majesty herself has ordered a hearing into this matter."

Nicholas started. "The Queen?"

"Aye. Don't look so surprised, man. Did you think I came to pay you a visit?" Leicester chuckled, adjusting his doublet. "Let's go."

Nicholas drew a deep breath. "As you say, my lord."

Leicester stood aside to let him proceed out the door, and he patted him on the back as he passed. "Be of good cheer, Nicholas. You have friends in very high places."

The spartan chamber was, if anything, even more bleak than Nicholas's cell. A long wooden table and six chairs were the only furnishings. The two occupants of those chairs surprised him. Walsingham fixed him with a steely eye as he entered, flanked on both sides by guards, with Leicester bringing up the rear. "Lord Talcott."

"Sir Francis." Nicholas inclined his head.

"I believe you know your accuser, Sir John Makepiece."

Nicholas's eyes slid over to Sir John, who had the grace to appear uncomfortable. "I do."

"You dispute the charge against you?"

"I do."

"And what have you to say in your defense?"

Nicholas turned to Leicester. "Is this a court, my lord? Is this to be my venue of justice?"

Leicester sat down opposite Walsingham. "Think of this as a hearing, Nicholas. We do not come to condemn you. But the story you tell is quite fantastic, as I'm sure you'd agree if you were seated in our place. So tell us, Nicholas, as you told me. What is your answer to Sir John's charge?"

"I answer with a question, my lord." Nicholas drew himself up and looked at Sir John. "What were you doing in that church?"

At that, Sir John started. "I—I was told to watch for you, sir."

"By whom?" Walsingham's voice was colder than the stones of the Tower.

"By your own agent, Master Warren, Sir Francis." Sir John met the other man's eyes with the fearlessness of one who knew he walked with the Lord.

Walsingham's face paled, then flushed an ugly purple color. "Wait here." He stalked to the door, opened it, and spoke rapidly to the guards. "Bring me Master Christopher Warren. Now!" He looked back over his shoulder. "It seems all roads lead us to Master Warren. We'll soon get to the bottom of this, I promise."

Leicester nodded. "What did he tell you to look for, Sir John?"

"He said that Lord Talcott and his leman would be there, and that they would be meeting with an agent of the King of Spain."

"And did you see them thus?"

Nicholas's face flushed. "Mistress Olivia is not—"

Leicester waved an airy hand. "Calm yourself, Nicholas. 'Tis not the matter at hand. Go on, Sir John. Did you see them meet with anyone?"

"A dark-complected man—he looked like a Spaniard—dressed as a priest. I saw them meet with him. And then later, I saw the man come to the tavern at which they stopped, and leave after but a brief time."

"So all you really saw, Sir John," said the earl, leaning forward, "was a conversation or two? You saw nothing pass hands?"

Sir John flushed. "It was clear to me—They found the plans on Talcott's person—"

"But you can't say how they came to be there?"

Sir John opened his mouth and shut it. "I cannot, my lord."

Leicester shrugged. " 'Twould seem to me of no matter, Sir Francis, whether or not this Master Warren is found.

Sir John witnessed nothing but a meeting or two—a meeting which could be chance—"

"But—" Nicholas began, then stopped.

Leicester winked as someone knocked on the door. "Enter!"

The jailer entered, wearing a puckered frown. He hesitated, looking uncertain.

"Well?" barked Walsingham.

"Master Warren, Sir Francis—we sent to 'is lodging, sir, as ye asked, and—" He glanced at Leicester, Nicholas, and Sir John in turn. " 'E's not there, sir. Landlord said 'e's gone. And all 'is belongings—young Jemmie's outside here, if ye wish to speak to 'im."

"Gone?" Walsingham repeated.

"Aye, m'lord. Quite gone."

Walsingham turned to Leicester. There was a long silence, as the four men gazed at each other. Finally Walsingham spoke. "This is most irregular."

Leicester threw back his head and laughed. "Irregular? Come, Sir Francis. Sir John corroborates Lord Nicholas— 'twas Warren who set this up—"

"Why?" demanded Walsingham. "What earthly reason—"

" 'Twas my father's fault," said Nicholas quietly. "He saw Warren's father burned. My brother Geoffrey reminded me when he came last week. 'Twas in the realm of the late Queen, Mary."

There was another long silence and then Sir John cleared his throat. "And the sins of the fathers shall be visited upon the children—yea, even unto the seventh generation."

The hour was late when Nicholas walked into the little tavern. He ducked his head beneath the low door and stood for a moment, just inside the door, looking around. Alison, sitting next to the hearth, noticed him first. She nudged Olivia, who flew into his arms with a little cry. For a long moment, they stood still, holding each other tightly, until finally Geoffrey gave a discreet cough. "And we're all very glad to see you, too, Nick."

Nicholas raised his head and released Olivia. He reached for his brother, and the two embraced. "I should've listened to you, Geoff."

"Aye, you should've," Geoffrey agreed. "After all, I'm the brilliant one. You're just the good-looking one."

Olivia gazed up at Nicholas. Even in the warm wash of firelight, his face was tired and gaunt after just a few days in that terrible place, and she shuddered to imagine what a prolonged confinement could do to a man or woman. He smiled down at her.

"Does this mean you're free to go?" asked Alison, ever practical.

Nicholas nodded. "We'll leave at first light tomorrow, Mistress Alison."

"About time," she sighed. "Because the day after that—" She broke off as Geoffrey nudged her.

"It's time we all went home," said Nicholas. He looked down at Olivia as he spoke and a quiver went through her.

He's asking me for an answer, she thought. He's safe now. And what am I going to do?

"So what are you going to do?" asked Alison, as she helped Olivia out of her gown. She stood back to let Olivia step out of the folds of the dress, then hopped onto the bed with a little bounce as Olivia bent to pick up the heavy garment.

"About what?" Olivia asked carefully.

"You know what about," Alison replied. "We have to talk about this, Livvie."

Olivia sighed. She climbed onto her side of the bed. "I know."

"Are you sure you love Nicholas? Enough to give up everything you have for him?"

Olivia hesitated. "He asked me to marry him."

"And what did you say?"

"I didn't say anything. The guard came and told us time was up."

It was Alison's turn to hesitate. "Do you want to marry him, Livvie?"

"I think I do."

Alison grabbed Olivia's hand and squeezed. "You have to be very sure about this, you know that? You won't be able to come back—"

"For another forty years, I know."

"So you think you want to stay here? And marry Nicholas?"

Olivia gently pulled away from Alison and walked to the one window. A soft breeze blew in from the street, bringing with it the odors of the stables, and the kitchens. "You know, it's funny, Allie, but I could never imagine a life beyond my father. After he died, and I could see the end of his work in sight, I could just never imagine doing anything—"

"That's not true, Liv, you talked about drama school, about being an actress—"

"I talked about those things. But I could never see myself doing any of them. The whole future seemed so—so blank. Until we came here. And I can see myself here, married to Nicholas, the mother of his children—oh, Allie, maybe this all sounds crazy to you, but it's like—here, I feel I have a life. Back there—back there, I don't feel as though I have much of anything at all."

"What about me?"

"Well, of course, there's you, but—but you have your own life to live, Allie. You know exactly what you want and how to get it, and you know where you belong and—" Olivia broke off and glanced out the window. Below the window the watch cried out, " 'Tis twelve of the clock, and all is well." Olivia turned back to Alison with a sad smile. "I've never really known any of those things."

"But you feel you belong here?"

"Strange as that might sound, Allie, I do."

"Then you should stay here." Alison gave her a sad

smile of her own, and a tear slipped down her cheek. "I'll miss you."

Tears filled Olivia's eyes. "Oh, Allie, I'll miss you, too." With a little sob, she rushed to Alison's side and the two friends hugged each other tightly, tears rolling down their cheeks.

Finally, Alison drew back. She sniffed loudly and wiped her face on her sleeve. "Well. Now that that's settled, there's just one more thing."

"What's that?" Olivia managed to say, wiping away her own tears on the hem of her shift.

"Convincing Geoffrey he belongs in the future with me."

And through her tears, Olivia giggled. "Somehow, Allie, I don't think that's going to be a chore at all. Not at all."

"You want to do what?" Nicholas turned incredulous eyes on his brother. The setting sun slanted across the table in Nicholas's study as Geoffrey shifted uncomfortably on his feet. Nicholas's unexpectedly prolonged absence had meant that he'd been closeted in his study with Miles ever since their arrival at Talcott Forest that afternoon.

"You heard me, Nicholas." Geoffrey's voice was even, but his eyes danced with suppressed excitement.

"But—but, Geoffrey, that means you'll never come back—you'll be trapped there—"

Geoffrey broke out laughing. "Oh, Nicholas. From the way Alison's described it, I don't think I'll be trapped at all." He broke off at the stricken look on his brother's face. "Don't you see, Nicky?" he asked softly. "You don't need me here. You need Olivia. And Dee's quite clear—two people have to go through the maze, or it won't work. There's not enough mass to trigger the mechanism otherwise."

"How noble of you." Nicholas met his brother's gaze with a wink.

"All right, I admit it. I find Alison as attractive as you

find Olivia. I'm not sure she'll ever consent to marry me—but following her to her own time is a first step."

Nicholas leaned back in his chair. "Then, go, Geoffrey. With my blessing." The two brothers exchanged another long look.

"Thank you, Nick. That means a great deal to me."

Nicholas smiled wryly. "At least then I won't have to worry that you'll be burned at the stake."

At the door, Geoffrey turned back with his hand on the latch. "You know, Nicholas, I wish I could tell you I'm sorry for all the trouble I caused you, but under the circumstances, I don't think I can."

Nicholas nodded slowly, a small smile playing at the corners of his mouth. "Under the circumstances, I don't think you have anything to apologize for, either."

He found her waiting in the garden, where the last rays of the setting sun shone in long yellow beams through the hedge of the maze. "You talked to your brother?" She spoke over her shoulder as he approached.

"Yes. And you spoke with your friend?"

"Yes." She turned to face him, smiling.

"So it's all settled, then?"

"It seems to be." She nodded.

"Are you sure?"

There was a long pause while she considered her answer. "Yes," she said at last, a smile spreading across her face like the light of the rising sun. "Are you?"

He smiled back at the happiness in her eyes. "Yes," he replied at once. "Never surer."

The dark figure stole through the thick shadows beneath the trees. The moonless night was still—without the great house, all was quiet beneath the cloud-studded sky. With a catlike agility, the figure scaled one of the trees that gathered so closely to the house. With a knife, he jimmied the frame around the small square window and pushed it outside. It caught almost soundlessly in the leaves below.

Christopher Warren slithered through the window. He wore only a tight-fitting black doublet over his black hose and boots, and his sword was strapped tightly to his back. He sheathed the knife as he crept silently through the halls of the sleeping house.

He passed the room where Olivia lay sleeplessly beside Alison. She shifted on her side, then lifted her head off the pillow when she thought she heard a footstep outside the door. She listened. The footsteps sounded as though they were going away from the door. She rose up on one elbow and glanced over her shoulder at Alison. As usual, Alison slept peacefully, her face pillowed on her hand.

Olivia slid out of bed and tiptoed to the door. She slipped the latch up and peered outside. Yes, that was the creak at the bottom of the steps. Was Nicholas as sleepless as she?

She shut the door and stole down the hallway, listening to the faint footfalls, which walked quickly in the direction of Nicholas's study.

Warren walked with purposeful steps through the house, grimly focused on the task at hand. His fingers closed on the hilt of his sword, the palm itchy to plunge it into Nicholas's chest. He pushed open the door of Nicholas's study. Beyond the study lay Nicholas's bedroom. Maybe the bitch would be with him. And he'd slay two birds with one sword. He laughed silently at his own black humor and stepped into Nicholas's bedroom.

"Who's there?" Nicholas's voice was cold, alert and wary.

Warren blinked, momentarily dismayed to find him awake. With a cry, he rushed in the direction of the shadowy bed, and the white-clad figure within it.

Nicholas rolled away when he saw Warren's dark shape coalesce out of the shadows, the raised sword shining in the starlight. He reached for his own weapon and landed on his bare feet on the other side of the bed. "Warren, you're mad."

"Am I?" Warren hissed, stepping away from the bed. In the shadows, Nicholas could see the silvery blade glimmering. He moved warily away from the corner, easing toward Warren to give himself more maneuverability. His own sword jerked up instinctively as Warren rushed in to attack.

With a great cry, Nicholas leapt to the offensive, and the blades crossed and rang. "You came to let me kill you, Warren?" he spat at the other man.

"I'll see you dead." Warren reversed his attack, lunging at Nicholas's chest. Nicholas parried and riposted, his short nightshirt billowing. The tip of Warren's blade caught in the fabric, ripping a slit across the shoulder and catching in Nicholas's flesh. He cried and twisted away, thrusting his hilt at Warren's sword.

The clash of weapons, the thud of footfalls, and the sporadic cries brought Olivia speeding into the study. She paused, horrified, in the doorway, staring at the two men fighting in the dark bedroom. Without a word, she turned on her heel and sped down the hallway, up the steps toward Geoffrey's room. She hammered on the door until he opened it, his hair tousled, his nightshirt rumpled. "Geoffrey, come quickly, please—Nicholas is fighting someone—please—"

He stared at her a moment as her words registered, then reached for his own sword and dashed down the stairs. "Get Miles," he cried.

Olivia rushed into the kitchens, where a low fire glowed in one of the wide hearths.

Geoffrey paused in the doorway, assessing the situation. The two men were fighting at very close quarters, circling around each other, slashing at each other in the barely adequate light. As his own eyes adjusted, he realized Nicholas was slowly losing the upper hand, as Warren forced him closer and closer into the corner. He waited for just the right second, then leapt into the fray.

The two brothers were closing in on Warren when the bright glow of a lantern fell over their shoulders, illuminating Warren's sweat-slicked face. "Lord Nicholas!" cried Miles, entering the room with Jack on his heels.

Warren raised his sword to block a blow of Geoffrey's, and in that moment, Nicholas lunged. The blade pierced the thick leather doublet and slid between Warren's ribs. His eyes widened in shock, then he crumpled to the floor.

Nicholas backed away as Miles, Jack, and Olivia crowded closer, all talking at once.

"Are you all right, Nicholas?" Olivia's voice rose above the rest.

He turned and reached for her with his left hand, his right still gripping the hilt of his sword. He pulled her to him, and she clung to him carefully, fearful that he might be hurt. "Are you all right?" she asked once more.

"I am," he said against her hair. "I'm quite all right. A few scratches, nothing more." He looked at Geoffrey. "Thank you."

"It was Olivia who came to get me."

"How did you know?" Nicholas asked, as Miles gently took the sword out of his hand and tried to coax him to the bed. Jack had summoned Janet, and now she bustled in, with a tray full of ointments, to assess the wounds.

"I heard someone go by in the hallway—I thought it might have been you—" she blushed unexpectedly. Nicholas smiled, and Geoffrey hid a grin.

"I see," he said with a wink, as Janet pushed him to sit on the bed.

"Come, come, Lord Nicky, you've got more than a scratch or two on you—Jack, don't stand there gaping—fetch Ned and Tom from the stables to move this one—" She indicated Warren. "He lives?"

"Aye," Miles said, looking up from where he crouched beside Warren's prone body. "But the blade went in deep—I doubt he'll survive."

"See to him, Miles," said Nicholas. "The man's mad

with grief and hate. If he recovers, he can answer for his crimes, although I'm not sure he's really responsible."

With a muttered assent, Geoffrey directed the men to carry Warren to the hall, where a makeshift pallet had been set up. Janet finished binding the last of Nicholas's wounds. A sling, which Janet had insisted upon, and Nicholas had protested was unnecessary, bound his right arm to his chest, and a white strip wound around his chest. She straightened up with a sniff. "Now mind you don't go moving about, Lord Nicky. They'll open up again, and I must have a look tomorrow, when I can see better. Imagine—attacking good folk in their beds in the middle of the night! It's not Christian."

She bustled away, and Olivia and Nicholas were alone. "You thought it was me, hm?"

"I thought it could've been you," she said, feeling embarrassed once more.

"Tomorrow night it will be me," he replied, reaching out to finger one long dark curl. He picked up the silky strand and brought it to his mouth. She moved just a little closer, as the now familiar heat flared deep. It spread through her body in a slow, steady wave. He smiled at her, and she drew closer. His left arm closed around her, and she melted into his embrace, her mouth soft beneath his kiss. "But tonight," he whispered, his breath hot against her ear, "tonight, you'll stay with me."

"And all the nights after that," she murmured, as he drew her mouth to his once more.

Epilogue

"AND YOU SAY you found this painting at a pub in Kent?" William Danecourt peered over his spectacles at Alison and Geoffrey. "Which your friend—Miss Olivia Lindsley—tentatively believes to be the Dark Lady? Someone named Olivia, Lady Talcott?"

"Yes, yes," said Alison. "As I explained to you on the phone, we happened to see this picture on our way to Talcott Forest, where Olivia was planning to do some research. She's finishing up the work for her father—the late David Owen Lindsley?"

"Ah." Danecourt lifted his pale blond brows. His tailored gray suit and crisp blue cotton shirt belonged on a man twice his age, thought Alison, who guessed him to be about twenty-four. Despite his youth, he seemed as stuffy as the portrait of his father appeared to be, which hung in the tastefully furnished foyer of "Danecourt & Son—Appraisors of Antique Artifacts." Olivia said they were the best in London.

"Look, would you just take a look at it for me? Tell me what you can about the painting? I know your father's not here, but could you—?"

"Certainly, Miss O'Neill." He bent over the painting

with a magnifying glass, surveying it carefully.

Alison glanced at Geoffrey. He was looking very comfortable in rumpled khakis and a denim work shirt. They'd been in the twentieth century for over a week now, and Geoffrey was settling in remarkably well, and far better than she'd been able to adjust to the sixteenth. He certainly seemed to be enjoying himself, except for their being in the awkward position of having to make explanations regarding Olivia's disappearance. As for culture shock, he was adapting quickly.

Danecourt murmured to himself several times, then turned the portrait over. He ran his fingers over the canvas, then frowned when he reached the bottom. "Hm," he said.

"What is it?" Alison asked eagerly.

"This is somewhat odd. . . ." He ran his fingers over the lower portion of the canvas back. "It almost feels as if there's a packet of some sort behind this. As if this. . . ." He cut the canvas carefully along the bottom of the frame. "Look here. Just as I thought. It's a double canvas. There's something under here."

Alison squeezed Geoffrey's hand. She knew in her gut that Olivia had left some message, something tangible. . . .

"Hm," said Danecourt again, as he lifted a slim leather packet from between the two layers. "What's this?"

"What do you suppose it could be?" Alison asked, but even as she spoke, she knew the answer.

"Would you like to open it?" Danecourt asked.

"No, no, that's okay. You go ahead." She clutched Geoffrey's hand tighter.

Danecourt's long pale fingers swiftly unwrapped the thin leather. Within lay a sheaf of parchment sheets. "I say, what have we here?" He picked up one and began to read it silently. He put it down, his mouth working silently. He read another, and then another, and his eyes grew wider and wider, and Alison wanted to giggle. "Oh, my God." He took a short gulp of air. "Oh, my God. Oh. My. God." He took a deeper breath, then, without looking at either Alison or Geoffrey, dashed out of the room, calling, "Melissa! Melissa! Where's that number my father left?"

Alison looked at Geoffrey. "I knew she'd leave something there somehow. I just didn't want to damage the painting in any way."

"What is it?" he asked. "Don't you want to know?"

"I know what it is. It's the play that Shakespeare wrote for Nicholas—well, for Olivia, really. His first play. The one the acting troupe performed at Greenwich. That no one ever knew about, until now. He gave it to her before we left London."

"Ah." Geoffrey touched the yellowed parchments carefully. "So amazing."

"Yeah. It was. The whole thing's been really amazing."

"There's something written on the back here, Alison." Geoffrey was peering into the opened canvas backing. "Here, on the portrait's real back."

"What's it say?" She leaned over to have a look, then smiled as she read the words. " 'And they lived happily ever after.' That's Olivia's handwriting," she murmured. "I guess sometimes fairy tales do come true."

"What do you mean?" asked Geoffrey. He gently touched the side of her cheek where a tear had slipped unheeded down her face.

"Well, that's how they always end, you know. With what she wrote there: 'And they lived happily ever after.' "

He drew her to him, and wrapped his arms around her, holding her close. She felt her head slip naturally into the hollow of his chest, and felt a deep sense of comfort, of belonging and acceptance. Well, why not, she thought with a silent chuckle. We've known each other over four hundred years.

"Happily ever after?" he murmured as he bent his head to kiss her. "We should certainly endeavor to do just that."